To our delego neighbors —

SHUNNED

Fool Me once A Novel

Paul J Wotten
2019

Paul E. Wootten

To the women in my life -
Mom, Jill, Lynnea, Alison, and Kelcy.
Your strength is found in these pages.

And of course, to Robin, with love

PROLOGUE

"Gateway Hotel and Convention Center. This is Hassan. How may I direct you call?"

"Suite 1501."

"It's three in the morning here in St. Louis, sir. Are you certain you want me to connect you with that guest?"

"I'm sure."

"As you wish."

Four rings. Five. Seven. A loud crack jars the line when the phone is picked up, dropped, and retrieved.

"Hullo." The voice is husky. Sleep-filled.

Male.

"Who is this?" The caller zeroes in.

"Who's this?" The groggy voice answers.

"Zane Hardesty."

The line goes dead. Zane dials again.

"Gateway Hotel and Convention Center. This is Hassan. How may I direct you call?"

"I called a moment ago. 1501. The call didn't go through."

"I'll reconnect."

The phone rang once.

"Hello?"

"Penny."

"Zane? Why are you calling so late? Is everything—"

"Who answered the phone before?" Zane spoke softly, belying the rage simmering underneath.

"Before? I don't know what—"

"Who is he?"

"What do you mean?"

"Penny, talk to me, or I'll have someone at your door in ten minutes."

Whimpering. The sounds she made when she started to cry.

"Wh-wha-du-do-"

"Penny." Zane's voice was quiet, controlling. "Here's what you're going to do. Are you listening?"

More whimpering.

"Are you listening?"

"Mmhmm."

"Get packed and out of there. Start driving back to Kansas City. Do not stop except to get gas."

Sobbing.

"I can't—"

"Be back here by seven."

"Zane, it's not what—"

"Leave now or I'll have somebody come and get you."

2

In the background over Penny's bawling, Zane heard the voice from before. He couldn't make out what was said, but Penny's shrieked response came through loud and clear.

"No, you can't! He will—"

Zane had heard all he needed to hear.

"You better get moving, Penny."

"Zane, I'm sor—"

Zane gently hung up.

SATURDAY

Day One

"Are there further comments to share with Adam before we vote?" Melvin Proffer glanced around the conference table.

Adam followed the chairman's gaze down one side of the table and up the other, willing the good karma to continue. The positive comments of the fifteen board members had taken the edge off any uncertainty he'd entered the room with an hour earlier.

The location helped. The meeting room at the Ocean Sands Hotel was roomier, the conference table bigger than the cramped conference room at Ocean City Memorial Hospital. It was Saturday; the meeting was closed to the public, and board members were relaxed. Most had eschewed professional attire for weekend wear. A bartender kept glasses full. Melvin insisted it be that way.

Still, it was hard for Adam to control the butterflies when his contract was the lone item on the agenda. A lot was riding on the vote about to be taken. Moving here fifteen months ago was a big gamble; career suicide his former colleagues said. Ha! They had to drive three hours to play in the ocean.

"Adam, are you happy here?" Steve Cronin, seated near the opposite end of the long table, leaned forward to make eye contact. Cronin was a Philadelphia transplant who'd shelved his Ph.D. two decades earlier, bought a boat, and now chartered deep-sea fishing excursions.

"Very happy," Adam replied. Who wouldn't be? While his friends in Annapolis endured hour-long commutes, he watched sunrises over the Atlantic during four-mile runs on the beach.

"Think you'll stay awhile?" The question came from Adele Sweet. Adele was like a lot of locals who wanted newcomers to fall in love with Ocean City life. She shouldn't have worried.

"Remember where we come from, Adele. I'm from West Virginia and Brooke grew up on the beach—"

"*Myrtle* Beach," she snapped. "Overcrowded, overhyped, and overpriced."

Laughter mixed with the tinkling of bottles and glasses. The board was more relaxed than Adam had seen them.

"We love the lifestyle. Jack's excited to start kindergarten in a couple months. We certainly don't miss the Western Shore traffic." Affirmative nods all around. Most locals loved the money brought in from Washington and Baltimore, but couldn't imagine living there.

"People tell me you're a good listener, Adam." Lindsey Rickover, the newest trustee, sat directly to his right. A researcher for the Maryland Department of Health, Lindsey was young, smart, and always prepared. Some suspected she might eventually become board chairman.

"Hilda Mays said you went to her husband's funeral," another board member said. Adam smiled, pleased that Hilda, an LPN at Memorial since its opening a decade ago, had the ear of at least one board member.

The comments continued to flow.

"You went by Andy Glasscock's room after his cancer surgery."

"You eat in the cafeteria every day. Our last administrator didn't know where it was."

"Tisha Lattimore said you know her by name."

"Who's Tisha Lattimore," another board member asked, drawing derisive laughter from the others.

"What?" Adele retorted. "How can you not know Tisha? Reed Lattimore's wife? You've lived here how long?"

"Reed the plumber?" the chastened board member asked meekly.

"That's the one. Tisha works in housekeeping."

Board members continued to share comments and anecdotes, one-upping each other's stories and rebuking colleagues for not knowing people they were supposed to know. Adam felt blessed to be there. It was so much different than Annapolis

Medical Center, where everything was buttoned down and formal. This board liked each other and, more importantly, they liked him. From the first day, it had felt right.

"Dr. Wong or Dr. Fitz, do you have anything to add?" Melvin took advantage of a lull in the conversation to pull in the physicians on the board. Daniel Wong was an Emergency Room physician, and Stephanie Fitz a family practice doctor.

"All good here." Dr. Fitz, a happy-go-lucky sort, was revered by her patients.

"We could use more money in ER," Dr. Wong replied. Sour, quiet, burnt-out Dr. Wong. Bringing this up during a board meeting was unnecessary, but typical. He and Adam saw each other every day. Adam sipped his beer, curious to watch this play out.

"Have you made your needs known to Adam?" Melvin asked.

"Our needs haven't changed in years. Supplies, equipment, staff."

"In all fairness, Dr. Wong, you should put that in writing," Steve Cronin said. "Adam can consider your requests and perhaps bring them to us."

Go Steve!

Dr. Wong nodded, then turned his sour gaze back to the stack of papers in front of him. Melvin gulped from his wine glass before addressing the board.

"Other comments?"

"I think we're ready to vote," a board member said.

"Me too," added another.

"Okay then, can we have a—"

"Melvin, may I say something?" Cliff Leake owned the local Toyota dealership. It wasn't like him to slow things down. He and Adam were friendly, and Cliff hadn't indicated anything was amiss.

When Melvin motioned him to proceed, Cliff started to get to his feet, but thought better of it.

"This isn't as much a criticism as a suggestion."

Oh boy.

"Adam, you do an outstanding job. I'm very happy. It's just..." Cliff stopped for a moment, considering his words. "When you're on television, or I hear you on the local radio stations, you don't come across as... in charge."

Adam met his gaze, but said nothing. Peripherally he caught a couple board members nodding in agreement.

"Like when we opened the new pharmacy last month, both Salisbury stations interviewed you, and you seemed... I don't know how to say it..."

"Shy." Lindsey Rickover said.

"That's it, I guess," Cliff said. "Maybe you could take a course in public speaking, learn to project an image of... leadership."

Adam nodded. Where was this coming from?

Lindsey cleared her throat.

"If you could be more like you are today."

"Yes! Exactly," Cliff said. "You're relaxed; you're smiling, not uptight. If that could be more evident on television, I think the hospital would benefit."

"What's the difference, Adam?" Lindsey asked.

Adam considered his response. He knew that he tended to get stiff when a microphone was thrust in front of him. Small gatherings were much easier. It wasn't a new problem. He'd suffered bouts of stage fright back in high school. Over time, he'd learned to compensate, to find ways to overcome the shyness.

And the best way was right in front of him. Adam touched his beer glass as he scanned their faces.

"It's hard to say, Lindsey. Just shyness I suppose. I'll seriously consider what you've said, Cliff."

"I apologize if I offended you. Like I said, you've done a marvelous job."

"Do you expect him to become somebody he's not?" Adele snapped, always one to get to the heart of the matter.

"Not at all," Cliff said, raising his hands. "It's not about changing. I'd never want that. It's more about... adapting."

"Let's get on with this," Melvin said, adjusting his expansive girth in a chair that looked overmatched to the task. "I trust you're ready to vote, and vote in favor of the recommendation I made when we came together."

Adam marveled at Melvin's skills. While all fifteen trustees were motivated, successful people, Melvin was the real mover and shaker. A fiercely loyal native with a body as large as his personality, nothing got done at OC Memorial unless Melvin was on board. And when it came to a contract extension for the hospital's young Chief Executive Officer, Melvin was enthusiastically on board.

###

They were supposed to talk about sugar beets. It was July, and that was what migrant workers picked in July.

Theresa Traynor cherished the fifteen minutes she spent on the phone with her father each Saturday. There usually wasn't much new to talk about. His lifestyle had been the same for the past decade: follow the harvest. Spring lettuce in California, early summer artichokes in Oregon, Washington State sugar beets in July. While he'd sometimes join the migrant farmers in the fields, most of Papa's time was dedicated to making sure they were taken care of. A grant he'd secured through the federal government ensured the migrants had proper nutrition, medical care, and education. You wouldn't find a migrant worker within a hundred miles who had anything but good to say about Professor Harvester Stanley.

But today they weren't talking about sugar beets. Papa and Aunt Joy weren't even in Washington State.

"We should be in Cape Girardeau tomorrow night, just in time for evening worship."

"Aunt Joy, do you feel like going to church?" Her voice was tired, not as sing-songy as usual.

"Sweetie, if I can't go, your Papa can do enough worshippin' for both of us."

That didn't sound good at all. They weren't young anymore. Papa was seventy-eight; Aunt Joy sixty-nine. The twenty-hour drive from Central Washington to Aunt Joy's house in Southeast Missouri would be punishment for anyone, let alone an elderly brother and sister in a cantankerous fifteen-year-old car.

Please Lord, keep a close watch on them.

Aunt Joy had been feeling run down for several weeks. Nausea and a persistent cough followed, concerning Papa to the point where he felt it would be best for her to take some time away from the fields to rest and recuperate at home. Before today, they hadn't said anything to Theresa, didn't want her worrying. Sometimes they still thought of her as a child.

"Papa, has Aunt Joy made an appointment to see a doctor?" Like always, Aunt Joy had chatted for a few moments before handing the phone to Papa.

"Doc Greene will get her in Monday."

Not that cloudy-eyed old sawbones. The smells of rubbing alcohol and mercurochrome flooded back from the few occasions Grandpa had taken Theresa to see Doc Greene. "Papa, please promise me you won't take her to Dr. Greene. Find a doctor for her at the hospital in Cape."

"Baby Girl, Doc Greene was good enough to get Joy and her kids through the measles, a couple broken arms, and a bout of scarlet fever. I think we can trust him."

Arguing was pointless. "Promise me you'll make sure she gets taken care of. Would you like me to come out and look after her?"

"Oh no, Cookie," Papa said, calling her by his favorite nickname. "I'll stay with her. You need to tend to your law practice, and Miles needs you."

He had a point. Work was piling up. Theresa sat down on the sofa, glancing at the stack of case files she'd brought home to work on while Miles played golf and politicked for more church parking.

After extracting a promise from Papa to call if Aunt Joy's health changed, she hung up and opened the first case file. Worry and prayer gave way to weariness. Too many hours working, not enough sleep. Still, there was much to be done. So much. She laid her head down and stretched out on the sofa. A five-minute nap would do the trick.

Even the uncrowded parts of Ocean City are crowded.

Eric Stover's words came to mind as Adam waited for a break in traffic. Ocean Highway was bumper to bumper. Twenty minutes to cover thirty blocks from the Ocean Sands to the spot on the beach were The Group gathered. Eventually, a sympathetic driver slowed enough for Adam to squeeze in. An illegal U-turn two blocks later had him headed in the right directions.

Four blocks wide, one hundred and fifty blocks long, shortcuts in OC were few and far between. Sometimes the gridlock could be maddening. Sometimes, but not today. A good performance review, a two-year contract extension, and a raise could take the edge off a stroll across the Sahara.

Each east-west street dead-ended at the beach, allowing a glimpse of the surf as he drove. How could anyone not love living here? The beach lifestyle more than made up for the traffic. Besides, after Labor Day, locals pretty much had the place to themselves.

Adam lowered the window and took in the smells. Sea salt. Sun tan lotion. Pizza and French fries. Brooke would be ecstatic at the guarantee of two more years living full-time in a place where others came to unwind. She had stayed home with Jack since they arrived, shuttling him from one activity to another Her plans after Jack started school in the fall were up in the air. They were on several adoption agency lists, including the one that had helped with Jack's adoption. They'd hoped he would have a little brother or sister by now.

The Group would be happy too. Adam couldn't wait to tell them. Big Mike would joke about not having to break in a new family. Nosy Eric might ask how big a raise he got. The wives would chatter among themselves, happy their cadre of mamas and kids was staying intact.

After wheeling his white Lexus into the lot of a small hotel owned by a Rotary Club friend, Adam placed a parking permit in the front window and headed toward the beach. The feel of hot asphalt on bare feet made him step gingerly toward the sand at the end of the street. A teenage couple passing by smirked at his discomfort.

The beach was packed, but it didn't take long to spot the bright green canopy, a little further up the beach than usual, but easily recognizable. Weaving through mini settlements of beach towels, swim toys, and baking bodies, Adam made his way toward the canopy. Some people complained about it. It was a bit garish and bigger than anything else on the beach, but it provided enough room for four families. Getting closer, he could make out *Big Mike's Produce* on the canopy's top, along with an address and phone number. Actually, Big Mike wasn't big at all. Mike Lusk and his wife Megan were one of four couples in the Surfside Fellowship Small Group with Adam and Brooke. Their 'uh-oh' son Brody, who arrived eleven years after siblings Angela and Little Mike, was fast friends with Jack.

Adam spotted The Group before they saw him. As always the women were clustered in a circle of beach chairs on one side of the canopy while the men sat on the other. Forrest Delaney and Big Mike were in the middle of an animated discussion, undoubtedly about the Orioles-Yankees series starting Monday night. Two empty chairs were between them, one for Adam and the other for Eric Stover. Glancing toward the beach, Adam saw Eric boogie-boarding a wave, his face shining with pleasure like the kids around him. Eric was a big man who carried his extra weight around his mid-section. His pasty white belly and jolly disposition gave him a Santa-like quality that kids were drawn to.

And there were plenty of kids among the four couples in The Group. Eric and Denise Stover had six, though only the youngest four usually came to the beach on Saturdays. Forrest and Julie Delaney's two kids, and Brody Lusk brought the number to seven, not counting Jack.

Jack.

Stumbling and almost falling over from the force of a wave, Jack and Adam spotted each other simultaneously. The boy's eyes lit up as he started running. Eric didn't notice the boy's hasty exit from the water – so much for keeping an eye on the kids.

14

Jack zipped through the crowd as fast as his five-year-old legs could take him, stumbling over a set of hairy tanned legs, but quickly recovering and charging ahead. In the afternoon sun, his bright red hair seemed electric.

The kid was perfect.

The kid was his.

"Dad!"

Adam swept him up and carried him toward the canopy.

"We have a surprise for you!"

"I can't wait."

The others noted his arrival and quickly formed a makeshift receiving line. Big Mike took a spot in the center, next to Brooke. He was holding a large poster board sign.

Congratulations Adam! We love you!

Brooke broke away from the group. She hugged Adam, planting a big wet kiss on his lips while the others applauded.

"How'd you know?"

"I've got friends in high places, brother." Eric Stover had made his way back to the tent, his white belly dripping. He hugged Adam, soaking his blue M.R. Ducks shirt to the skin.

"Eric called Mr. Proffer," Brooke said.

"Melvin and I go way back," Eric said. "He didn't tell me everything. Just that things went good and you'd be around for a while."

Adam laughed. "So much for closed meetings."

"It's Ocean City, man. Nothing stays quiet here," Forrest Delaney said, thrusting out his hand.

"What would you guys had done if the news was bad?"

"We knew it would be good," Big Mike said. "After some of the knuckleheads that've run that hospital, you look like a champ."

"But, just in case," Eric said, reaching for the sign, "We were ready."

He flipped it over.

Farewell Adam!

The afternoon melted into the slow routine Adam had come to love. Good food prepared by the wives, with fresh watermelon compliments of Big Mike. Conversations under the canopy broken up by short trips into the water to play with the kids. Jayden Delaney, Forrest's ten-year-old son, was helping Jack learn to ride a boogie board. Jack seemed unafraid of the breaking waves. The kid was really something.

Just before five, with the sun tilting in the sky behind them, Big Mike pulled the adults into a circle, spouses seated together. Adam moved his chair next to Brooke's. She squeezed his hand and winked. Big Mike offered a prayer on behalf of The Group, then excused the kids to play along the shoreline. It was understood that Jared and Libby Stover, at fourteen and twelve, would be in charge and that none of the kids would venture beyond the break. Truth be known, Jared and Libby were more trustworthy than their father.

Brooke reached into her bag, pulling out Adam's familiar tan leather Bible and handing it over. Adam brushed the sand off the cover. It had become a lot more worn in the year they'd attended Surfside.

Pastor Miles preached the word and expected the congregation to follow along.

This part of the weekend get-togethers had taken some getting used to. At first, it was hard to ignore the looks The Group received from people around them, the smirks, the occasional comment. The others didn't notice or didn't care. Listening to Big Mike share about the way people lived in Jesus' time, Adam realized he had reached a point where he didn't care either.

The thought of being part of a church small group was terrifying at first. Now, Adam couldn't imagine life without them. Big Mike and Megan were their best friends. They went out together when the Lusks could break away from the market. They did less socializing with the Delaneys and Stovers. Julie Delaney's job as a realtor and position on the advisory board to the Maryland Black Caucus required a lot of evening hours. The Stovers tended to stay to themselves, and Denise was hard to take sometimes.

Before concluding, Big Mike asked for prayer joys and concerns. Brooke praised God for allowing Adam to have a job he loved and a board that appreciated him. Megan Lusk asked for prayers for Little Mike who'd just broken up with his girlfriend. Megan had become Adam's favorite among the wives. She was the surrogate mom to everyone else, and even though she worked side-by-side with Big Mike at the produce market, she always had time to pick up other group members' kids and remember special events and dates.

"Anything else?" Big Mike asked.

Denise Stover tapped Eric on the arm. "Aren't you going to say anything?"

Eric rubbed his neck and glanced away.

"Go ahead. They need to know," Denise said softly.

Eric raised his head and looked uncertainly at the others.

"Does everyone know Melody Atkins?"

They did. Forty-something, sang in the praise band, couple of kids. Husband who liked to play golf.

"She was fired from her job this past week for stealing."

Julie leaned forward. "She managed that waterpark down by the Route 90 Bridge, right?"

Megan nodded. "Splash Down Park."

Adam watched The Group absorb the news. Forrest seemed most troubled, probably worried that Melody Atkins might contact him for legal advice. That happened sometimes, past and present church members asking him to be their lawyer in cases that left him in uncomfortable positions.

"What does Pastor Miles say about it?" Megan asked.

It was understood that Megan's question was meant for Eric. As one of Surfside Fellowship's three elders, he was on the frontline when dealing with situations like this.

"Pastor advised her to admit she was guilty and take her punishment."

"That's a tough position," Forrest said. "An attorney would tell her to plead innocent and seek a plea-bargain. She's likely to see some jail time otherwise."

"Well, if she's guilty, she's guilty," Denise Stover said.

"There's no doubt she took money," Eric added. "She told Pastor Miles that much. It's just a question of how much and for how long, and Melody isn't sure."

"Should we even be talking about this?" Adam asked.

"Adam, we're all part of the same family," Denise said sharply. "We agreed to support our church." Denise had an edge about her that made her hard to warm up to. Maybe it was Eric's job with the water department or the fact that neither of them went to college, but Denise always seemed to be overcompensating, trying to come across as somebody important in a group that didn't put any emphasis on that kind of thing. She definitely got social mileage from Eric's being an elder.

"So what happens now?" Brooke asked.

"Pastor Miles told Melody that she wasn't welcome at Surfside until she repents," Eric said. "It'll be brought up at the membership meeting tomorrow night."

"Ugh." Adam shook his head.

"What?" Denise retorted, staring daggers at him.

"Those membership meetings," he said. "The last several have been brutal."

"Pastor Miles feels they're necessary," Eric said. "Church discipline is everybody's responsibility."

"We're messing with people's lives, Eric." Adam glanced around the circle. Why wasn't anyone else saying anything? "This Melody, for example, Surfside is going to blackball her tomorrow night, even after she's stepped up and admitted her mistake. Forrest, what happens if her confession gets back to the prosecuting attorney?"

"As church business, it shouldn't." Forrest's body language said loud and clear, don't get me in the middle of this. Though he worked as an attorney, Forrest was the softest-spoken member of the group.

"And nobody thinks it will get out?"

Eric shook his head. "Pastor Miles feels a strong stand is necessary. Stealing is stealing."

"This is why I hesitate to get involved," Forrest said. "The law and God's Law don't always agree."

"It doesn't seem to bother Theresa Traynor," Julie Delaney said. "She takes all kinds of cases."

"Theresa even takes divorce cases," Big Mike said. "How can she do that, Forrest?"

"And how about those legal workshops she does?" Megan added.

Forrest was a man looking for a hole to crawl in. Five years earlier, he and the pastor's wife had started work within a week of each other at a lily-white, men-only law firm, bringing color and diversity in a move local pundits said was fifty years overdue. Forrest was a friend, but Adam knew that Theresa Traynor ran circles around him as a lawyer.

"It's not our job to question what the pastor's wife does or doesn't do," Eric said.

"No," Adam said quietly, "we're too busy questioning Melody Atkins."

"Well," Brooke started slowly, "I'm not the expert here, but it seems Melody could confess and repent to Pastor Miles, but hold out on a plea bargain in the court case." Megan and Julie nodded their agreement.

"That's splitting hairs," Eric said.

"I agree," Denise added.

"So, you're saying Melody will be kept out of Surfside?" Brooke's concern showed in her eyes. "Like shunned or something?"

"It's a choice she's making by not going to the authorities," Eric replied.

"I'm not voting to kick her out," Adam said. "I don't want any part of this. I'll either not go or I'll abstain, just like I did with Patrick and Anna.

Silence. Uncomfortable silence. Six months, and their names were still taboo.

"They didn't die, you know."

"Adam." Brooke's voice was pleading.

Denise stood up. "It's time for you to accept the responsibility that goes with being part of the church body." Adam wasn't sure how much more of Denise he could take.

Fortunately, the kids returned.

Theresa awakened to the softness of Miles' kiss on the nape of her neck.

"Mmmmm."

"Hey, Tee, you been asleep long?" Miles kneeled by the couch as he whispered in her ear, his head close enough that his dreadlocks tickled her face.

Theresa took a deep breath to shake away the cobwebs. "What time is it?"

"Just after eight."

"Then I've been asleep for... six hours." The realization caused her to sit up, spilling several files to the floor.

"Gotta catch up some time," Miles said, getting to his feet. "I'm gonna find something to eat. You hungry?"

"Yeah, let me help you." Theresa stretched and followed him to the kitchen. After scrounging through the refrigerator, he pulled out a leftover pot roast their twice-a-week housekeeper had made two days earlier. Ten minutes later they were seated at the large island that divided the kitchen.

"How was golf?"

Miles snorted. "I'll never be any good, but these old boys don't care. They just like doing business anywhere but the office, especially in the summer." He stabbed a chunk of roast and jammed it into his mouth. "I think we're going to get a break on that municipal parking lot across Coastal Highway. Surfside pays a flat weekly rate, and we get one-hundred and twenty-five spots from seven to noon each Sunday."

"How will people get across the highway to the church?"

"I'm still working on that," Miles said with a wink. "If we can get a crosswalk put in, the problem will be taken care of, but it's hard to get the city to agree to more crosswalks."

For the next ten minutes the conversation meandered from crosswalks to sound system problems to chair rental for Surfside's monthly service on the beach. Miles did most of the talking, with Theresa interjecting the occasional question or comment. This had become the norm in recent months, as Surfside's attendance at its Sunday Celebration service continued to grow. Theresa was proud of her husband. In five years, Surfside had grown from five families in a hotel conference room to over 1,500 attendees in the summer. The legend of Pastor Miles Traynor extended well beyond Ocean City to the metro areas from which weekenders and vacationers flocked. In a feature article last summer, a Baltimore Sun reporter wrote that Surfside Fellowship had become as much a part of the Ocean City experience as Trimper's carousel and Thrasher's French fries. A large new sanctuary, completed two years before on beachfront land formerly occupied by a motel, was a testament to Surfside's explosive growth. The crowning touch was a glass wall behind the preaching platform, allowing passers-by on the boardwalk to view the worship service. They were exciting and heady days, but also a time of concern. At least for Theresa.

"Papa called today." Miles had stopped to take a breath, allowing Theresa a chance to jump in.

"Is everything good with him and your aunt?" Miles asked. "Let's see, they're in... Oregon?"

"Actually, they're on their way back to Missouri. Aunt Joy's been sick."

Miles looked up from his plate.

"What's wrong?"

"They'll find out this week."

Finishing off the last of his roast, Miles reached across and started eating from Theresa's plate.

"I've said it before, Tee. They're too old to be living that migrant lifestyle."

Theresa sighed. "I know, but what else are they going to do? Following the crops is what Papa chose after retirement."

Miles stretched out his arms. "We've got plenty of space here."

He was right. Two people, no kids, and a four-bedroom house in one of West Ocean City's nicest subdivisions. Miles believed they should always push the limit of what they could afford. "God will provide," he said. While Miles had complete trust in the Lord, Theresa put some of hers in the extra hours she billed by working sixty-hour weeks instead of the fifty-hour workload of most attorneys at Talbot, White, and Enke.

"I'd love to have them close by," she admitted.

"I know you would," Miles said, stroking her hand. "Let's take a minute and pray for your Aunt Joy's health and that maybe God'll work something in their heart to make them want to settle down."

These were the moments when she remembered why she'd married him. Away from the pulpit and congregation, when he wasn't having to be Pastor Miles, he had the kindest heart of anyone other than Papa. They'd met in law school. Miles outperformed her academically, but didn't have his heart set on becoming an attorney. It wasn't until they attended a megachurch service in Chicago while they were dating that he saw with clarity what he wanted to do with his life. Within a month, he had dropped out of law school and enrolled in a second-tier theology school where he completed three years of coursework in two, all while working part-time for a small urban church and delivering pizza fifteen hours a week.

And sweeping Theresa off her feet and to the altar.

That was seven years ago. Since then, they'd graduated and gotten on with their careers. Theresa was doing well at the law firm, often handling high profile cases, while Miles was soaring far beyond anything people expected of the inner-city Detroit kid who never knew his father.

Still, sometimes when she thought about it, Theresa missed the simpler times.

# # #

After an evening of television, Brooke got Jack ready for bed while Adam checked the mail. The usual: flyers offering discounts on parasailing, miniature golf, and all-you-can-eat buffets, stuff locals wouldn't consider doing in July. Those went into the trashcan by the back door. Stepping back into the kitchen, Adam peeked at the electric bill. The air conditioning would need to be dialed back a couple degrees. The only other mail was a plain white envelope addressed to *The Wife of Adam Overstreet.*

"Anything good?" Brooke asked as she came into the kitchen and rummaged through the snack cabinet.

"A very high electric bill and something for you."

Brooke glanced at the envelope, then pulled a chocolate chip cookie from a box and stuffed it in her mouth.

"Probably another invitation to join the Garden Club or the Ladies' Benevolent Society," Brooke said.

"I just wish they'd take time to learn my name. Put it on my stack with the electric bill. I'll look at them tomorrow. Let's go to bed."

Brooke's 'stack' was a running joke between them. Their kitchen had a built-in desk with a half-dozen cubby holes. Brooke had enthusiastically agreed to manage their checkbook, pay bills, and handle any correspondence. She'd gone as far as labeling the cubby holes and buying an expander file. That was a year ago. Today, the cubby holes were full of loose pieces of paper, some of Jack's smaller toys, and a variety of bric-a-brac. Bills and other correspondence wound up on Brooke's stack, which was sometimes a foot high before she sat down to deal with it.

Unless they had a date night lined up, they usually were in bed by ten on Saturday nights. It was quality time. Jack was down for the night, and church didn't start until nine-thirty. Having resisted the urge to put a television in their bedroom, Adam and Brooke's options were limited to conversation, reading, or love.

"It's so sad about Melody Atkins," Brooke said, snuggling close.

"Who?" Adam glanced up from the Grisham novel he was hoping to finish, then laid it aside.

"Melody Atkins. From the praise band. The lady in trouble at work."

"Something about that bothers me. Doesn't it you?"

"Yeah, I feel bad when things like that happen to people we know."

"Did you actually know her?"

Brooke smiled. "Sure I did. She came to some of the women's activities. She has the prettiest auburn hair."

Adam stretched. "I struggle with giving people the cold shoulder. Aren't we supposed to be about forgiveness?"

Brooke pulled her brown hair away from her eyes and propped her head up with her arm.

"She wouldn't get the cold shoulder if she was honest about what happened."

"Yeah, Brooke, but from what Eric said, she already confessed to Pastor Miles. It would seem the church could stand by her during the trial."

"Adam, she's entered a plea of innocent. That's not being honest."

Adam smiled faintly, then shook his head.

"What?" Brooke said.

"Like I said at the beach, a plea of innocence isn't so much a statement of honesty or dishonesty as it is a way to work toward a lesser punishment. Juries can be brutal. It's probably in her best interest to plead innocent and hope for a plea deal as the trial gets closer."

"Well, I don't like that part of it," Brooke sighed. "I think God would want her to admit her guilt and take her punishment."

Adam nodded. "In the end I'm sure she will."

"And I guess that's when she can come back to church."

Adam pulled back the sheets and got up, startling Brooke with his sudden movement.

"Are you mad?"

"Hungry. You want another cookie?"

Moments later he was back with a half-dozen cookies. He handed two to Brooke.

"Guess what?" Brooke's eyes were dancing.

"Melody Atkins gave you a hundred bucks?"

Brooke giggled and punched his arm. "Wrong."

"You better tell me."

Brooke rolled over so she was looking down at him, face to face.

"The cashier at Food Lion said Jack looked just like me."

They laughed.

"Did you tell her?"

"No way!"

"Did Jack hear her?"

"He was picking out some candy."

"I guess it's true what they say," Adam said. "The longer people are together the more they look alike."

"I think they say that about dogs and their owners," Brooke giggled, "but I'll take it."

Adam yawned. "It's time for Jack to have a brother or sister. I wish I knew why it's taking so long. Forrest said he'd help with the paperwork if that would speed things up."

"Yeah," Brooke said, snuggling close. "Then he told Julie who immediately called me."

Adam shook his head at the innocent breach of confidence.

"I mentioned it to Pastor Miles a couple weeks ago," Brooke continued. "He said we should come see him. He can offer us spiritual guidance."

"What kind of spiritual guidance do we need?"

"He thought that if we prayed together we might be able to conceive naturally rather than having to adopt."

Adam stiffened.

"Brooke, we've been through that. I can't have kids."

"I know, but still—"

"Did you tell Pastor Miles that?"

Brooke hesitated.

"Well, yes. I thought—"

Adam sat up. "Why Brooke? What business is it of his if we have a baby, adopt a baby, or whatever?"

From the look on her face, Adam knew he'd reacted harshly.

"He's our pastor, Adam. We can trust him with things like this."

Adam felt a tightness in his chest. He swallowed and rubbed the back of his neck.

"The key is we, Brooke. It should be we trusting Pastor Miles. Not just you."

"You don't trust him?"

"It's not that. It's..." Adam struggled to find the right words. Brooke was quick to trust, quick to accept. Adam hadn't grown up in church. He tended to keep things to himself. Still, he had to admit, she had a point. If you can't trust your pastor, who can you trust?

Brooke's eyes clouded with uncertainty. Adam laid back down and pulled her close.

"You're right. We... I... need to be more open about these things." He smiled quickly before adding, "You have to admit I'm doing better with The Group."

Brooke nodded, her concern replaced by a sly grin.

"Yeah, buddy, it only took you a year."

Adam turned her face toward his.

"Hey, better late than never."

He moved closer and softly smothered her response with a kiss.

SUNDAY

Day Two

Fog from a machine enveloped the darkened stage as a lone musician played a bluesy introduction on the keyboards. The fifteen-hundred-plus in the expansive auditorium grew quiet.

Then, wham! A rainbow of colored spotlights illuminated the stage; the keyboard's tune shifted to something up-tempo, contemporary. As the fog lifted, guitars, horns, woodwinds, and drums fused seamlessly, bringing worshipers to their feet, clapping to the hard beat.

"Surfside! Are you ready to worship our Almighty God?"

The clapping morphed into fervent shouting and applause. Two large projection screens came to life with the words to a familiar praise song.

"Then . . . let's . . . worship!"

Sunday morning at Surfside Fellowship. Lights, cameras, emotion.

And at the epicenter, Derby Hatfield.

In his late thirties, with a shaved head and happy countenance that some said reflected God's light, Derby had been part of an up-and-coming hip-hop act out of Cleveland until realizing that his music was encouraging kids to do things they shouldn't be doing. Raised in an inner-city church that saw music as something more than songs in a hymnal, Derby sought out an opportunity to put his musical gifts to work. A chance meeting with Miles Traynor had brought him to Ocean City three years ago.

Adam would be the first to say that Derby's music ministry could move mountains. After ripping through a couple up-tempo selections, the praise band slowed for a traditional church hymn. It was during these slower moments when Adam most felt God's presence, a reminder of how important it was to be still and know Him.

In addition to Pastor Miles and Derby, Riley Wenger served as Executive Pastor. They formed Surfside's leadership triumvirate, though it didn't take a genius to know that Miles ran the show. Riley, a buttoned-down studious man in his mid-forties, was similar to Adam in personality, but it was Derby whom he'd grown closest to. It started a few months after the Overstreets' arrival in Ocean City. Derby's eight-year-old son was dealing with health issues that required a short stay at Memorial. Adam came upon Derby in the hallway, and they'd enjoyed a few minutes of light conversation. Since then, Derby would show up at Adam's office every few weeks to take him out for lunch. Their conversations might touch on religion but more often focused on the Orioles, Ravens, or Derby's hometown Cleveland Cavaliers. They also talked about their kids. Derby had six and hoped for more. His wife, Aloe, kept house and homeschooled.

From his perch behind the keyboards, Derby brought the congregation to a period of silent meditation. For several minutes the only sounds in the darkened auditorium were the occasional cough or rustling of paper. Then, a single voice echoed through the sound system.

"Amen."

As if by magic, the musicians had cleared the stage and a podium appeared. Pastor Miles Traynor, resplendent in a bright white suit over a dark blue pullover, examined his flock. Most were dressed in their Sunday best; an expectation Pastor Miles had set in recent years. "God deserves your first and finest," Adam remembered him saying. "Be it the first fruits from your labors or the finest clothes you can afford. Bring it to him." The admonition had troubled Adam initially. Wasn't God accepting of people no matter how they looked? Still, he had to admit, the pastor was on to something. The members' dress code made it easy to spot visitors, usually in beach attire; and in the case of summer services at Surfside, there were lots of visitors.

And it was mainly because of Pastor Miles.

Adam had seen few people who could move an audience like him. His charisma was off the charts. His knowledge of the Bible was impressive to someone like Adam who, if he had to be honest with himself, would admit he'd never read the Good Book all the way through.

Though Pastor Miles was quick to credit God and the Surfside congregation, Adam knew that the church wouldn't have been built without the preacher's vision and drive. First, it was the land acquisition, a parcel of prime OC beachfront, formerly the home of a run-down 1950's motel. The owner, an elderly widow, deeded the property to Surfside in return for a church-paid lease on a small apartment where she could live out her days. Some likened the acquisition to Moses parting the Red Sea. The property could easily have fetched a couple million dollars on the open market.

Then there was the building. Members were asked to double their tithes and offerings for two years. Most had willingly committed. Others ponied up after some gentle arm twisting. The rest moved on to other churches. As this happened before Adam and Brooke moved to OC, they hadn't been asked to make a similar commitment.

After welcoming more than five hundred guests, Pastor Miles got down to business.

"I've got a bur in my bonnet," his voice rang out over several dozen speakers mounted to the auditorium's walls and ceilings. "Do you want to know what that bur is?"

Shouts of "yes, preacher!" and "bring it!" echoed in reply.

Leaning heavily on the large white podium, Pastor Miles flipped through his Bible, his dreadlocks obscuring a view of his face until he looked up again.

"Open your Bibles to the Book of Luke, Chapter 9." The riffle of pages throughout the auditorium followed. Adam lagged behind Brooke, who seemed to know instinctively where every book was.

"This is an important point in Jesus' ministry," the pastor continued. "He's sending his disciples out into the world." He stopped for a few beats and scanned the audience. "Up until now these followers had stayed close to Jesus, but now he's throwing them out of the nest."

More amens followed.

"Jesus was very wise," Miles said, then smiling and winking he added, "After all He is..."

"God!" Adam jumped at the thunderous response, then chastised himself for not following closer.

"Now notice in verse five, Jesus tells the disciples, 'if people do not welcome you, leave town and shake the dust off your feet as a testimony against them.'"

Closing his Bible, Pastor Miles walked to the edge of the stage. Anticipation built as the congregation waited for him to continue.

"You want to know what the bur is in my bonnet?"

"Yes!"

"That bur is the public schools that our children attend."

Murmurs of agreement followed. Adam leaned in.

"Think about this: what would Jesus tell his disciples if they came to him and said, 'Father, we're staying in a place where we're not allowed to talk *about you*?"

Pastor Miles paced across the stage waiting for quiet.

"Father, we're staying in a place where we're not allowed to talk *to you*."

Adam scanned the auditorium, looking for a familiar face. Several rows to his left he found him. Dr. Thomas McIlhenny, local superintendent of schools. McIlhenny and Adam were in Rotary together and served on a couple civic committees. Tom was staring down at his open Bible. His discomfort was obvious.

Almost as if reading Adam's mind, Pastor Miles continued.

"Dr. Tom McIlhenny, where are you? Tom, raise your hand."

The superintendent lifted his hand. The effort appeared painful.

"People, we know Dr. Tom. He's been a member of Surfside for a year or so. He is a Christian through and through."

Affirmative responses filled the air.

"We love Dr. Tom, don't we Surfside?"

More positive response. The superintendent's face turned crimson.

"I know that if Dr. Tom could, he would allow God into our public schools. Wouldn't you, Tom?"

Tom smiled weakly, then put his head back down.

For the next twenty minutes, Miles put the public education system on the stove and turned up the heat. He shared his belief that the founding fathers never intended for God to be left out of school and how liberals had shoved Him out, creating a system that not only didn't educate kids, but hurt them spiritually.

The congregation ate it up. Pastor Miles' furor became their furor. Adam noticed Brooke's enthusiastic nods of agreement as he laid out his challenge to Surfside.

Oh no.

That was Theresa's first thought as Miles began to rail against public education.

Please God, give him the insight to consider what he's about to say.

Too late.

Twenty minutes after quoting the book of Luke, Miles laid down his challenge.

"Let's build our own school, where God comes first."

Certainly a good and noble idea, Theresa thought. But...

"Let's start raising funds this fall, in November."

This made her uneasy. Some members were still struggling to catch up financially from the building project a couple years ago.

"Double tithing."

From her vantage point at the end of the front row, Theresa glanced over her shoulder as Miles made this pronouncement. Some affirmative gestures, but quite a few raised eyebrows and double takes. Couples seated together started to whisper between themselves.

"Surfside Fellowship School. Grades kindergarten through eight. Planned opening in three years."

Theresa was unable to see Dr. McIlhenny, the local school superintendent, but she could imagine how he must be receiving this news. To be asked to financially support a church school that would pull students from the public schools was probably more than he could digest.

Then it got worse.

Miles moved to the edge of the stage, the way he always did when he had something important to say. He calmly looked around, willing everyone to put their eyes on him. He was, Theresa thought, a most compelling figure.

"In the meantime, if you are capable and have the time, I encourage you to consider homeschooling your children."

Oh, boy.

"You and only you know the spiritual needs of your children." Miles opened his Bible.

"You want proof? Look no further than Proverbs 22:6."

After a few beats, he continued. "Read it along with me. Read loudly. Own these words of God."

Another pause before a thousand voices read in unison, "Train up a child in the way he should go, and when he is old he will not depart from it."

Despite the response, it was obvious to Theresa that some in the auditorium were not following along with Miles' plan.

What's more, she was one of them.

###

Surfside's auditorium had five exits, and Miles made a point to be at a different one each week, shaking hands and putting names with faces. It was his preference to have Theresa with him; they had a system that worked well. If someone approached that Miles didn't know, he would nudge Theresa. If she knew them, she would say something that allowed him to give the impression he did too.

"Miles, isn't it great news that Jose and Margaret are expecting?"

"Margaret, when is the due date?"

Inevitably Margaret would gush about the pending arrival, while Jose puffed out his chest. Later both would tell their friends how Pastor Miles and Theresa spoke to them and remembered they were expecting.

When it came to Adam and Brooke Overstreet, Miles recognized them immediately, or at least Brooke.

"Good to see you today, Brooke," he said, embracing her warmly, then shaking Adam's hand and high-fiving their son Jack. Then, in a quieter tone he said, "What do you think of our plans for providing a Christian education here at the beach?"

"Pastor Miles, I'm so excited." A smile frozen on her face, Theresa watched silently as Brooke waxed enthusiastically about the idea. Adam was considerably more reticent.

39

"I'm glad we have your support," Miles said, then turning to Adam added, "Perhaps we can get one or both of you involved in the planning process."

"We'd be delighted," Brooke said quickly. Theresa was certain that Miles would prefer having the administrator of the local hospital on the planning committee rather than his stay-at-home wife. Even though he'd only been here a short time, Adam Overstreet's name meant something in Ocean City. Still, most of Miles' attention went to Brooke.

Sensing the growing impatience of the line behind them, Theresa watched Adam place his hand on his wife's arm and lead her out the door. He had remained noncommittal to Miles' overtures, and she thought he'd done a masterful job of it.

"Keep your eye on number seven." Big Mike pointed to a boy stretching in the outfield. "He's gonna be the Orioles shortstop in three years."

Adam looked closely at the kid. He didn't look old enough to be out of high school, let alone playing minor league ball.

"Scrawny, isn't he?"

"Most are at this level," Big Mike replied. "Kid's name is Levi Stafford. First-round pick a year ago. He tore up the Rookie League. By the time he gets to Baltimore he'll be two inches taller and twenty pounds heavier."

Adam studied the kid and tried to see what got Big Mike so excited. He didn't look much different than Big Mike's seventeen-year-old son. Both were tall and gangly. The biggest difference he could see was that Levi Stafford was playing baseball, while Little Mike Lusk was working the counter at his family's produce market.

Adam took in Perdue Stadium, home of the Delmarva Shorebirds, the only professional baseball team within a hundred miles. It was a cozy ballpark just off Highway 50, a half hour from Ocean City. Big Mike and Megan came to a dozen games a year. This was the first time they'd invited Adam and Brooke to join them. They were so happy for the getaway that they'd sprung for a sitter to watch Jack and the Lusk's son, Brody.

"How'd you get such good seats?"

"Snappy White farms near Pittsville. He has 'em. I've bought string beans from him for years."

Brooke announced that she was starving, so Adam took orders and headed for the concession stand. When it was his turn to order, he scanned the menu.

"Four hotdogs, two large Diet Cokes, a large Dr. Pepper... and a large light beer."

Brooke wouldn't like it, but in the heat and humidity it would be worth it.

The game was getting underway as Adam returned to his seat. The beer in its distinctive tall plastic cup stood out like a sore thumb. Sure enough, Brooke's smile vanished.

"Adam, really? On Sunday?"

"It's a baseball tradition, sweetheart. Beer and baseball go together."

Adam doled out hot dogs and sodas. Megan and Big Mike seemed unbothered by his decision to imbibe.

"I gotta say, it does look good," Big Mike said as he took a sip of his Dr. Pepper.

"You want one?"

"Nah, ain't had one in years," he laughed. "I'd probably be a slobbering drunk after a few sips."

As the game progressed, Adam started to notice little things about the minor leaguers. He watched a lot of Orioles games on television and had attended many in person when they lived in Annapolis. Minor league ball was new to him. The players were raw, but you could pick up little things.

"You're right about Stafford," Adam said after the kid made an off-balance throw to beat a runner going to first. "He goes to his left really well."

"Some folks say he has range like Belanger," Big Mike said, referring to an Oriole great of the 1970's. "Biggest difference is, he can hit."

The game entered the sixth inning with the Shorebirds and Lexington Legends tied at three. Adam and Big Mike dissected player strengths and weaknesses, while Megan and Brooke talked about their kids. Adam made another trip to the concession stand, but stuck to soda.

Adam wanted to ask Big Mike's opinion of Pastor Miles' message, but the time hadn't yet presented itself. Finally, during a lull in the seventh, he saw his opening.

###

The picture started to come together for Theresa as she and Miles had lunch with Evan and Leta Fulkerson. Like many OC locals, they'd delayed lunch until almost three, allowing the crowds to thin out. By now many weekenders were starting to pack up for their returns to the city. The busiest restaurants were often less than half-full.

The Fulkersons had chosen a pricey steak restaurant in West Ocean City. Their table was in a corner, away from prying eyes and ears. Theresa quickly understood why.

She quickly understood a lot of things.

"I thought you did a marvelous job presenting the idea, Miles," Evan said over a glass of wine.

"I did as well," Leta added. "For the first time I really feel like we might have an opportunity to provide our local children with a quality education."

The Fulkersons were a study in contrasts. Evan was in his mid-fifties, a bachelor until he'd met Leta twenty years earlier. A decade older than her husband and twice divorced, Leta's family had been heavily vested in Ocean City real estate before Leta's father started selling it off in the 1970's. Leta continued in her father's footsteps, to the point where the Fulkersons no longer owned anything, but had more money than they knew what to do with.

Their interest in education had started four years earlier, when Evan ran for the county school board on a platform of ridding Worcester County schools of incompetent teachers and administrators, while instilling appropriate values in all students. He lost by seven votes, emboldening him to make another run a year later. When it became clear to voters that the values Evan sought to instill in their youth were evangelical Christian values, the margin of defeat widened. As Surfside grew, Evan and Leta began attending and contributing large sums of money. Their interests in education and their membership at Surfside had finally converged. Theresa quickly figured out this wasn't the first time they had discussed the topic with Miles.

"What's the next step?" Evan asked.

Picking at his salad, Miles replied, "We need to determine who to get on board first. There are people at Surfside who have a lot of influence. We need to bring them into the loop."

"Can we help?" Leta said. "We know a lot of people."

And most of them think you're a couple of looney tunes, Theresa thought. Why in the world was Miles attaching himself to these nuts?

"We'll definitely need your help," Miles said quickly. "But for the time being, allow me to get things moving behind the scenes."

"We'd like to be involved in naming the school," Evan said.

Miles looked up quickly. This had caught him off guard. It shouldn't have.

"What were you thinking?"

Evan and Leta shifted in their seats.

"Well," Evan replied sheepishly, "We were thinking, 'The Fulkerson School.'"

Miles flashed a smile that Theresa knew was fake, his way of buying time in a difficult situation.

"Your name should certainly be prominent at some level," he said. "Naming the school after you might be difficult, given we're soliciting funds from our entire church body."

Frowns crossed their faces. Leta was the first to recover.

"How much do you see the entire project costing?"

Miles' mouth twisted as he did the math in his head.

"Four, five million, depending on the price of land. Maybe even six."

They didn't miss Theresa's gasp.

"What's wrong, sweetheart?"

Why was Leta Fulkerson calling her sweetheart?

"Miles," Theresa said slowly. "We just ended a five-million-dollar building program. Isn't this asking a lot of the congregation?"

"Didn't Pastor Miles tell you, sweetheart? Evan and I are contributing six-hundred thousand. That will take a lot of the financial pressure off the members."

"Well, that's certainly generous of you," Theresa started speaking before knowing for sure where she was going. What she wanted to say was that, if local gossip was right, the Fulkersons were worth somewhere in the range of twenty million. Six hundred grand was chump change, especially when they wanted the school named after them.

Instead she closed her mouth.

"I was kinda surprised by it," Big Mike said.

"It'll be hard for us." Megan overheard Adam's question. She and Brooke were tuned in as well. "Especially the home schooling part. I wouldn't want to pull Little Mike out of school for his senior year."

"Nah, there's no way." Big Mike said gruffly. "He has soccer, prom, graduation. It's asking too much."

"What about Brody?" Brooke said.

"We considered homeschooling years ago," Megan said, "but our work schedule is a killer through mid-October. We're not as busy in the winter, but how appropriate is it to cram a kid's entire schooling into five months?"

"Yeah," Big Mike said, "and I can't get by at the store without Megan, even during the slow season."

Adam fidgeted, glanced at the game, then spoke.

"The idea of homeschooling Jack just... bothers me. I mean, think of the fun times we had in school. He'll be missing that."

"What fun times?" Big Mike laughed. "I hated school."

"I do like the concept of a Christian education," Megan said. "I've seen the inside of these schools. There are a lot of Godless people; more than a few of them are teachers."

"Seriously, Megan, look around you. There are Godless people everywhere." Adam motioned to the surrounding seats. "Some of these people aren't Christians. It doesn't mean we should separate ourselves from them."

"But we're adults, Adam," Brooke said. "Jack's not ready to face the things he's going to deal with in school."

Adam breathed a sigh of exasperation. "It's kindergarten, Brooke. What's he going to face?"

"You'd be surprised," Megan said. "Some kids see things at home that they shouldn't have to see, then they go to school and talk about it."

"Your kids have turned out pretty well, Megan."

Big Mike nodded. "They have. It's taken a lot of work and a lot of influence. We watch who our kids hang out with, keep them busy at the store, limit down time."

"I still think homeschooling is a possibility," Brooke insisted. "I have the time, and I think with the church's support, I can do well for Jack."

They turned their attention back to the game as Lexington took a five-two lead. A critical error by phenom Levi Stafford set the stage for a three-run homer by the Lexington centerfielder.

"You know, Adam, its best to pray about what Pastor Miles is proposing. God'll give you the answers you're looking for." Brooke and Megan had moved on to other topics, and Big Mike kept his voice down.

Adam studied his friend. "Do you accept everything you hear at church?"

Big Mike's brow furrowed, his expression pensive.

"I wish I could say I do. I certainly try. The hardest is Pastor Miles' belief that our store should be closed on Sunday."

Adam's breath caught. "What?"

"Yeah. I see his point, but—"

"You do?"

"Yeah, it's what God wants, but we do a third of our business on Sunday, especially Sunday morning. People run by the market, grab some fresh fruit for breakfast, then later in the day on their way out of town, they stop again. It's our busiest day."

Adam could see this was an issue Big Mike was struggling with. Still, this was Mike and Megan they were talking about. The same people who went out of their way for others, whether they knew them or not. Truth be told, Big Mike Lusk was as close to his mental image of Jesus as anyone he knew.

The Orioles' series finale against the Texas Rangers was tied at one-all going into the bottom of the seventh. Stretched out on the large leather sofa, Miles' eyes had barely strayed from the large-screen television since lying down an hour before. Theresa, seated in a matching recliner, had tried to initiate conversation, but to no avail. Rather than try again, she opened her work files and began prepping for a jury trial the next morning in Georgetown, Delaware. A wise-guy DC kid had mouthed off when an Indian convenience-store cashier was too slow for his liking. One thing had led to another, and the kid shoved him against a wall of liquor bottles. The cashier's arm and back were bruised and a thousand dollars' worth of booze had crashed to the floor. Theresa expected a plea bargain, but none was offered, so tomorrow she would appear with the young man who she hoped would exhibit enough remorse to avoid thirty days in the Sussex County Jail.

It was seven-fifteen when Theresa heard the Orioles' announcer signing off. Miles was lying in the same position; his eyes closed. The rhythmic rising of his chest and barely audible snore told her it was better to let him sleep. If today was like most Sundays, he was out for the night. Theresa watched how much work and worry he put into preparing for Sundays, how he wanted everything to go off without a hitch. The result was usually the same, with Miles hitting the wall for fourteen hours of sleep, interrupted only when he moved from the couch to the bedroom.

Unfortunate, Theresa thought, because she wanted to talk more about his plans for a new school. Discussing it on the way home had been out of the question, as Miles was replaying the meeting with the Fulkersons. That was the way he did things, going over them in his mind again and again. Sometimes he would ask her opinion, but more often he kept his thoughts to himself.

It hadn't always been that way. Sunday afternoons in the early days of Surfside were filled with the kind of back-and-forth conversations she cherished. They would talk a little, pray a little, then talk some more. Back then, Miles was so concerned with doing everything in the Lord's time. She didn't sense that so much anymore, but then how could she, given the way he kept things to himself.

A few months before, Theresa had stopped by Surfside to take him to lunch. He was late getting back from a meeting, and Riley Wenger invited her into his office. Riley was Miles' hand-picked Executive Pastor, a man with deep Biblical understanding who served as an excellent counterbalance to Miles' broad-brush approach.

After a few moments of small talk, Riley had leaned forward and lowered his voice.

"Theresa, can I ask you something... it's personal, so feel free to say no."

Knowing Riley as she did, Theresa hadn't hesitated to allow him to continue.

Riley pursed his lips as he ran his hand over his bald pate. Theresa could see he was reluctant to continue.

"It's probably a silly question, but does Miles share much with you about Surfside?"

Theresa considered the question before answering.

"Well, I guess, Riley, but certainly not things that should remain confidential."

"No, no, I don't mean confidential stuff," Riley raised his hands. "I just mean... stuff."

"Well, Riley, I mean... sure... to a point... I guess."

Riley nodded.

"Is there something more to your question, Riley?"

Sitting back in his chair, Riley clasped his hands in front of his chin, exhaled, and continued.

"We just don't talk as much as we used to here at church. Sometimes I get worried."

Theresa knew exactly what he meant. Miles had become the same way at home, but she wasn't going to get that personal.

"Have you talked to Miles?"

Riley checked his watch, suddenly in a hurry to end the uncomfortable conversation.

"It's probably nothing. I mean Surfside is still growing in leaps and bounds."

The discussion ended when they heard Miles return and greet one of the church secretaries. Theresa hadn't forgotten the encounter, and it had left her feeling concerned for Miles. If he wasn't talking to Riley, who was as trustworthy as the day was long, and he wasn't talking to her, then... who?

On the way home from the game, Adam felt a pang of guilt about how little he had worked with Jack on the fundamentals of baseball. After the Lusks left, he took Jack to the backyard, and they attempted to play catch. It was quickly apparent that Jack needed a better glove than the plastic giveaway they'd gotten at Camden Yards last summer. For as much difficulty as he had catching the tennis balls they were playing with, Jack displayed a pretty good arm. Adam kept increasing the distance between them until Jack's throws started to bounce.

"You're going to be a pitcher."

"I want to play lacrosse like Jared," Jack said as another ball nicked off his glove and headed for the bushes that separated the back yard from their neighbors.

Jared Stover was Eric and Denise's fourteen-year-old son. He was a terrible lacrosse player.

You can't make a million dollars playing lacrosse, Adam wanted to say, but instead he headed toward the bushes to help Jack find the ball.

Once all tennis balls were accounted for, they returned to the house. Brooke had prepared grilled cheese sandwiches and coleslaw. Jack wolfed his down and headed into the living room. They heard the television come on.

Adam picked up his son's plate and took it to the dishwasher. He noticed the stack of mail on Brooke's desk. The letter addressed to *The Wife of Adam Overstreet* was still on top, unopened.

"I'll get to it tomorrow," Brooke said, following his gaze.

"It can wait," Adam said as he returned to the table. "Why mess with bills and mail on Sunday?"

"This *has* been a really fun day," Brooke said, coming up behind him and wrapping her arms around his waist. "Don't you just love Megan and Big Mike?"

"I do," Adam said, taking the last bite of his sandwich while Brooke swirled her glass of iced tea.

"I feel like God led us to the perfect place," she said. "Our home, our church, and The Group; they've all got it so together. I hope we can be as Godly as they are someday."

Adam sipped his tea.

"They're good people, but everybody has problems, honey. I think if you were to see inside Forrest and Julie's house, or the Lusks', or even Eric and Denise's house, you'd see problems."

"I don't think so," Brooke said. "I think they're at a point I hope we can get to someday."

Adam almost laughed, but caught himself. It came out as a snort.

"What?" Brooke looked at him closely.

Adam picked at the tablecloth. "Nobody has it all together. Nobody's perfect."

"I didn't say they were perfect."

Adam knew he was venturing down a path where he didn't want to go. Still, for whatever reason, he continued.

"Look at Big Mike. Did you know the church is leaning on him to close his store on Sundays? It's really tearing at him."

"Maybe he should," Brooke said quickly. "Everyone should observe the Sabbath."

"How about the people who work at the ballpark? How about the people who wait on us when we go out to lunch after church?"

Adam saw her stiffen. He asked himself if this discussion was worth it, then decided to end it if she did.

She didn't.

"Maybe our world would be better if we went back to observing the Sabbath. All businesses close. Ballplayers get the day off, everybody."

Adam laughed, a bit too loudly.

"Can you imagine what Ocean City would be like if every business on the boardwalk closed on Sunday? This would be a ghost town."

"And that's bad how?"

"For crying out loud, Brooke, this city is built on tourism. You can't pull the plug on the biggest day of the week."

Brooke sat her glass down with a thump and rose from the table.

"Well, I disagree," she said tersely. "Are you going to the membership meeting?"

"I'll stay here with Jack."

"They have childcare. Jack loves it."

"I'll still stay here. I have no desire to get involved with kicking people out of church."

"Suit yourself," Brooke said. "But I'm going."

MONDAY

Day Three

Adam had mastered completing his morning routine without waking Brooke or Jack. Up at six and out the door for a four-mile run across Ocean Highway and south along the beachfront. For most of June and July the sun was already above the horizon as he passed condos, hotels, and breakfast joints. Shortly before seven, he would quietly return home and whip up the protein shake that was his daily attempt at healthy eating. Then it was shave, shower, and out the door by seven-thirty. Most of his suits were variations of the same theme. Dark grays, navy blues, and the occasional brown. Sometimes he would coordinate jackets and slacks, but regardless of the combination, he always wore a tie.

Pausing at the bedroom door, he looked at Brooke, burrowed under the sheets. Stubbornly, he had immersed himself in television after she'd gotten home from church the night before, then stayed up long enough to ensure she would be asleep when he came to bed. He now wished he had made things right. Brooke was an idealist, always had been. She saw the silver lining in all situations, trusted everyone and anyone, and loved Adam with a tenderness he'd not experienced before her. Last night's disagreement would be forgotten, he was certain of that, but still he wished he'd made amends.

"Love you, sweetie," he whispered. She didn't budge. It would be another half hour before she'd stir.

Outside, Adam spotted the telltale signs that the birds in the trees in front of their house were awake and active. Winterset Drive was a great location, just off Coastal Highway and tucked into an enclave of similar homes. The lack of a garage and constant noise from Coastal Highway seemed a fair trade for a home two blocks from the Atlantic. It was those wintry mornings when Adam's routine had to be extended to scraping ice off his car, and mornings like this when the birds used his car for target practice, that he wished they could have spent a bit more for a house with a garage.

Still, it was a good life. They had a nice home that didn't overextend their finances. Brooke got to stay home with Jack. They could eat out now and then and have a decent social life. All in all, Adam was happy he'd bypassed opportunities in the Baltimore area to come to OC. His big-city colleagues who predicted the Eastern Shore would be career suicide couldn't have been more wrong.

Traffic was non-existent, and the drive to Ocean City Memorial took ten minutes. Most of the vacationers in town on Mondays had arrived the day before and were in for the week. At seven-forty they were still sleeping off the excitement of their first night at the beach.

Ocean City Memorial was located on a narrow parcel of land near Route 90, the northernmost of two highways that accessed Ocean City from the west. An amusement park had previously occupied the location. The sand-colored building was long and tapered on the end closest to Assawoman Bay. The bay view to the west was beautiful, while the northern view overlooked a trailer court. Peeks of the ocean were possible from the hospital's third floor. Adam pulled into the parking lot and located a spot far from the employee entrance. He had eliminated his predecessor's designated parking spot soon after arriving. Many viewed this as a sign that he didn't want preferential treatment. The truth was he didn't want people to be able to know when he was at work, out of the office, or on vacation.

Inside, he followed a series of hallways leading to the corner of the first floor that housed the executive offices. Unlike Annapolis, with its two dozen executives and directors, the executive team at Memorial consisted of Adam, a Chief Financial Officer, a Director of Human Resources, and four overworked secretaries. Memorial's Directors of Medicine and Nursing shared office space on the second floor, close to patient rooms.

"Good Morning, Adam."

Vicki Passwaters, a professionally dressed and coiffed blonde in her late fifties, had been Memorial's Executive Assistant for nine years. She had survived five CEOs, and Adam had liked her immediately and could tell she felt the same.

"Good weekend, Vicki?"

"Yes, it was, but not nearly as good as yours. Congratulations on the contract extension. I expect you to be here to fulfill the entire three years."

Adam grinned. "Melvin talked to you."

Vicki got up and gave him a quick hug.

"He called me Saturday afternoon, said to draw up the new contract and get it ready for his signature by Wednesday." When Vicki stepped back, Adam saw tears in her eyes, despite her attempt to conceal them.

"Don't be sad, Vicki. I'll do my best not to get in your way the next three years."

She beamed as she wiped her eyes.

"I'm happy they found somebody who really wants to be here. It's been so different since you arrived, more settled and less drama." She playfully punched his shoulder. "Try not to mess it up, okay?"

Adam patted her arm as he headed for his office. Within ten minutes he had checked the day's schedule, fired up his desktop computer, and started reviewing proposals for new appliances for the hospital cafeteria. The morning sailed by with only a few quick interruptions. At eleven-fifteen the reminder alarm on his computer sounded. Rotary started at noon. The forty-five-minute lead gave him a chance to make the rounds before heading out.

"Adam, Brooke called a couple minutes ago. She said she needed to speak to you right away." Vicki handed him the phone message as he was walking out. She looked at him quizzically. "Is everything okay? She sounded distressed."

Adam thought back to the night before. It wasn't like Brooke to carry ill feelings into the next day, but maybe this was the exception.

"All's good," he smiled, stuffing the message into his jacket pocket. "I'll call her on the way to Rotary."

Adam prided himself on being on a first-name basis with each of the two hundred and forty people who worked at Memorial. He made frequent walking rounds of the facility, stopping and chatting briefly with people he encountered. His rounds were initially viewed with suspicion by staff unaccustomed to seeing previous CEOs outside their office. Now, most thought nothing of it, allowing them to open up about whatever was on their minds. Occasionally, Adam would also stop by patient rooms for a quick hello and offer of assistance. Most mumbled their thanks and went back to whatever they were doing. A few had complaints that he would always follow up on. Then there were the lonely or afraid who needed someone to talk to. On a few occasions, he'd prayed with them. The rounds weren't part of his job description, but Adam would no more give them up than he would lunch.

And lunch on Monday meant Rotary at Marty's Dinette. The running joke was that every restaurant the North Ocean City Rotary settled on for its weekly noon meetings invariably went out of business. After the last closure, several restaurants said thanks, but no thanks to hosting the forty-five Rotarians. The exception was Marty's. Like its owner, Marty Lucchesi, Marty's was nothing fancy. The meeting room was cramped; the food plain, but good. The one thing they could count on was that Marty's Dinette would be there next week. It had operated continuously since 1977, staying open even during the slow winter months when many OC restaurants shut down.

Passing through Marty's main dining area and its decades-old Formica tables and red vinyl chairs, Adam entered the meeting room in back. Marty's daughter-in-law Carla passed him as he moved to his regular seat.

"Meat loaf, hon?"

"Yes, Carla, and mashed potatoes. Gravy over everything."

"You want gravy on your pie, hon?" Forrest Delaney was already in his seat, his falsetto a weak impression of Carla's cigarette-ravaged voice.

Adam offered his hand to Forrest, yanking it away just as his friend reached for it. He squeezed in next to Forrest, careful not to shake the spindly table and knock over water glasses. Forrest sat to Adam's right. On his left was Jimmy Crowder, an Ocean City slumlord and one of the funniest guys Adam had ever met.

"Send anyone to prison today, counselor?"

"No one who didn't deserve it." Most of Forrest's work with Talbot, White, and Enke took place in offices and boardrooms, yet Adam persisted with the same tired line.

Dinner plates arrived, and conversations jumped about as members talked among themselves. The North Ocean City Rotary was still a male-only organization, an arrangement most members would tell you they liked. It allowed the jokes to be a little bawdier and the laughter to be a little louder.

"I wonder where Tom is," Forrest said, nodding to the empty chair across the table where the school superintendent usually sat.

"After yesterday, who knows?" The words were barely out of Adam's mouth when Tom McIlhenny stomped through the door.

"Are your ears burning, Tom?" Forrest asked.

"My ears have been burning since yesterday morning," McIlhenny answered brusquely.

"Nah, I meant—"

"Can I talk to you guys after the meeting?" McIlhenny said, cutting Forrest off. "I need to blow off steam, maybe get some advice."

Adam and Forrest nodded their assent before steering the conversation to safer subjects.

#

Theresa stopped at a Burger King drive-through on her way from Georgetown to Rehoboth Beach. Her case that morning had started to run off the tracks when her client, the kid from DC, showed up late. If that wasn't enough, he angered Judge Mendoza by claiming that the confrontation with the Indian shopkeeper could have been avoided if the guy spoke better English. Theresa watched Judge Mendoza's eyes widen, then cloud over in a haze of fury. The son of Mexican immigrants, the Judge sent Theresa's client a clear message that his actions and stupidity would not be tolerated in Sussex County. The smirking know-it-all was escorted from the courthouse in chains, off to serve a thirty-day sentence at the Keogh-Dwyer Correctional Facility.

Talbot, White, and Enke had its headquarters in Salisbury, with satellite offices in Ocean City and Rehoboth Beach. Theresa divided her time between the two beach locations. Her court appearances were usually in Snow Hill or Salisbury on the Maryland side of the line, or in Georgetown for cases in Delaware. Occasional trips to the Eastern Shore of Virginia were thrown in for good measure. Some in the firm looked upon her vagabond schedule with disdain. She liked the diversity. Some of her best work came from representing poor Eastern Shore farmers and watermen being taken advantage of by one big system or another. She'd won some significant cases and gained the respect of the firm's partners.

As she was crossing the bridge into Rehoboth Beach, her phone rang. The display showed it was her father. A moment of dizziness came over her as she reached for the phone.

Relax. It's going to be okay.

Lord, your will be done, but please watch over Aunt Joy.

"Hi, Papa,"

"Hey, Cookie, how're you doing?"

"I'm fine. I've been in court all morning. Just got out a little bit ago. How's Aunt Joy?"

"She's gonna be fine. Doc Greene said she had a touch of pneumonia, but she's starting to get over it. He thought we'd be good to get back on the road in a few days."

Doc Greene, that old coot. Patience, Theresa.

"Papa, did Doc Greene perform any tests?"

"Sweetie, doctors like Doc Greene don't do tests. They just know."

"Promise you won't rush to get back to Washington, Papa?"

Theresa heard him chuckle.

"Course not, Cookie. Your Aunt Joy's all I got, except you and Miles."

Theresa relaxed.

"How is Miles? I haven't heard from him in a while."

Well, he's pushing his entire congregation to double-tithe for a new Christian school after they just finished double-tithing for a new church sanctuary. We don't really talk much.

"Miles is good, Papa. He sends his love and hopes you and Aunt Joy will come see us."

"We sure will, Cookie. Maybe this winter. I need to spend a few days at the university, anyway."

"I hope so, Papa. I love you."

"Aunt Joy and I love you too."

# # #

"Totally ambushed me, then called me out and made me look like a fool."

McIlhenny was hot, no doubt about it. He barely waited until the last of the Rotarians were out of the room before letting go. Adam had never seen him like this. He was usually unflappable.

"I don't think it's as big a thing as you're making it out to be." Forrest's tone was gentle, soothing. Adam imagined it worked well with clients. It wasn't working so well on Tom McIlhenny.

"Forrest, how can you say that?" McIlhenny's breathing was ragged, like he had just run a couple miles. His eyes were large, his pupils dilated. "The man put me in an impossible position."

"You had no idea it was coming?" Adam asked.

"None at all," the superintendent thundered. "He came by last Wednesday with questions about homeschool requirements. That was it. It was an ambush, Adam, I'm telling you."

"Perhaps you should visit with him," Forrest said. "Maybe if he understands where you're coming from, he'll reconsider."

McIlhenny's laugh was hollow.

"Word on the street is that the Fulkersons... you know who they are?"

Adam and Forrest nodded.

"Weirdos," McIlhenny continued. "Evan ran for school board, almost won, then started going off the deep end. Anyway, word is they're ready to pony up some significant cash to help jumpstart the campaign."

"I still think you need to have a face-to-face with Pastor Miles," Forrest said. "He likes you, Tom. He said so."

"Right before he threw me under the bus."

"What are you going to do, Tom?" Adam could only think of one thing, but maybe the superintendent had other ideas.

He didn't.

"I'm leaving the church. I can't keep going there and acting like I support an effort to pull students from my schools."

"Maybe it's just the lawyer in me," Forrest said, "but I still think there's some middle ground that can be reached."

"Any middle ground went out the window this morning," McIlhenny said testily as he reached into his briefcase. Pulling out a newspaper, he unfolded it to show Adam and Forrest the front page.

"This is the Monday *Daily Times*."

They gasped at the headline.

OC CHURCH SAYS 'ENOUGH' TO LOCAL SCHOOLS

A subheading, in slightly smaller font, went further:

Surfside Church to Open Christian School

"This is why I was late," McIlhenny said, folding the paper and returning it to his briefcase. "Three school board members have already called. I missed a call from another during the meeting."

"What are they saying?" Adam asked.

"They're mad," McIlhenny snapped. "They're mad at Miles Traynor. They're mad at Surfside." The superintendent stopped to gather himself before continuing, his voice quieter. "They're mad at me."

The meeting with Tom had chewed into a half-hour of Adam's afternoon schedule. While that frustrated him, it paled to what he felt for the school superintendent. They both answered to board members. Adam knew how fickle they could be, how their opinions could change like the wind. School board members were upset that their superintendent's church appeared to be out to get them. Tom, caught unaware, couldn't offer any reasonable explanations.

The buzzing of his cellphone brought Adam back to the moment, reminding him he hadn't gotten back to Brooke. He expected the call to be from her, but the display showed it was Vicki.

"Hey."

"Adam, are you coming back to the office soon?"

"I'm on my way. Tom McIlhenny and Forrest Delaney needed to visit with me after the meeting."

"Hurry back. Melvin got here twenty minutes ago. He's waiting in your office."

"What's up with Melvin?"

"I don't know," Vicki had lowered her voice. "I thought he wanted me to put your new contract together, but he didn't have it with him."

"Okay, Vicki. I'm pulling into the parking lot right now."

Adam was returning the phone to his pocket when he heard the beep indicating voicemail.

Checking the display, he saw he had missed four calls from Brooke. She would have to wait. Fortunately, she understood how his life could get busy quick.

Adam breezed into the waiting area. Vicki smiled uncertainly and nodded toward his office. He opened the door and found Melvin seated across from his desk.

"Good afternoon, Melvin." Adam shook off his sport coat and tossed it across an empty chair. "Hot day."

"Sure is." Melvin wasn't his usual chipper self. Adam could see it in his face and the way he hunched over, elbows on the desk. Adam pulled out his chair and sat across from the large man, waiting for him to speak first.

After a few uncomfortable moments, Melvin opened a file folder containing an envelope and two sheets of paper. One appeared to be an original, folded to fit the envelope. The other was a copy.

"I got this in the mail this morning and didn't know what to do with it. I finally decided to bring it here and show it to you."

"I'll be happy to look at it, Melvin," Adam said. "What is it?"

Melvin pulled out the photocopy and pushed it across the desk. Adam picked it up and examined it. Hand-written. Large, blocky text, most likely a man's handwriting. It looked familiar, but Adam couldn't be sure from where.

When he began reading, he thought his heart might stop.

Three weeks ago, at a medical meeting in St. Louis, your CEO, Adam Overstreet got drunk and spent the night with my wife Penny. Penny says she never wants to see him again, but I thought you should know the kind of person who works for you. Please don't reach out to me or my wife, as we are trying to save our marriage.
Zane Hardesty

The first time Adam read through the letter, he was filled with disbelief. The second time, anger. Then, reading it a third time, a creeping reality set in. This looked terrible. His mind cycled through a variety of responses. He raised his head to look at Melvin.

"Lies."

Melvin exhaled and appeared to relax.

"But why?"

"I wish I had an answer for you, Melvin. I will have an answer soon."

Melvin loosened his tie, sweat forming on his upper lip and forehead.

"Something like this could..." Melvin raised his hands, as if surrendering. "Do you even know this..." Picking up the letter, he scanned quickly. "Zane Hardesty?"

Taking a deep breath, Adam said, "Yes, well... not really. I don't know him, but I know Penny."

Melvin arched his eyebrows.

"I went to college with her. We dated for a year, but I can assure you there's nothing between us; there hasn't been since our junior year of college."

Adam felt like he was defending himself. It wasn't a good feeling.

"Did you see her at the conference her husband says this all...?"

"Yes, there and at least a couple conferences a year. Penny works for a company that sells medical billing software. She's usually at the product expos, making sales presentations, that sort of thing, but nothing like what her husband is describing happened."

Melvin was a good man, a gregarious happy sort, and Adam could see that dealing with this was difficult for him. More than anything, Adam wanted to get the meeting over so he could find out what Penny Hardesty and her husband were trying to do to him.

"Look, Adam," Melvin said, sitting forward and leaning his heavy girth on the desk. "As we said Saturday, you've proven yourself to be a good man and a good CEO. I believe you when you tell me nothing happened. You've never given us a reason not to trust you."

"I appreciate your support." Adam responded, then waited for Melvin to continue.

Melvin picked up the original of the letter. "For now we'll keep this between us. Do what you need to do to take care of it; maybe find out why this woman would say something happened when it didn't."

"Thanks, Melvin. I think I can have this issue resolved by the end of the day."

"That's not necessary," Melvin said, pulling himself from the chair, "but don't take too long. I feel bad about keeping it from the rest of the board."

Melvin huffed and puffed his way from the office, closing the door behind him. Adam slumped in his chair, picking up the file with the photocopy. The envelope caught his attention as it fell to the floor. Reaching for it, he noticed again that the handwriting looked familiar. Not just the style, but how it appeared on the envelope.

Vicki knocked, then opened the door. Adam barely heard her as he examined the envelope.

"Adam, Brooke is on the phone. She said she needs to speak to you immediately."

The Board President of Adam Overstreet's Hospital.

"Adam, you really need to take Brooke's call. She sounds almost hysterical."

The Wife of Adam Overstreet.

Adam snatched the phone from its cradle.

"Brooke, I'll be there in ten minutes."

###

"What are you doing up here on a Monday?" Theresa asked, sticking her head into Forrest's office.

"Traffic court. Wilmington guy trying to avoid losing his license."

"Thank goodness for the out-of-towners," Theresa said. "Their indiscretions are our bread and butter."

"Anybody else around?" Forrest asked.

"I've only been here a couple hours, but nobody that I know of. Clarice said Stovall had a trial this morning in Kent County, but nobody's seen him."

Talbot, White, and Enke's Rehoboth Beach location was less an office and more of a temporary stop-by for the bold few willing to venture into Delaware to handle cases. The office secretary, Clarice Chaney, answered the phones, kept the calendar, and doled out legal advice on the side.

"Have you seen this?" Forrest asked, holding up the *Daily Times*. Theresa grabbed it and scanned the headline. She whistled softly, then started to read. Forrest put his feet on his desk and sat back.

"What do you think?" Theresa said, laying the paper on the desk.

"I think your husband is an astute man of God. If he feels this is the direction in which we need to go, I support him."

Theresa's thoughts drifted to the faces she'd observed in church as Miles made his pronouncement.

"I guess we'll see how much support there really is."

"There's certainly one person who's not on board. I just got back from meeting with him."

"Tom McIlhenny?"

Forrest nodded. "He's leaving the church."

"I don't see that he has a choice if he wants to keep his job."

"He feels like he was ambushed," Forrest said.

"What do you think, Forrest?" Feeling her tone was a bit harsh, Theresa promised herself she'd rein it in.

Forrest raised his hands over his head and stretched.

"Theresa, I was a rebel for way too many years. I fought and kicked my way out of more churches than I can count. All I know is, since I made a choice to follow Pastor Miles, I've been more at peace than at any time in my adult life."

This disturbed Theresa. Forrest had been a lion in the courtroom when he started with the firm. Lately he'd become selective about what cases he took. Some colleagues whispered that he was going soft.

"It's not Miles you're supposed to follow Forrest. It's God."

"I know, I know, but Miles is the first pastor who's made me feel like I want to be part of the solution rather than part of the problem."

"And you think a new school in Ocean City will be a solution?"

Forrest pulled his feet from the desk and sat up straight.

"Are you cross-examining me, counselor?" he said with a grin.

"Not at all," Theresa said, heading for the door. "Just remember that there are lambs of God and lambs headed for slaughter. Keep your mind about you, Forrest. God gave you that big brain for a reason."

It was the longest ten minutes of his life.

Would Brooke be overcome by anguish, crying hysterically?

Would she have tossed his clothes into the front yard? That had happened to someone in their neighborhood recently.

Would the locks be changed?

Would she be packing suitcases?

As he pulled off Ocean Highway, Adam could see his front yard. There were no clothes littering the lawn.

He parked, approached the front door, and twisted the knob. It opened.

He heard no crying. There were no suitcases sitting beside the door.

He allowed himself a quick sigh of relief as Brooke tore into the room.

"We have to do something! She cannot get away with this!"

Brooke waved a single sheet of paper as she stomped toward him. Instinctively, Adam flinched, but relaxed when she hugged him tight.

"Look at this letter. I can't believe someone would write it."

"I've seen it."

Brooke loosened her embrace, stepped back, and looked into his eyes.

"How?"

"One just like it was sent to Melvin Proffer."

Brooke's eyes darkened. "Why that... they cannot mess with my husband like this!"

Adam felt adrenaline draining away that he hadn't realized had surfaced. A metallic taste in his mouth remained. His shirt had grown damp under the arms. He also felt guilty. How could he have thought Brooke would suspect anything? She knew he and Penny had dated, but that was a lifetime ago, long before they met.

"Where's Jack?" he asked, suddenly aware that the house seemed quiet.

"I asked Megan if she could watch him."

"Did you tell her...?"

"Of course not," Brooke said, stifling a laugh. "I would never want her to know about something like this." She headed into the living room, taking Adam's hand and pulling him along.

"Why would he do this?" she said. "Do you think there are problems?"

Adam hadn't given much thought to why Zane Hardesty sent the letter. His thinking centered on what he needed to do to get it taken care of.

"No idea, but I'm going to call Penny and find out."

"Call her from here," Brooke said, handing him the phone.

Adam pulled out his cellphone and flipped through the hundreds of contacts he'd accumulated over the years. Penny Hardesty was among them. Her title, Vice-President of Sales. The company, MFS Account Solutions. He started to dial the number, then stopped suddenly.

"I need to think through what I'm going to say."

"Let me talk to her," Brooke said disgustedly. "I know what I'll say."

Adam held onto the phone while he thought. Brooke went to the kitchen and brought back two glasses of iced tea.

After a sip of tea, he dialed.

"MFS. How may I direct your call?"

"Penny Hardesty please."

"Can I tell her who's calling."

Adam considered making up a name, then decided to be direct.

"Adam Overstreet."

"One moment."

One moment became several as orchestral variations of seventies rock classics droned through the receiver.

"Do you think she doesn't want to talk to you?"

"I wonder if she even knows her husband wrote the note."

A couple clicks, then a voice came on the line.

"Mr. Overstreet, Mrs. Hardesty is in a sales meeting. I gave her your message. She said she'll have to get back to you."

"Will you tell her it's urgent that I speak to her?"

"I will, sir, but she asked not to be disturbed. Her meeting should be over by four-thirty." Adam checked his watch. It was three-fifteen, two-fifteen in Kansas City. He clicked off and looked at Brooke.

"She's not going to call you back."

Adam sat back for a moment and played things through in his mind. Then, it hit him.

"I think I have a way to get her to talk." He explained the plan, which met with Brooke's enthusiastic support. They waited fifteen minutes, then he dialed the number again. He handed the phone to Brooke, staying close enough to listen.

"MFS. How may I direct your call?" Good, a different operator.

"Penny Hardesty please."

"Who may I say is calling?"

"Brooke Simmons." Adam nodded. Using her maiden name was a good idea.

"Ms. Simmons, can I tell Mrs. Hardesty why you're calling."

"I'm a nurse from Myrtle Beach. I was given Mrs. Hardesty's name. She might be able to help me."

"Thank you, Ms. Simmons. I'll see if Mrs. Hardesty's available."

Brooke looked at Adam and shrugged. She *was* a nurse, at least when she was working. She *was* from Myrtle Beach. She *was* given Penny Hardesty's name.

In a few moments, the operator was back.

"Ms. Simmons, please hold for Penny Hardesty. Thank you for calling MFS."

Brooke and Adam high-fived, then she handed him the phone.

"Good afternoon. This is Penny."

"And this is Adam."

Silence.

#

Miles answered his phone quickly. "Hey Tee, what's up?"

"Have you seen today's paper?"

"I scanned the online version."

"Tom McIlhenny is getting a lot of flak from his board."

"I don't see why," Miles tone was sharp. "He didn't do anything wrong."

Theresa sighed. "Have you considered reaching out to him?"

"Reach out to him why, Tee?" Miles asked defensively. Theresa figured he was more aware of the damage he'd done than he let on. "Churches open schools all the time. It's not personal. It's about doing good by our kids. Surely the school board can see that."

"Tom McIlhenny has supported you, supported Surfside, supported the fundraising efforts, and now he feels he has no alternative but to leave the church."

"How do you know all this?"

"Really, Miles. This isn't Chicago. People hear stuff."

The line went quiet. Miles took a deep breath.

"Look, give it a couple days and it'll blow over. If things are still tense by Thursday or Friday, I'll reach out to him."

"Miles, I hope you've thought this through. It's not just a matter of getting Surfside's congregation to raise more money. Something like this can polarize a small town like Ocean City."

"Good," he replied. "If that's the price we have to pay, then so be it. Look, I got somebody waiting to see me, so I gotta go. You might want to look at Romans 12:12. It says—"

"I know what it says," Theresa said angrily, hanging up the phone. There were times when Miles forgot which Traynor knew the Bible best. While he was knocking around Detroit as a kid, running numbers and shoplifting from convenience stores, she was learning the Bible from her parents and grandfather. Miles had fervor, but he still had a way to go to catch up with Theresa. When it came to Romans 12:12, well, that one was easy.

Be joyful in hope, patient in affliction, faithful in prayer.

When she finally spoke, Penny sounded angry.

"Wasn't Zane specific enough? Don't bother us."

"Penny, you're making this up. I don't know why, but you're messing up my life in the process."

"I have nothing to say to you, Adam. What happened, happened."

"Nothing happened."

"Are you saying we didn't go to the casino together?"

Adam's stomach roiled. He glanced at Brooke. Her face was stony.

"With a group of people. Not just you and me."

"Do you not remember having drinks at the casino and the hotel bar?"

Adam felt the perspiration reappear on his forehead. It was suddenly very stuffy.

"We had drinks, Penny, but there were other people there. Nothing happened."

"Look, Adam, I can't talk about this, now or ever. You need to get past me."

Brooke pulled away from Adam's side, looking at him like an unwelcome stranger.

"Penny, for crying out loud, why are you doing this?" he pleaded.

There was no answer. The line had gone dead.

TUESDAY

Day Four

Fifteen years after leaving her parents' Pennsylvania farm, Theresa remained an early riser. The clock showed five-forty. She glanced across the bed where Miles' sleeping form was buried under two blankets. Typical Miles. Even in summer he kept the temperature in the house at sixty-seven. Theresa found it an endearing trait. He'd grown up in a neighborhood where middle-of-the-night gunfire was common, but air conditioning wasn't. That meant open windows and the unending risk of violence entering the house. Being able to close the windows, turn up the A.C., and burrow under a pile of blankets was a luxury she never begrudged him.

She shuffled into the living room, grabbed her Bible, and fell into the recliner. She had made a promise to herself to read through the Old Testament this year. It was late July and she was breezing through Ecclesiastes. Finishing by Christmas wouldn't be a problem. As best she could remember, it would be the fifteenth time she'd read the Old Testament cover to cover. Miles was more of a New Testament preacher, but Theresa received comfort and encouragement from the prophets of old.

When she opened her Bible, the photograph she used for a bookmark fell into her lap. Papa and Mama at a party celebrating their twenty-fifth wedding anniversary. It was taken at the church in Cape Girardeau, Missouri, where Grandfather Meekins grew up. Despite a quarter-century of marriage, it was evident in the yellowed photo that a spark of love was alive and well. You could see it in the way Papa placed his hand over Mama's as they cut the anniversary cake, and the way she glanced at him from the corner of her eye. Barely in the photo, four-year-old Theresa beamed up at them. She had come to live with them seven months earlier, and it was their first family photograph.

Theresa pulled out her prayer list and moved through it line-by-line, occasionally crossing off a name as she went. At the end of the list she added Aunt Joy, said a special prayer for her, and was about to put the list aside when she had another thought. She picked up the pen and wrote.

Miles/Christian School

As always she spent a few moments praying for her husband; for God to continue to bring wisdom to him, and for herself, that God would allow her to be the wife that Miles deserved and needed.

Having lost track of time, she glanced around the room before her eyes settled on Miles' phone on the end table next to her. Six-thirty. Good, she still had plenty of time to get showered, dressed, and out of the house in time for the thirty-minute drive to Wicomico County Circuit Court. She was representing a forty-something woman whose husband sued for divorce more than two years ago. It shouldn't have dragged out this long, but the husband had attempted to hide a couple million in assets and at least two long-time girlfriends from the prying eyes of the court. A settlement was still possible, and knowing Judge James' reputation, the husband's attorney would be encouraging him to accept.

Theresa rarely said much at home about cases like this. Miles was adamantly opposed to her representing divorce clients, regardless of their situation. She got it. The Bible said divorce was sin. Still, as an attorney she felt some divorce laws were unjust. Men and women could work hard to attain a certain standard in life, only to have it ripped away. As an attorney, Theresa worked to make sure her clients got the representation they deserved. This was particularly important when kids were involved.

Miles' phone beeped as she returned it to the end table. Low battery, she thought, picking it up to take it to the charger in the bedroom. The battery bar on the display was at one-half. It was a text message. The sender was Brooke Overstreet. Theresa could only read the first few words.

Pastor Miles, I need to see you today. Adam has gotten into trouble and...

###

"Scott Ramirez, please. Adam Overstreet calling."

While waiting to be connected, Adam wracked his brain about the night in question. As best he could remember, a couple dozen people took the hotel shuttle to the casino. Once there, they went their separate ways. The group on the trip back to the hotel had dwindled to six. Five of them headed to the hotel bar for drinks.

"Hey, Adam, how ya' doing, buddy?"

Adam had rehearsed his answer several times. He was ready.

"Good to hear your voice, Scott, I'm in a bit of a spot actually."

"What's the problem, man?" Scott chuckled. "Vacationers crowding your favorite restaurant?"

"It's a lot more than that." Adam stood and moved away from his desk, stretching the cord as far as he could. The office door was solid oak, but he didn't want to risk Vicki hearing this conversation. "Can I trust you with something personal, Scott?"

"No question," Scott said, his voice serious. "You know you can."

It was a silly question. Scott was Executive Director of a hospital in Wheeling, West Virginia, close to where Adam grew up. Since meeting at a hospital leaders' convention two years ago, they'd talked and emailed often. Their friendship had deepened when Scott ran into some board discontent a few months before and called on Adam to help him navigate stormy seas. The man was as trustworthy as the day was long.

Adam took a deep breath and plunged in.

"You know Penny Hardesty, right?"

"Sales lady? We had drinks with her in her company suite in St. Louis."

"Yeah, that's her." Adam told Scott about the letters to Brooke and Melvin and the phone call the day before.

"I know you better than that, Adam. I'm sure your board does too."

"Right now, they don't know about this. Only Melvin, my board chairman... and Brooke. Melvin's giving me time to set this thing straight. That's where I need your help."

"I'm certainly willing to vouch for your character, man. You did a good turn for me when I ran into trouble."

"Well," Adam started slowly as he sorted out how to ask. "What I really need is someone who saw me in that suite and knows that I didn't do what Penny's husband is saying I did."

The line went quiet.

"Scott? You there?"

"Yeah, I'm here. I'm thinking back to that night. Adam, I left before you did. When I left, you and that loudmouth guy from Oklahoma City... what's his name?"

"Rodney Sharpe." Adam had Rodney's name and phone number in front of him. He was the next person he would be calling.

"Yeah, Rodney... when I left the two of you were still there, and Penny of course. I can certainly attest that I saw nothing happen during the time I was there."

"I was hoping..." Adam's voice trailed off as he considered what he was about to ask. Getting anything more would require Scott to change his story, something he would never ask his friend to do. But if Scott volunteered...

"Like I said, Adam, I'll write a letter, make a call, whatever it takes. During the time we were together, nothing happened. We had some drinks and that was it. Now you were wasted, but if anything were going to happen it would have more likely involved Rodney Sharpe. That guy's as slimy as a worm in the rain."

Ouch. Adam knew he'd had quite a bit to drink, but *wasted*?

"I appreciate it, Scott. I'll get back to you if I need some backup. Hopefully I can take care of this without pulling you in."

No sooner had he rung off when Vicki stuck her head in.

"Have a minute?"

Adam waved her in. He had gotten past her when he arrived, but she was too smart not to know something was up. He rarely closed his office door, yet today he'd been holed up for two hours.

"Is there anything I can help you with? You look like a lost child."

He'd hoped to take care of things without involving Vicki. It wasn't that he didn't trust her. Her honesty and loyalty were beyond reproach. More than anything, he didn't want her to be disappointed with him.

And that made him mad. Mad at Penny Hardesty and her husband for putting him in this position. Mad that he was having to spend time chasing alibis. Mad that he had to share the whole unsavory business with someone he respected as much as Scott Ramirez. Mad that he now had to call Rodney Sharpe, a greaseball most people went out of their way to avoid.

Adam glanced at Vicki, then stared at his desk, holding his head in his hands. For a second he thought he might cry. He lifted his head and hit the desk with his fist. Vicki jumped.

Then he told her everything.

#

"Howdy, Adam! What are you doing calling this old cowboy?"

Rodney Sharpe spoke with the twang of an Oklahoma plowboy, which always struck Adam as ridiculous. He had mentioned growing up in Ohio and attending college in Illinois. There was no way the accent was real. Still, he had to give the man credit. He had somehow gotten four promotions in five years in Oklahoma City, a fact that he shared proudly and often. He was Chief Operating Officer for one of the largest hospitals in the state, but that didn't change the fact that Rodney Sharpe was a difficult man to like.

"Rodney, how've you been?"

"Been good, bud. Real good. Second quarter numbers are coming out in a week, and I think that the boys here are gonna be real happy with ol' Rodney."

Did it all by yourself, huh, sport? Adam wanted to ask.

"Good to hear, Rodney. You're certainly making things happen down there."

"Ain't that the truth. Say, bud, how are things in... what's the name of that little town you live in?"

Keep your wits about you Adam. You might need this guy.

"Ocean City. Things are pretty good, but I've run into a problem and may need your help."

"Sure enough, Adam, you guys need a consultant? I do a little of that on the side, you know."

"Not so much a consultant, Rodney. It's a personal matter."

Rodney whistled. "Trouble at home? I hope fooling around with little ol' Penny in St. Louis didn't come back to bite you in the shorts."

Adam almost dropped the phone.

"What do you mean?" he asked sharply.

"What do I mean?" Rodney chuckled. "I've been trying to get alone with that one for years. She invites guys up for drinks, then picks the one she likes best. I thought it was me this year; I mean, nobody ever figured you to be a skirt chaser."

Adam felt nauseous.

"Rodney, I can assure you nothing like that happened."

"Okay, buddy, whatever you say. I'll back you to the hilt. Is the little lady giving you grief? Just have her call me."

"Penny's husband sent letters to my wife and my board chairman. He's saying things happened that didn't. I'm in a real bind."

"You don't usually drink that much do you, Adam?"

"Not really, why?"

"It shows. Between the drinks in the hotel bar and the drinks in Penny's suite, you got a little too much in ya. It happens, brother, trust me. It happens."

"I'm sure it does happen, but, in this case, I remember the night clearly."

Rodney snickered. Adam was starting to hate the sound of his condescending cackle.

"Okay then, what were you doing when I said I was leaving?"

"Uh..." Adam replayed the scene, realizing for the first time that it was hazy. "I was standing by the couch. You came over, shook my hand, and said something I don't remember."

"Yeah, I said the better man won tonight."

Then Adam remembered. It had seemed such a stupid thing for Rodney to say at the time. The meaning had been lost on him.

Rodney continued. "Then Penny walked me to the door. She patted my backside and said maybe another time Rodney. I need to talk over old times with my friend Adam."

#

The day had started badly and was becoming worse. Getting anything done was impossible. Vicki checked in frequently, but there was nothing she could do.

Adam forced himself to eat lunch in the hospital cafeteria. Two family practice doctors cornered him to complain about a rift with a group of OB doctors who were overruling their decisions. Adam had heard both sides of the story and was working with Memorial's Medical Director to iron out the issue. This was a conversation he would usually have gone out of his way to avoid, but given the other things going on in his life, dealing with a confrontation that didn't directly involve him was a relief.

Vicki handed Adam two phone messages when he returned to the office. He flinched when he glanced at them. Melvin Proffer and Brooke.

He called Melvin first, assuming he wanted an update. The board chairman answered on the second ring.

"Hello, Adam. Hold on a minute so I can step out."

Adam heard voices, then a door being closed.

"Sorry. I'm at the State House. The Senate is going back and forth on a piece of erosion legislation that'll impact our beaches if it passes."

"I didn't mean to interrupt. Want to talk later?"

"No, no. I was just wondering how you were doing."

"I've had better days, Melvin. I hoped to have this matter resolved, but I'm not getting any cooperation."

"Yeah, I know. I got an e-mail from the guy who sent the letter, Zane what's-his-name."

Adam didn't think his stomach could clinch up any more than it already was. He was wrong.

"He said you've been harassing his wife, and he wants it to stop; said you called several times yesterday, then some more this morning."

"Melvin, put yourself in my place," Adam's voice echoed off the office walls. "I have a woman and her husband saying I did something I didn't do. I'm trying to find out why, and I keep running into roadblocks. I'm going nuts here."

"Son, I hear you," Melvin's voice was softer. "This'll get worked out. What you can't do is go after her so aggressively that her husband takes out a restraining order."

Adam exhaled. "I'm sorry I snapped. I'll figure something out."

"Were there other people there who can vouch for you?"

"Maybe. I'm in contact with a couple guys." Adam stopped short of telling Melvin about his earlier conversations.

"We'll talk more tomorrow," Melvin said. "I have to get back inside."

Was Melvin in his corner? It seemed that way, but how much he could count on the chairman was yet to be determined. Melvin was, above all else, a politician of the first order. Ocean City had made him a wealthy man, but it was his political savvy that kept him at the top of the heap. Adam couldn't expect he would do anything to tarnish his image.

Adam returned to his desk and pulled the keyboard of the desktop computer close. He had just entered *wrongly accused* in the search bar when Vicki rang in.

"Brooke's on the phone. You want to take it?"

No! I want answers before I talk to her again.

"I'll take it."

"Hey, Brooke."

"Adam, how are you doing?"

"I've been better. Penny's husband threatened a restraining order if I try to contact her anymore."

"I think I have an answer that might help."

It felt like Brooke had turned on a light in a dark room. Adam hadn't felt anything close to hope since Penny hung up on him the afternoon before.

"I can use the help, honey. I'm struggling."

"I made an appointment with Pastor Miles. He'll see us at three-thirty."

Ugh.

"Brooke, what can he do for us?"

"He can give us spiritual guidance. Help us pray through this. Have you even prayed once since this came up?"

Adam was loath to admit he hadn't. Not once.

"Brooke, three-thirty is so early. I can't just leave work—"

"You can't leave work a couple hours early to save your marriage?" Brooke's sharp tone left no room for argument.

###

The more he thought about it, the more Adam felt the meeting with Pastor Miles might help. Once the pastor heard what had happened, once Adam laid out the entire story, he would undoubtedly help Brooke see he was telling the truth.

He rushed home in time to change into jeans and a comfortable shirt. Brooke was cool, but at least she was speaking. The support she'd demonstrated the afternoon before had waned as the evening progressed. At some point between one-thirty and three, the only ninety minutes Adam found sleep, she'd left their bed and taken refuge in Jack's room.

"Were you able to make any headway?" she asked on the drive to Surfside.

"Not really. It seems to be coming down to one of those my-word-versus-her-word things."

"Adam," Brooke's tone had acquired an edge. "It can only come down to that if the two of you were alone."

"Well, it's not—"

Brooke raised her hands, cutting him off. "Let's just wait until we can talk to Pastor Miles. I may not want to hear this twice."

Adam slumped in the car seat. "Brooke... honey, I need your support."

"And you have it," she said cautiously. "At least to the point where you chose to drink and go to a casino. You know my feelings on both those things."

Indeed, he did. In fact, when it came to gambling, the feelings were mutual. They had never stepped foot into the nearby casinos in Harrington or Dover. Adam had enjoyed playing blackjack in his early twenties, but the desire to lose money had long passed. Still, when the chance to get away from the monotony of the conference in St. Louis had presented itself, he hadn't declined.

###

Adam was relieved that the only person in the office was Pastor Miles' secretary, DeeDee, who was as discreet as the day was long. They were barely seated before Pastor Miles strolled out of his office, dressed in tennis whites. He shook Adam's hand and hugged Brooke.

"One of my pastor buddies kicks my butt every Tuesday at five," Miles explained, noticing Adam's appraisal of his attire.

Once they were seated in his large office, Miles asked permission to say a short prayer. After the amens, he turned to Adam.

"Brooke texted me during the night about some issues at an out-of-town conference. We talked a bit more on the phone today, but I want you to know, Adam, that I'm here for both of you. You're good members and supporters of Surfside and I want to be sure you receive the spiritual care you deserve."

There would be no small talk. Pastor Miles was getting down to business.

Adam nodded. "Thank you."

The pastor continued. "I've found the best way to work through marital problems is to be direct. I understand, Adam, that some things happened that you regret. Tell us the entire story. Don't leave anything out. This will help Brooke get her head around what happened and allow you to clear your conscience and move forward." Pastor Miles paused for a moment to let his request sink in.

"Is this acceptable?"

Again, Adam nodded. The pastor faced Brooke.

"And Brooke, I ask that you listen to Adam's explanation. No questions, no raised eyebrows, just listen. He deserves a chance to get this out, just like you deserve a chance to hear it. This might be hard, but I'll ask you to refrain from harsh judgments until everything's on the table."

"I can do that," Brooke said softly, reaching out and squeezing Adam's hand.

Adam took a deep breath and charged ahead.

"I'd been in meetings all day. Things wrapped up, and I didn't have dinner plans. It was my third time in St. Louis, and I'd learned it was better to tag along with a group, especially since I didn't have a car."

He took a breath and continued.

"A friend of mine, Scott Ramirez, asked if I wanted to join a group going to one of the riverboat casinos. Anything sounded better than hanging around the hotel, so I went along. The hotel shuttle took us. The group leader, if you could call her that, was Penny Hardesty. Penny is a sales rep for a company a lot of hospitals use. It wasn't uncommon for her to sponsor trips like this."

Brooke was looking at him, nodding her head almost imperceptibly.

"As Brooke is aware, I've known Penny since college. We dated for a year. It was a long time ago."

Pastor Miles leaned forward. Adam felt his eyes boring in.

"Like I said, it was a long time ago. Anyway, when we got to the casino, people went their own ways. Penny gave everybody fifty bucks in casino chips. I planned to give mine to Scott or one of the other people, but forgot. A half-hour passed, and I was walking around, looking in the shops and restaurants, then decided to try my luck at blackjack."

Adam smiled weakly, embarrassed to be sharing this with his pastor. His stomach was in knots. He thought about skipping some of what happened, then remembered Pastor Miles' admonition.

"I played blackjack for a while, how long I'm not sure, maybe an hour. I went through the fifty bucks pretty fast. They only had five-dollar tables."

That was stupid. Why did I add the part about the five-dollar tables, like they're going to need to know that the next time they go gambling in St. Louis?

"Anyway, I bought another fifty in chips and played some more. Eventually, Scott came to get me; he said the group was headed back. I cashed out and joined them on the hotel shuttle."

"You blew fifty dollars of our money?" Brooke's outburst was quickly shushed by Pastor Miles.

"Remember our agreement," he said, signaling Adam to continue.

"We got back to the hotel. It was dark, so it was probably nine or nine-thirty. A couple of people headed to their rooms, but most took Penny up on her offer of a free drink in the lobby.

"I had a beer and a mixed drink. Scott was sitting with me. So was a guy from Oklahoma, Rodney Sharpe. We talked hospital business. Scott was having some labor issues. Rodney didn't have any problems, but he thought he was good at solving everyone else's."

Adam expected at least a smile of commiseration. Brooke and Pastor Miles didn't offer any.

"So maybe another half-hour passed, and Penny invited us to her suite. Her company provides it so she can make presentations there. Anyway, Scott, Rodney, me, and a couple other people went up."

"Men and women?" Miles asked.

I thought we were holding our thoughts and comments to the end.

"Hmmm," Adam gave the appearance of trying to remember something that he knew fully well.

"All men, as best I remember."

Pastor Miles nodded. Brooke's lips were pursed. She tottered a bit in her chair.

"We went to the suite. It was a living room with two or three doors leading off to other rooms. Penny gave us some company information, a list of product updates, and offered us more to drink. Some of the guys had more, others didn't."

Seeing their expectant looks, Adam answered the unasked question.

"I had a couple more cocktails... and a beer. Definitely more than I should have had."

Brooke continued to watch him, but her posture had changed. She turned her body slightly away; less open, more guarded.

"It was close to eleven, and guys started leaving. Scott left with one of the guys I didn't know. Then somebody else left. Finally, it was just me, Rodney, and Penny.

"I was getting real sleepy, but the alcohol was keeping me planted in the chair I was sitting in. I made a couple moves to leave, but Penny started asking me questions. Stuff about the hospital, our revenue projections, that kind of thing. Eventually Rodney got up and said he was calling it a night."

The better man won tonight.

"I got up to follow him. Penny asked me to stay; she said she had something to go over with me."

Adam thought Brooke might start to hyperventilate. He figured it was best to press on.

"I thought she wanted to ask me some more questions about Memorial, but instead she asked if I ever thought about her."

Pastor Miles' breath caught. There were tears in Brooke's eyes. Adam reached for her hand, but she pulled it away.

"I told Penny I was married... happily married, and never thought about her in any way, shape, or form."

Pastor Miles relaxed slightly. Adam thought he detected a slight smile.

"The next thing I remember, I was waking up in my room – alone – with a fierce headache. I decided to skip the last couple meetings, so I slept a few more hours, then flew home."

The office was silent. Adam felt an immense sense of relief. Now perhaps Pastor Miles would help get things back on track.

"I know how hard that was to share," Pastor Miles said slowly. "And, Brooke, I know how hard it was to hear." Both nodded.

"Now before we go any further, Adam, I want to make sure we've covered everything. Is there any part of what happened that you've left out, either to protect yourself or to keep from hurting Brooke's feelings? If so, let's not hold back now."

Adam studied their faces, buying time. It would be easy enough to stop, probably better for everyone.

"Adam?" Pastor Miles pressed.

Just leave it.

"I sense there's more."

Was he that transparent?

"Well," Adam said slowly. "There is one more thing."

#

Theresa smelled him before she saw him.

It was just after seven when Miles came banging through the kitchen door. Theresa had gotten home early enough to prepare his favorite meal, and even over the aroma of sizzling bacon she smelled him.

"Whooo hooo! Breakfast for supper!"

Miles made a beeline for her, but Theresa held her arms out to ward off his sweaty embrace. He cackled loudly and pecked her on the cheek.

"How was tennis?"

"Terrible as always," Miles said, grabbing a piece of bacon and sticking it in his mouth. "Adrian had a bad day at work, and he took it out on me."

"I can tell," Theresa grinned, examining him from head to toe.

"Yeah, I'm pretty sweaty," Miles said. "I hope I don't stink."

They stared at one another for a moment, then Miles grinned broadly. It was a running joke that he couldn't smell his own stink.

"Get a shower before the drapes start to smell," Theresa said, shooing him away from the bacon. "I'll have dinner ready when you get done. Pancakes, bacon, and eggs."

Miles headed for the master bedroom, leaving behind a trail of funk. His love of breakfast food was, as many things in Miles' life, a result of his childhood. Early on he'd confided that most mornings at home had started with off-brand cereal. When money was scarce, the flakes were doused with water rather than milk. When there was no money at all, Miles and his siblings didn't get breakfast. After hearing the story, Theresa made breakfast for supper a couple times a month. Miles devoured it like a choice steak.

Fifteen minutes later they were seated at the kitchen table, tearing into the meal.

"How was your day?" Miles asked.

Theresa refrained from telling him about the divorce case.

"Good overall. I was in Salisbury most of the day. I got back to the office around three. How about yours?"

Miles wiped syrup from his face. "The Overstreets were in today. They have problems."

Theresa flashed back to the message on Miles' phone. Rather than ask, she waited him out. Confidentiality was a big thing in their professions, but they'd shared openly with each other over the years. Sometimes Miles could shed light on legal issues Theresa had missed. More often, she was able to help him think through things he was dealing with.

"Adam Overstreet got himself into a mess at a convention."

Theresa went from surprise to disbelief as Miles related the story. The Adam Overstreet she was hearing about was far from the one she knew from church and the occasional civic meeting, but she knew she shouldn't be surprised. People sometimes act differently away from home. She'd represented a man three years earlier who was fighting a wrongful termination suit. She had it in the bag until it came up during discovery that he'd used his company credit card to purchase dozens of adult movies in the hotels where he stayed for business trips. He was a well-respected husband and father of four. He was also a sex addict. Drinking and gambling didn't seem nearly as egregious.

Then Miles dropped the bomb.

"He kissed her?" Theresa felt her skin prickle.

"Adam says she kissed him, and he left immediately."

Theresa exhaled. "Thank goodness for that."

"I don't think he's telling the truth."

"Why? He was forthcoming with everything else." Theresa pushed her plate away and placed her arms on the table.

Miles shook his head. "Adam said he told the woman not to kiss him, then the next thing he remembered was waking up in his own bed." Miles hesitated before continuing, "Six hours later."

"He blacked out?"

Miles nodded.

"And you think he's making it up?"

Miles shrugged. "I'm not supposed to make judgment calls, but I think there's a lot more he's not saying."

Theresa cupped her hands around her water glass. She felt terrible for Brooke Overstreet, but also felt something for Adam. It was a tough spot, and oftentimes people in similar situations found themselves guilty until proven innocent. Based on what Miles said, Adam didn't have many avenues left.

"I wish you'd been there, Tee. You always have a way of seeing through things."

Pastor Miles hadn't believed him.

He didn't say as much, but Adam could read it in his body language. Everything changed after he admitted to the kiss. Pastor Miles angled his chair toward Brooke, as if he were surreptitiously moving to offer support. The way he took her hand in his when they were leaving; it was all there.

Thankfully, Pastor Miles intervened on his behalf when Brooke insisted she wanted him out of the house until things were sorted out. There would be little chance to resolve things if they were apart, he'd said. It would hurt Jack, too.

They'd returned home, sent the sitter on her way, and tried to act as normal as they could in front of Jack. Brooke had rebuffed Adam's attempts at anything more than basic conversation. He was unsure if Jack noticed the frostiness, but doubted it. Jack was pretty wrapped up in Jack.

It was only after they tucked him in for the night, turned off the light, and closed the door that the charade ceased.

"Is there anything you need from the bedroom?" Brooke's tone was drained of emotion. Adam went into the closet of the master suite and took out a couple suits, underwear, and other incidentals. Brooke stood by the door, waiting for him to finish. As he passed her on the way out, she'd shrunk back against the wall. Outside the bedroom door, Adam turned back to face her.

"Brooke, I promise I'll make—"

The door closed in his face.

WEDNESDAY

Day Five

Usually Adam would marvel at the view as he crossed Maryland's Chesapeake Bay Bridge. For once, however, the choppy blue expanse dotted by sailboats, yachts, and the occasional Navy vessel went unnoticed. He was on a mission to close the 145-mile gap between Ocean City and Baltimore as quickly as possible.

The idea came in the night. Many ideas had come to him in the night; some rational, others as far-flung as catching a plane out of the country. In the end, he'd decided to take a day off and go see Jasmine Fleece, a Baltimore attorney of some repute whose firm represented Adam's former employer.

There were certainly any number of qualified attorneys on the Eastern Shore, but the Delmarva Peninsula was a small, tight-knit world, and the last thing Adam needed was for word to get around that he was consulting a lawyer. He'd considered calling Forrest Delaney, but quickly discounted it. Forrest was a friend. It needed to stay it that way.

Jasmine had answered her cellphone at seven-twenty and told him she had an hour available just before lunch if he wanted to make the trip. Three years had passed since he last visited the firm, and he took a couple of wrong turns before locating the North Charles Street address.

A secretary he vaguely remembered escorted him to Jasmine's office. In the past, he would have teased her about how appropriate her last name was for the legal profession, something she'd undoubtedly heard often. Today there would be no levity. Jasmine Fleece was good, and she was expensive, and Adam would be footing the bill.

Barely five feet tall, the stocky but stylish fifty-something lawyer showed Adam to two chairs arranged at right angles in a corner of her office. Once seated, he wasted no time pouring out his story. Ten minutes later, he sat back, exhausted from the effort. He expected Jasmine to ask if there had been more than the single kiss, but she surprised him.

"What do you want from me?"

Adam looked at her curiously.

She leaned forward, laying aside her legal pad.

"You've told me what happened. What do you want me to do?"

"Make it go away."

"Adam, I can't make something that really happened go away. This isn't a traffic ticket."

"Yeah, but it's the things that didn't happen that are screwing up my life. My wife is struggling to believe me. My board will struggle, too, if it gets that far."

Jasmine put the tip of her pen in her mouth and stared at a spot on the wall, just over Adam's shoulder.

"You could sue her for slander, but that would cost a bundle and be hard to win."

Adam shook his head. "I don't want a lawsuit. I just want everything straightened out."

"You can't force her to take a lie detector test. You could take one, but there are questions about reliability."

"Can we file suit without it becoming public?"

Jasmine shook her head. "Unfortunately, no. The filing will be public, as would the trial."

Adam's cheeks burned, the frustration was becoming overwhelming. Jasmine could see it too. She reached over and squeezed his hand.

"Let me call Mrs. Hardesty. I'll try to scare her into backing down. I'll toss some surefire legal terms at her: slander, defamation of character, that kind of thing. If that doesn't do the trick, I'll threaten to talk to her employer. That might get us someplace."

Adam's heart quickened. Another ray of hope, perhaps?

"Thank you, Jasmine. I'd like that."

It was noon when he left Jasmine's office. With no desire to return to work and Brooke not speaking to him, he started walking. Cutting across Fayette to Light Street he headed south. Ten minutes later he passed the *USS Constellation* at Baltimore's Inner

Harbor. Following the harbor walkway a few more minutes brought him to Charm City Eatery, a favorite of his and Brooke's when they lived in Annapolis.

Once seated, Adam looked over a menu that had changed little in the months since he'd been there last. A college-age waitress approached.

"Welcome to Charm City Eatery. Can I get you something to drink? Some wine perhaps, or a beer?"

Adam's mouth watered at the thought of a cold beer. It was in the upper eighties, and the temperature and several-block walk had left him with a real thirst.

Two hours into the meeting and Theresa hadn't said a word.

Miles had asked her to attend the weekly meeting of the Surfside pastoral team. She didn't much care for staff meetings, a dislike shaped by the monthly free-for-alls that the managing partners of her firm called team-building. But as a favor to her husband, she had agreed to attend and help review contracts for a parcel of West Ocean City real estate that Miles hoped would be the future home of Surfside's Christian School.

Staying in the background was her way. It wasn't that she was anti-social. She'd laughed often, especially when Derby Hatfield spoke. Derby was funny in a biting, sarcastic way that sent her into hysterics.

Executive Pastor Riley Wenger interjected a comment here and there, but was content to let Miles and Derby do most of the talking. A decade older than the others, Riley was more of a thinker. On the occasions when he had something to say, Miles was quick to give him the floor.

Derby sat down after a spot-on imitation of an Ocean City councilman's distinctive waddle. Congregants would have been surprised at how their pastoral team let their hair down behind closed doors. At no point would they ever say or do anything that would be dishonorable to God. Miles would've put a stop to that immediately, though Derby's waddle was pushing the envelope.

When they reached the agenda item titled *Pastoral Concerns,* Miles related the entire saga of Adam and Brooke Overstreet, a conversation that surprised and troubled Theresa.

"I can't imagine anything happened," Derby said, his concern evident. "I know Adam pretty well. The dude's madly in love with his wife."

"Don't underestimate the power of strong drink," Miles said.

"The man drank enough to pass out," Riley spoke for the first time. "That means he was drinking some serious booze."

"Not necessarily," Derby said. "For some people it doesn't take a lot."

Miles turned to Theresa.

"Do you care to add anything, Tee?"

"Innocent until proven guilty."

"I don't agree," Riley said. "I like Adam, too. But he got himself into this situation. The gambling is one thing, and we don't want to overlook it, but he drank to a point where he lost control. I tend to believe the woman's story that the intimacy went beyond kissing."

"Me too," Miles said. "As much as it pains me, I think there was more."

Theresa was about to come out of her seat. She took a breath to calm down. "So you pronounce him guilty and that's it?"

Miles shook his head. "It's just us here, Tee. We're not pronouncing anything. We need to help this family, and the best way to do it is to get Adam to take responsibility for his actions."

"What if he didn't—"

Miles looked at her sharply, raising his hand.

"I visited with Brooke earlier today. She's crushed. It's all I can do to keep her from throwing him out."

"What happens next?" Derby asked.

"I suggested they meet with their small group, tell them everything, and get their support."

Are you sure it won't get all over town? Theresa wanted to ask, but smarting from Miles' rebuke, she remained mute.

"What about confidentiality?" Riley asked the question for her.

"It's a good group," Miles said. "Eric Stover, Denise, the Lusks, Forrest and Julie Delaney." He turned to Theresa. "You work with Forrest, sweetheart. He'll be solid, don't you think?"

Sweetheart? Miles knew cutting her off earlier was a mistake.

"He'll be fine," she said quietly.

#

Feeling guilty for being away all day, Adam stopped by the hospital and put in a couple hours. It was seven when he got home. After another game of catch with Jack in the dusky light of the backyard, they watched an hour of television, Jack close by his side. Brooke remained in the room with them, joining the conversation, friendlier than the night before. Any illusions of a breakthrough were dashed, however, once Jack was in bed.

"Do you need anything out of the bedroom?"

"I went to see a lawyer friend in Baltimore."

Adam thought he saw a flash of hope in her eyes.

"What did he say?"

"She. Jasmine Fleece. Her firm did a lot of work for us in Annapolis. She's going to contact Penny. Try to get her to tell the truth."

Tears welled in her eyes. She wiped them away quickly. Being angry was as unnatural for her as flying would be for an elephant. Seeing an opening, he forged ahead.

"I ate lunch at Charm City Eatery. A lot of memories there."

Brooke smiled faintly, then caught herself.

"Did you have a beer? Maybe a few?"

Ouch. He hadn't seen that coming.

"I thought about it," he replied, smiling shyly. "I stuck to tea."

Brooke stared at him for a moment before backing into their bedroom.

"If only you'd stuck to tea in St. Louis," she said, closing the door.

###

"Late for someone to be stopping by," Miles said, pulling himself from the recliner at the sound of the doorbell. Theresa put aside the magazine she was reading and turned down the television as the ten o'clock news was coming on.

"Come back to the living room, Tom." Theresa stood as Miles returned, Tom McIlhenny following. The superintendent looked as if he'd just boxed fifteen rounds.

"Hi, Dr. McIlhenny," Theresa said. "Miles, I'll leave you two alone."

"That's not necessary, Mrs. Traynor," McIlhenny said. "I won't be here long."

Miles offered the superintendent a chair. Theresa sat on the sofa and took a long look at McIlhenny. His friendly, self-assured aura was missing. He had a haunted look as he slumped in the chair, nervously rocking back and forth.

"Pastor, you did me a bad turn last Sunday when you railed against our schools."

Miles grew stiff. He wasn't used to being put on the spot, particularly the last couple years as Surfside had grown, and his decisions seemed without fault.

"Tom, you know how I feel about you. Nothing I said was personal. I thought I made that clear."

"Tell that to my school board. I just left an emergency meeting, and they've got me in their crosshairs."

"About what?"

"Between Sunday and today, eleven families pulled their kids out of school to begin homeschooling. That's thirty-one students in four days. They all attend Surfside."

"C'mon, Tom," Miles laughed nervously. "Thirty kids are a drop in the bucket. You won't even miss them."

"Perhaps, but if others follow your directive, we could lose as many as seven hundred. That's ten percent of our student body. Do you have any idea what that would do to our public schools, Pastor Traynor?"

"Wait a minute, Tom." Miles shook his head. "I never gave a directive. That's your word. People are free to make their own choices."

"Is that what you really think?" McIlhenny leaned forward, his eyes boring into Miles. "With all due respect, I think you underestimate your authority."

Miles waved his hand dismissively. "I think you're *overestimating* my authority. People don't jump because I say jump." He turned to Theresa. "Tee, help Tom understand that he's worrying unnecessarily."

Theresa focused her attention on McIlhenny.

"Thirty kids already?"

"Thirty-one. Fourteen today."

"What's that mean to the school district, Dr. McIlhenny?"

McIlhenny rubbed his temples. "Just the kids that left this week cost us over thirty-thousand dollars in state aid. That's not much, but when you consider that as many as seven hundred could leave, we're talking serious fund shortages. We would have to cut staff, extracurricular programs, maybe a lot more."

McIlhenny took a breath. "But there's more to it than that. The school board looks at the bottom line, but I look at the children. There are parents who've got no business homeschooling their kids. They work long hours or struggle academically themselves. Their kids will pay."

"It's only until we get our school off the ground, Tom. We'll do good by the kids."

"Pastor, what do you know about operating a school?"

Miles was taken aback by McIlhenny's frankness.

"I understand the role God should be taking in our children's lives, and, quite frankly, Tom, your schools fall short in that area."

The air seemed to have been sucked from the room. McIlhenny got to his feet.

"I won't be returning to Surfside. It pains me to say that. I've benefitted greatly from the friendships I've made there. In this case, however, you're wrong. You're making decisions without regard to the consequences. Children will be hurt because of what you said Sunday morning. I can't stand by and watch that happen."

Miles stood, mouth agape as the superintendent let himself out.

"Do you believe him?" Miles said, staring at the front door. "All he's worried about is his precious job."

"He made some good points."

Miles wheeled around. "How can it be wrong to want a quality Christian education? Tell me that, Tee. Tell me."

"It's not wrong, Miles, it's just... you need to consider the effects of what you say. Dr. McIlhenny wasn't off base when he called it a directive. Did you look around when you started talking about homeschooling and another round of double-tithing? People were scared, Miles."

A fury flashed across his face, but he pushed it away.

"People need to spend more time on their knees and less time second-guessing God."

Theresa picked up her magazine and headed for the bedroom.

"Is it God, Miles? Is it really?"

FRIDAY

Day Seven

Adam, I took Jack to the National Zoo. We'll stay overnight and be back in time for small group tomorrow at noon. It's important that you be there too. Pastor Miles thinks we should talk to The Group and get their input and support. Eric arranged for a sitter so we can have everyone over here. Brooke.

Adam read the note a second time, went to the bathroom, and threw up.

The past two days had been more wait-and-see. He'd tried to get back into a routine at work, but it was difficult. It felt at times as if he were watching a reality TV show in which he was the star.

And now he was going to have to tell his story once again, this time to The Group. How many times had he already given his account?

There was Brooke, of course.

And Melvin, though only part of the story.

And Pastor Miles.

And Vicki.

And Scott Ramirez.

And Rodney Sharpe.

And Jasmine Fleece.

And tomorrow night he would recount it again, for the Lusks, the Delaneys, and the Stovers.

It was almost enough to make him give up. Just say it happened. Do what it took to make it right. Move on.

But could they move on? Could Brooke? Could Memorial's Board of Directors?

He didn't think Brooke would leave him, but that didn't mean things could be like before. There had never been a divorce in her family, and Adam doubted she would want to be the first.

Still, there was one problem.

He didn't do it.

He was certain of it.

If he could only account for those missing hours.

Glancing out the back window, he saw the scruffy lawn. It had been over a week since he mowed, back before all of this started.

After changing into old shorts and a t-shirt, he was going out the kitchen door when he had another thought. It was a little after six. Brooke and Jack would have left the zoo by now. They were probably staying with Brooke's college friend, Lindy. Retrieving his phone from the kitchen, he punched in Brooke's cell number. It clicked to voicemail.

"Hi, it's me. Just calling to make sure you made it to DC okay. Tell Jack I love him and I'll see him tomorrow." Adam was about to click off when he had another thought. He placed the phone back up to his ear.

"I love you, Brooke."

The phone was in his pocket for less than ten seconds when it rang.

The call was from the 667-area code, more common to the Baltimore area.

"Adam, it's Jasmine Fleece."

"Jasmine. I figured I wouldn't hear from you until next week."

"I know it's after hours and you're probably home with your family, but I have some information."

Adam felt shaky. He willed himself not to get too hopeful, but it was hard.

"I talked with Mrs. Hardesty yesterday. It was a good conversation. I told her about your difficulties, about the trouble at work and at home, and asked if there was anything she could do to help."

The shakiness increased. "And she said?"

"Somehow, she and I connected. She seemed genuinely sympathetic. Her exact words were, 'I wish I hadn't gotten Adam into this.'"

Adam sat down heavily on the sofa. Was the end in sight?

"I asked her to help me set things straight. She said she wanted to, but couldn't talk openly at work. She asked if I would call her back today."

"And you did?"

"Several times, but it was just an hour ago that she returned my call."

"Did she admit that nothing happened?"

"Adam, it was the strangest thing," Jasmine said. "When we talked today, Mrs. Hardesty's tone was completely different, like I was talking to another person."

His heart sinking, Adam croaked, "Go on."

"It's like she was reading from a script. She said you took advantage of her and stayed most of the night."

"That did not happen!"

"She said that you need to accept the truth and move on."

"The truth? Jasmine, the truth—"

"And, Adam, I have to tell you something else. During the conversation today, I had a feeling there was someone else on the line. Perhaps Mr. Hardesty, but I don't know. It was just a feeling, but at times it sounded like two different people breathing into the phone."

The tears came faster than he could control them.

"I didn't do it," he sobbed, disconnecting the call.

SATURDAY

Day Eight

Miles was ticked. It showed in his body language when he returned from the Saturday morning Elders' meeting. He glared at Theresa as he stomped past, but said nothing. She went back to the work files she'd been reviewing at the kitchen table. Twenty minutes later, as the hall clock chimed eleven times, he reentered the kitchen and stood beside the table. Peripherally, she could see him glowering at her.

"Tee, why don't you help me out more?"

Theresa took a deep breath and looked up, preparing herself for the latest chapter of an on-going disagreement.

"We've discussed this Miles. I—"

"Do you know how it looks when my own wife won't come to Women's Outreach meetings?"

Theresa knew there was no point in arguing, so she said nothing.

117

"I'll tell you how it looks – bad! For you and for me."

"Miles, lower your voice."

"I don't get it," he snapped. "We got ourselves a church that's growing faster than anyone can imagine. I'm working sixty hours a week, and I can't even get you to come to a two-hour meeting on Saturday morning."

Remaining calm, she stood and faced him.

"We had this conversation years ago. Do you remember what you said then?"

"Different time, Theresa."

"Same us, Miles. Do you remember what you said?"

He flinched. He remembered.

"Women's Outreach is getting by fine without me."

Miles raised his hands. "Yeah, but... oh, never mind. I'm sorry, Tee. It's not you that's got me upset."

"No," Theresa said, "I'm only the recipient of your ill-mood."

His shoulders slumped. His voice grew quieter.

"I'm sorry. Really."

Theresa returned to her work, knowing this conversation wasn't over.

"Melody Atkins is causing trouble."

"Melody, the praise team member?"

"Yeah, she got fired for stealing from Splash Down Park. Turns out she had a sick kid and no insurance. The company dropped the charges and hired her back."

"That happened fast."

"This past Wednesday. Now the paper has picked up the story. She's talking about how her company is giving her a second chance, but her church turned its back on her."

"Oh, no, Miles. I remember her prayer request some time ago, but hadn't heard anything else."

"That's just it. The kid was sick a year ago. It's just the last several months that the bills came due and she started taking money."

"Didn't she explain that to you?"

Miles hung his head. "Maybe she tried."

"Maybe?"

"People are always offering excuses for the stuff they do. Who do you believe?"

Theresa grabbed his hand.

"If you remember nothing else from law school, at least remember there are two versions of the truth. The actual truth is someplace in between."

"Tee, if I spent all my time chasing alibis, there'd be no time for the important stuff. I'd be preaching to the same fifty people every week." Miles took a glass from the cupboard and filled it with water. When he turned around, she was watching him.

"Sometimes maybe getting bigger isn't the best thing," she said. "Not when people get hurt."

#

The Group knew something was up. They didn't usually move inside from the beach until fall. Forrest and Julie arrived first. Adam greeted them quietly. Julie's hug was a little firmer, like she knew he was going through tough times. Adam showed them into the living room, noticing for the first time that the place was a mess. He hurriedly picked up a few of Jack's toys, then went to answer the door. Megan and Big Mike came with snacks, and when Adam couldn't find a serving tray, Megan shooed him from the kitchen.

Still no Brooke.

The Stovers showed up right at noon. Both were tight-lipped, making Adam wonder if they'd already heard.

"Brooke should be here any moment," Adam said as the others grabbed snacks and made themselves comfortable in chairs or on the living room floor. Conversation was strained. Big Mike shared a story about a competitor who was the target of an attempted stick-up as he'd left work the night before. The group oohed and aahed; violent crime was rarely an issue in Ocean City, even during the busy summer months.

Twenty-minutes later, with the conversation starting to wane, Adam forged ahead.

"I'm sorry for bringing you here. Something's happened that Pastor Miles feels I should share with you." Adam took a deep breath and continued. "Brooke is supposed to be here. She spent the night in DC with a friend. I hope she's coming. Given what's happened, she may not."

"I'm here." Brooke had come through the front door in time to hear Adam's last sentence. She tossed her purse aside and entered the room.

"Traffic on the Bay Bridge was stopped." Murmurs of understanding for something everyone had experienced.

Brooke glanced around for a place to sit. Her eyes fell on the open seat on the sofa next to Adam before choosing a spot on the floor next to Denise Stover. Denise grabbed her hand.

"I dropped Jack off at your house," she said to Denise.

The Group turned their attention to Adam. He considered standing, but wasn't sure his legs would support him as he unpacked his dilemma again. Remaining seated, he recounted the day in St. Louis and Penny's accusations, watching the faces around him register a myriad of feelings.

"I'm ashamed of my actions and sorry for the hurt they've caused Brooke. I know I left that room after she kissed me. I know it. I remember feeling that it was wrong, and I left. How I got back to my room I don't remember. But I know that nothing more happened."

No one spoke. The only sound was Brooke's haggard breathing as she fought to keep her composure. Denise was hugging her. No one moved toward Adam.

Big Mike broke the silence.

"Let's go see this woman. She needs to tell the truth. I'll go."

"I will too." Adam was surprised that Julie Delaney spoke up. He didn't know her as well as the rest of The Group. Julie was shy, and Adam had wondered how she was so successful selling real estate.

Even after Adam cautioned them about the problems he and Brooke had experienced when they called Penny, and the about-face she had done on the phone with Jasmine Fleece, they were willing to go. After feeling so alone the past week, their support touched him.

"We need to get this straightened out," Big Mike said. "Adam, you've got my support." Megan and the Delaneys echoed the sentiment.

"You guys haven't said much," Forrest said to Eric and Denise.

"You know I love you, brother," Eric said to Adam. "You're in a bind and we need to help. Still, I want to make sure this isn't part of a bigger problem."

"What do you mean?" Big Mike asked.

"Drinking, gambling, going to women's hotel rooms—"

"Hotel suite," Julie interjected. "There's a difference."

"Semantics, Julie." Denise Stover said coolly.

"Adam, do you have a drinking problem?" Usually jovial, Eric wasn't beating around the bush.

"No."

"You passed out," Denise said pointedly.

"I did. That's never happened before. There's no doubt I drank too much that night, but you guys know me."

"I thought we did," Denise replied.

Eric leaned forward, his eyes bearing into Adam's. "What about Surfside's member covenant? You signed it."

Adam felt sweat forming on his forehead.

"It says you won't consume alcohol," Denise said.

"To excess," Big Mike said loudly. "Nobody says I can't have a beer once in a while."

"Look, Eric," Adam felt it was time to step in. "I failed. I drank too much. I gambled. I put myself in a position that brought shame upon me and hurt Brooke."

"You're right," Denise said, pulling Brooke close. "You've hurt your wife badly."

"But you didn't commit adultery," Julie said, getting to her feet. "We owe it to Adam to help him prove his innocence. This could cost him everything. I say let's go to Kansas City and see if we can appeal to this woman."

"Fine," Denise said. "I just don't want us to get so involved in helping Adam prove his innocence that we gloss over the things he's done. Adam, you've sinned. You violated the church covenant. I, for one, cannot just let that slide."

"For crying out loud, Denise, who's glossing over it?" Megan said sharply. "What do you want? Should we burn him at the stake?"

"That'll be for the church leaders to decide," Denise said brusquely, glancing at her husband. Adam got the message. He was sure the others did too. Eric Stover was a church elder, one of the leaders who would ultimately decide how and if he should be disciplined.

"I'm willing to take whatever discipline is recommended," Adam said quietly. "I signed the covenant, and I'll abide by it, but I won't be disciplined for something I didn't do."

"That's all we can ask," Brooke said. "That's all I ask." Then, looking at her husband, she continued, "I want my marriage."

SUNDAY

Day Nine

Jack spent breakfast describing the animals he'd seen at the National Zoo. Adam reveled in his son's animated account of sea lions playing in their pool and his excitement at seeing koala bears. Though they'd continued sleeping in separate rooms, Brooke had gotten up and made breakfast. She seemed more relaxed, more her normal self. Perhaps it was the planned trip to Kansas City. Julie Delaney, Big Mike, and Adam planned to leave the next morning.

While dressing for church, Adam's phone rang.

"Mr. Overstreet, good morning, this is Gabe Slattery from the Daily Times."

"We already subscribe, but thanks." Adam started to disconnect, but the caller spoke first.

"No, Mr. Overstreet, I'm in the newsroom."

Adam felt a knot in his stomach.

"Mr. Overstreet, we've received word that a restraining order has been issued against you in Jackson County, Missouri. Would you care to comment?"

"I have no idea what you're talking about."

"It was filed on behalf of Penny Hardesty. I assume you know her?"

Fear gripped him, along with the realization that the story was going public.

"I'm sorry, but I can't comment until I know more about it."

Adam turned off his cell, stopping long enough to compose himself. The last thing he wanted was to let this spill over into the time he was about to spend with Brooke and Jack.

The Group tended to sit in the same seats each week, scattered about the church. As a result, they rarely said more than a quick hello on Sunday mornings. Adam was surprised to see Big Mike and Megan waiting for them near the back of the church, kids in tow.

"You're stuck with us today," Megan said as she hugged the Overstreets. "Let's find a place to sit."

"I made airline reservations this morning," Big Mike whispered to Adam as they headed up a long side aisle. "We're leaving Salisbury at ten-fifteen, layover in Charlotte, get into Kansas City at three-fifty. If it all works out, we'll go by her work and catch her before she leaves for the day."

"Great," Adam said. "How much do I owe you?"

"No rush on that. Let's take care of the important stuff first."

Adam considered telling him about the newspaper reporter, but decided not to. It wasn't the time or place, and he had no right to burden a friend who was already giving up two days of work to help him. He settled into his seat, with Jack on his right and Big Mike on his left. Brooke sat on the other side of Jack. To the world they looked like a happy couple. If only…

It was another of Miles' messages within a message. Every now and then he felt the need to go beyond preaching the word, to make an announcement or remind the congregation of something. Today it was the latter.

Theresa watched as he moved purposefully from one side of the stage to the other. In his hand was the church's membership covenant. He was talking about the need for the covenant, and he wasn't mincing words.

"Most churches don't worry about something like this," he said, waving the covenant over his head. "They're so glad you walk through the door they'll do anything to keep you.

"So you sinned? Oh, it's okay. We still love you. You sinned again? Oh, well, we aren't perfect." His tone was almost mocking.

"Church, you know what?" The auditorium was silent.

"It ain't okay!"

Scattered responses of 'amen' echoed as Miles slipped into the parlance of his youth.

"It ain't okay to keep sinning! It ain't!"

Referring to Romans Six, Miles insisted that habitual sin had no place in church. He challenged members to live up to the covenant they'd signed. Theresa knew where his comments were directed.

"You can't call yourself a Christian and be getting drunk!"

"You can't call yourself a Christian and steal from your employer, regardless of why you did it!"

"You can't call yourself a Christian and gamble away your family's money."

"You can't call yourself a Christian and put yourself in compromising situations."

Theresa knew Melody Atkins wasn't there to hear this frontal attack. She hoped that the Overstreets weren't either.

To Adam, it felt like the eyes of the entire church were upon him.

Oh, sure, they weren't really, but after the phone call from the newspaper and the number of times he'd had to tell his story, he wondered if the whole world knew.

The uneasiness among the adults seated around him increased as Pastor Miles continued his stern discourse. Adam couldn't bring himself to look around. Seated several rows ahead, Forrest Delaney looked uncomfortable too. A couple rows to the right,

Denise Stover was nodding vigorously as Pastor Miles intensified his diatribe.

It was near the end of the sermon, when Pastor Miles challenged members to live up to their covenant that Brooke started to cry, quietly at first, then more noticeable. Jack looked worriedly at her, unsure what to do. He hadn't seen his mother cry before. When she got up and left, Jack started to follow, but Adam pulled him onto his lap.

"It's okay, buddy," he whispered. "Mama's just sad. She'll be fine. She wants you to stay here with me."

Jack looked at him, then to the door where Brooke had exited. Adam pulled him close. The feeling of his son's trembling body made him more determined than ever to straighten things out.

MONDAY

Day Ten

Big Mike pulled into the Overstreets' driveway at eight-thirty. The sky was bright and beautiful, and Adam could smell the salt air as he picked up Jack and gave him a good-bye kiss. Brooke was chilly, but offered her cheek when he stepped toward her.

Forrest and Julie's house was a few blocks off the highway in West Ocean City. Julie was waiting on the front porch. Adam offered her the front seat, but she jumped in back.

Adam didn't know what might happen in Kansas City, but if prayers could move mountains, this would be a slam dunk. It needed to be. The newspaper was on his trail, and if the story went public, his innocence wouldn't mean much. He'd debated telling Brooke about the call from the Times, before deciding to keep it to himself for now. Another secret.

Vicki said she was praying for him when he called to tell her he was taking a couple days off. He needed to call Melvin sooner or later, but kept waiting and hoping for some sort of conclusion.

The plane was small, like all commuter planes out of Salisbury. It was a crowded flight, and the engines were loud, but they talked as best they could about how to handle things in Kansas City. Adam considered telling them about the restraining order, but since he hadn't seen it, decided not to.

As soon as they were in the Charlotte terminal, Adam stepped away and fired up his cellphone. His message light was blinking. He punched the access code and heard Vicki's voice.

"Adam, one of the Salisbury television stations was just here. They came in with cameras, wanting to talk to you. I told them you were out of town, but they turned on the camera and filmed the office."

Oh, no.

"I felt like a criminal, Adam, like on those news shows when they ambush the bad guys. They asked for a list of hospital board members. I gave them Melvin's name. I think they're going to call him. I don't know what's up, but it definitely has something to do with your problems."

Adam's heart sank. Why were they putting Vicki in the middle of this?

The second message was from Jasmine.

"Adam, the Hardestys have filed an ex parte order of protection against you on behalf of Mrs. Hardesty. Basically, it's a restraining order that prohibits you from going within a thousand feet of her home or work, or contacting them by phone. I've e-mailed it to your personal account. Someone has tipped off the press. You should be ready for whatever comes next. If you want me to assist with this further, give me a call and we can talk."

"Everything okay?" Big Mike came up behind him, slapping him on the back. Adam tried to hide the stricken feeling, but Big Mike saw it.

"Tell me," he said as Julie joined them.

"This is getting serious," Big Mike said, shaking his head.

Adam was incredulous. "It's been serious since last week, Mike. The woman is taking my life away from me."

"It definitely changes our strategy," Julie said, as they handed the gate attendant their boarding passes.

The plane from Charlotte to Kansas City was larger, and they shared a row. Given the restraining order, it was decided that Adam would drop Julie and Mike off at Penny's work, then find a place to wait.

"I like our chances there better than at home," Julie said. "If the husband is as irrational as we're hearing, it could be hard for her to talk."

"It makes me wonder if there's something more to this," Big Mike said. "Like he's forcing her to make these accusations. Adam, are you sure you don't know him?"

"Positive."

#

After arriving in Kansas City, they secured a rental car and got on the road. It was four-thirty when they left the airport for the downtown address of MFS Account Solutions.

At five-fifteen Adam pulled to the curb in front of a seven-story office building.

"I hope MFS is open until five-thirty," Big Mike said, getting out and opening the door for Julie.

"We'll call you," Julie said. Adam watched them head into the building before driving south on Grand Avenue. A few blocks ahead he found Crown Center, a hotel and shopping complex. Adam parked in the Center's underground garage and made his way to a large atrium inside. He bought a soda at the food court, then sat down to wait.

And wait.

And wait.

#

The call came at eight-thirty.

"Hey, Mike! Wow, that took a while. I'll come pick you up."

"Don't."

"What? Are you still talking to Penny?"

Big Mike was slow to respond. In the background Adam heard announcements being made over a loudspeaker.

"Mike? Where are you?"

"The airport. We're boarding a plane to go home."

Adam jumped to his feet, knocking over his chair. A custodian cleaning the area eyed him suspiciously.

"What happened? Why are you at the airport?"

"Adam, I don't know how to tell you this. We've heard enough. From the minute we got there, Mrs. Hardesty was nervous, afraid even."

"That's because she's lying!"

"She could barely talk to me, so I left her and Julie alone."

"What did she say? Tell me, Mike!"

"She's scared of you, Adam. She didn't want anything to happen in St. Louis, and now she's scared you're going to come after her. She said you keep calling and leaving threatening messages. She wants to forget about that night and try to work things out at home."

Adam's head pounded. "She is lying, Mike! I don't know why, but she's making all this up!"

"Look, man, I've gotta get on the plane. You need to step forward and own this before it's too late. You've got a son to think about."

Adrenaline at max, Adam kicked a chair, then picked it up and tossed it. The custodian left the area, as did a family sitting several tables away.

"Mike, please! Please!"

###

Adam merged onto Interstate 70 and floored it. Penny lived in Independence, a suburb about ten miles from downtown. The GPS said it was a twenty-minute trip, but he planned to make it a lot quicker.

Gripping the steering wheel, his anger was such that he hadn't yet developed a plan. Nothing had worked so far, and he wasn't beyond begging if it would make the nightmare go away.

Just past Kauffman Stadium, the Kansas City Royals' ballpark, Adam exited onto Noland Road. Two miles of fast food and car dealerships later, he turned onto a residential street, followed the GPS directions, and stopped in front of a tan split-level house, similar to others in the area. He turned off the engine and sat back, allowing his breathing to slow. This would likely be his only chance. He needed to make it good. When they were face-to-face, Penny would explain everything. She had to.

After allowing ten minutes to cool off, he climbed from the car and approached the front door. He rang the doorbell and waited. It was a couple moments before the door opened.

"Penny."

Recognizing him in the porch's dim light, she took a step back, started to speak, but caught herself. She glanced nervously over her shoulder, came outside, and closed the door behind her.

"Adam, you cannot be here." It came out more like a statement than a threat. Adam felt a small amount of hope.

"You're wrecking my life, Penny. I'm in danger of losing my family, my job, everything I have."

"I'm sorry... I didn't want it to get like this." Tears rimmed her eyes.

"Make it go away, Penny. Please, just make it go away."

Her eyes darted about, over her shoulder at the closed door, then past Adam to the street.

"You really need to leave. If Zane knows you're here he'll..."

"I'll happily leave. Just tell the truth about what happened in St. Louis."

"It wasn't supposed to be like this, Adam. It was supposed to be fun. But now it's a mess."

"My life is a mess, Penny. Give it back to me." Adam reached into his pocket, withdrew his phone, and held it out. "Call my wife and tell her I didn't sleep with you."

The offer of the phone caused a change in her comportment. She continued to look over her shoulder, but became more direct.

"There's nothing to talk to your wife about, Adam, unless you want me to tell her how you forced yourself on me."

Behind her, the door was flung open. A man in his forties, with a neatly trimmed beard and brown tortoiseshell glasses, glared at them.

"Penny, get in the house."

"Zane, please."

"Get in the house."

Penny silently squeezed past her husband. Before disappearing inside, she glanced back over Zane's shoulder. There was fear in her eyes. Somehow, Adam knew it wasn't directed at him.

"Hang around another couple minutes, Mr. Overstreet. The police are on their way." Hardesty's voice was amazingly calm given the situation.

"You and your wife are making a mess of my life."

"No, Mr. Overstreet, it is you who made a mess of our lives. We're trying to move past it, but it's been hard. It doesn't help when your lawyer calls or your church friends show up at Penny's work."

"It's all lies." Adam felt his heart racing.

"There were lies, Mr. Overstreet. But we're only dealing with the truth. And the truth is, you're a home wrecker. A womanizing home wrecker."

Adam stood mute, shaking his head vigorously. Zane Hardesty wasn't a big man, but Adam sensed he wasn't a stranger to confrontation.

"Now, Mr. Overstreet, I'm going back into my house and closing the door. The Independence police will be here shortly. If you're still here, they'll arrest you for violating a restraining order. Personally, I hope you are still here, but Penny feels you deserve an opportunity to leave on your own, so I'll honor her wishes. This time."

"Penny didn't say anything," Adam was starting to regain his senses and realized his chances were running out.

"I know Penny pretty well. Much better than you." Zane backed through the door and started to close it, not once taking his eyes off Adam.

"Good night, sir. Don't darken our doorway again."

TUESDAY

Day Eleven

Theresa was starting her afternoon in the Ocean City office when her cellphone went off. Her heart lurched when she saw it was her father. It was unlike him to call in the middle of the workday.

"Papa?"

His sobbing said everything.

"Aunt Joy?"

"Yeah, Baby Girl. I got up and had some coffee, thought she was sleeping late. I went back and checked on her a half-hour later, and she was gone."

"Miles and I will catch the first plane out, Papa. I love you."

"I love you too, Baby Girl. You and Miles are all I got now."

#

The commuter plane touched down in Salisbury a couple minutes before three, right on schedule. It was, Adam thought, the only thing that had gone right in more than a week. After leaving the Hardesty's house the night before, he'd returned to the airport, hoping to catch a flight home. Late flights to the East Coast were few and far between in Kansas City, however, and he'd spent a sleepless night at the terminal before catching the nine-fifty flight on which he was already booked. A dead cellphone added to the misery. He'd forgotten to pack a charger, and constant checks of e-mail and flight schedules wiped out the juice before midnight.

Inside the Salisbury terminal, Adam located a pay phone, inserted some coins, and called home.

"Hi, Brooke, can you come get me? I'm at the airport."

"Let me drop Jack off at the Stovers. I'll be there in an hour. We need to talk."

#

The hour after Papa's call was filled with details. Rescheduling meetings, requests for continuances, and the obligatory notification of the partners that she would be out of the office for a while. Everything handled quickly and impersonally via e-mail and on-line calendars.

It was when she was in Miles' office with the door closed that Theresa lost it. She sank into one of the large leather chairs across from his desk.

"What's wrong, Tee?" he said coming around and kneeling at her side.

"Aunt Joy" was all she could say before the emotions overcame her. Miles scooped her out of the chair and carried her to a corner sofa, holding her close. Theresa clung to him with everything she had, as if letting go might bring more bad news.

They didn't speak for several minutes. He stroked her hair and kissed her forehead as she let grief have its way. Eventually she sat up, pushed the hair away from her eyes, and straightened her shoulders.

"I told Papa we'd be leaving today. Can you get packed in the next hour or so?"

"I can't go today, Tee. It's impossible."

She sat up straighter, facing him.

"Papa needs us, Miles. He's hurting."

"He needs you, sweetheart. Not us, you. I'll get the things done here that can't wait and be on the first plane out in the morning. I promise." His tone was soft, but firm.

"But Miles, *I* need you."

"And you'll have me, Tee. There's so much to do here that I can't take a whole week off. I promise I'll rush to get everything done and be there for you."

"When?"

"As quick as I can."

Adam checked his watch and moved outside to wait for Brooke. His thoughts were jumbled, crashing together like clouds in a thunderstorm. He almost missed the familiar face passing by a few feet away.

"Theresa?"

The pastor's wife looked at him, surprised.

"Hello, Adam. I'm sorry. I was so deep in thought."

The typically self-confident, stylish Mrs. Traynor was wearing a simple pair of black shorts and a pink shirt. Her hair was mussed.

"Is everything okay?"

"Yeah, yeah, I... no, not really. My aunt died this morning." Tears came, and she seemed to cave in upon herself. Without thinking, Adam embraced her.

"Is there anything I can do?" he murmured, as she hung on.

"Thank you," Theresa said, pulling away suddenly. "I have to get to Cape Girardeau, Missouri."

"Would you like me to move your car?" Adam nodded at Theresa's light green sedan idling at the curb. Theresa looked at it, blinked, and shook her head.

"I guess I wasn't thinking."

"Go in and check your bag. I'll park the car and bring you the keys."

When he caught up to her in the small terminal, Theresa was waiting outside the security checkpoint. Adam gently folded the key into her hand.

"I'll pray for you and your father," he said quietly. "I remember meeting him last winter. He talked nonstop about you. I take it you and your Aunt were close."

Theresa flashed a tearful smile. "Aunt Joy is Papa's little sister. After Mama died, she became his anchor. He travels a lot and probably spends as much time at Aunt Joy's house as he does our family farm is Pennsylvania."

"Please give Professor Stanley my condolences," Adam said, embracing her again before she headed through security, tears streaming down her face.

Five minutes later Brooke swept to the curb in the family SUV. Adam opened the back door and tossed in his bag, then crawled into the front. Brooke kept her attention focused ahead.

"Not a good trip to Kansas City," he said.

"When are you going to confess about everything that happened?" Brooke's emphasis on 'everything' was a clear indication that she didn't believe him.

"You want me to confess to something I didn't do?" Whether from lack of sleep or overloaded emotional circuits, Adam wasn't backing down.

"I talked to Julie and Mike."

"What did they tell you?" Adam asked angrily. "Because they didn't tell me a damn thing. They left me sitting and waiting, then called and said I was guilty and they were going home."

"Penny told the truth. And it's time for you to do the same."

Adam thought his head might explode. "I did tell you the truth, Brooke. I went to a casino and gambled. I know I shouldn't have, but I did and I'm sorry. I drank more than I should have, and I'm sorry. I went to a suite with some other people, which in hindsight I shouldn't have done. I'm sorry for that. Then, I made the terrible mistake of being alone with Penny Hardesty. She came on to me. I pushed her away and got out. Nothing else happened! *Nothing else happened!"*

Startled by his response, Brooke took a deep breath, composing herself for her next barrage.

"And your sweater in her bedroom? What about that?"

"Sweater?" This was new territory. Adam wracked his brain, then remembered.

"I took the sweater with me when I went out that night. I must've left it in the suite. How it got into Penny's bedroom I have no idea. Penny didn't mention it at her house last night." The words were barely out before he realized he'd said too much.

"You went to her house?"

"To find out what caused Julie and Big Mike to leave so quickly. Brooke, I don't know what else to say. I did not do it. I'll do anything to clear myself, but I've run out of options. You must believe me. Please."

Brooke's cellphone chirped. She fished it from her purse.

"Yes. He's here." Wordlessly she handed the phone across the seat.

"Adam, it's Vicki. I've been trying to get in touch with you."

"Dead phone, Vicki. Can whatever it is wait until tomorrow?"

"Melvin called a special meeting of the Board of Directors for tomorrow morning at seven-thirty. He wants you there." Vicki's voice trailed off. "Adam, things aren't good here. The local television stations have picked up on your situation. Melvin is catching flak from the rest of the board. It's bad. They're going to have a hearing for you."

Adam clicked off and stared ahead. He needed someone to talk to. But who?

"I've been visiting with Pastor Miles," Brooke said.

"I'm glad you've got somebody to confide in, Brooke. It must be nice."

"Don't get angry at me because you messed up."

More silence.

"Pastor Miles thinks you should move out."

"And what do you think?"

"I'm not sure yet."

"Have you considered standing by me? Believing me?"

"Adam, I want to do that, but more and more keeps coming out. I'm not sure you're even the man I married."

It was on the second leg of her flight when Theresa's mind slowed enough to consider the airport encounter with Adam Overstreet. She smiled when she thought of how kind he'd been, especially with all he was facing. She'd heard most of the story during the church staff meeting. Since then, she'd picked up snippets from Miles. Restraining orders, a sweater left in the bedroom of his accuser. She could see the evidence stacking up. Still, Adam had sensed that she was in distress and willingly stepped forward to help. She shuddered to think about what would have happened if her car had remained in the airport drop-off zone, keys in the ignition. What kind of man saw past his own problems long enough to reach out to someone else?

Certainly not her husband.

WEDNESDAY

Day Twelve

Adam could have kicked himself for not calling Jasmine Fleece when he learned about the board meeting. Entering the conference room at seven-thirty, he realized he'd made a tactical mistake and would be facing this witch hunt alone.

Fifteen board members were seated in their usual spots around the conference table. It was rare when all were present, and Adam expected fireworks. Melvin sat at the head of the table, a television mounted on a cart over his left shoulder. Judging by the stacks of empty coffee cups, they'd been there awhile. Sitting to Melvin's right was Fletcher Gordy, the hospital's attorney. In his early sixties, Fletch was partner in a long-established Eastern Shore firm catering to corporate clients. He and Adam had become friendly, but it was obvious there would be none of the usual chitchat about family vacation plans or Fletch's first love, antique car restoration.

Adam took the lone open seat, at the far end of the table. Melvin got down to business.

"The reason we're here, Adam, is to conduct a hearing into your actions at a conference in St. Louis four weeks ago. We will review the evidence, then solicit testimony from you. You have the right to say as little or as much as you wish. You reserve the right to be represented by legal counsel if you choose—"

"What if I do want legal counsel? Will this meeting be postponed?"

Fletch Gordy leaned forward and cleared his throat.

"Mr. Overstreet, were you not contacted and apprised of this meeting by Mrs. Passwaters yesterday at..." Fletch pulled on his reading glasses and checked his notes, "three-forty in the afternoon?"

Mr. Overstreet? Mrs. Passwaters? This was as official as it got. Adam felt the butterflies in his stomach threatening to become something bigger.

"Vicki did call me about being here, but I didn't feel that legal representation would be necessary. Now it seems it might be."

"Since you were aware that this was a hearing and you didn't show up with legal representation, it is assumed you waived that right. It's part of the hearing process outlined in the hospital employee handbook."

Adam glanced around the table, looking for any sign of support. There was none. Steve Cronin was the closest thing to a friendly face in the room, and the best he could do was glance away when their eyes met. Adam felt naked and vulnerable. They obviously had evidence they planned to submit. All he had was the truth, and the truth hadn't been playing well lately.

"What if I get up and leave?"

Fletch sighed. "The hearing will go on, with or without you."

Adam held his palms up, signaling Melvin to proceed.

"I'll begin with a letter I received on Monday morning, eight days ago," Melvin said, opening a file.

"The letter you *did not* share with other board members," Adele Sweet said firmly.

"I did what I felt was right at the time." Melvin was on the defensive. "We've already talked about that."

Spotting an opening, Adam honed in. "You've already discussed the evidence? Are there minutes of that discussion?"

Fletch Gordy raised his hand sharply. "There's been no discussion of the evidence. You have my word on that, Mr. Overstreet. The only discussion involved Mr. Proffer's decision not to immediately forward the letter to the board. It's an internal matter." Then, turning to Melvin, the attorney said, "Can we get on with this?"

Melvin read the letter and summarized the discussion he'd had with Adam. His account was accurate, and Adam saw no reason to question it.

"The next piece of evidence is a news story that was broadcast Monday evening on television station WBOC in Salisbury." Melvin reached for a remote and turned on the television. The local news anchor read the lead:

A local hospital administrator is in hot water over his behavior at an out-of-town convention. WBOC's Stephanie Morrisey has the story.

A toothy blonde appeared on screen with Ocean City Memorial in the background.

Ocean City Memorial CEO Adam Overstreet has been served with a restraining order following an incident several weeks ago at a convention in St. Louis. According to sources close to the situation, Overstreet made threatening calls to a Kansas City woman after her husband sent a letter to the hospital's Board Chairman describing an inappropriate relationship between the CEO and the man's wife.

A close-up of Melvin came on the screen. The video was shot outside his office, and Melvin was sweating heavily as he read from a prepared script.

The board of Ocean City Memorial is conducting an investigation into actions attributed to Mr. Overstreet. We hope to get some answers in the next few days.

The reporter picked up the story.

We made repeated attempts to contact Mr. Overstreet, but were unsuccessful. A source tells WBOC that Mr. Overstreet was in Kansas City with friends attempting to resolve the matter. No word has been given as to whether a resolution was reached. We have been told that the investigative hearing will be held early Wednesday morning. For WBOC News, this is Stephanie Morrisey reporting in Ocean City.

Several board members glared at Adam. Melvin distributed photocopies of a news article.

"The final exhibit is this story from Monday's *Daily Times.*"

Skimming it, Adam noted that it contained much of the same information as the television news account. A glaring difference was the newspaper's assertion that Adam had used fear and intimidation to coerce Penny Hardesty to change her story, a tidbit obviously pulled from court documents used to secure the restraining order.

After giving board members a few moments to review the article they had undoubtedly seen before, Melvin said, "Adam, you have the opportunity now to call witnesses or present any evidence in your defense."

Adam looked around the table. "What can I say to make you believe this did not happen?"

"How about the truth," Cliff Leake spoke for the first time.

"Okay, Cliff, let's try the truth. I did not force myself on Penny Hardesty. I did not make threatening calls to her. There. You have the truth."

"What about the claim that you were in Kansas City the past two days?" Steve Cronin asked.

"True. Two church friends and I traveled to Kansas City to find out why Penny is making these claims."

"Any luck?" Steve again.

Adam shook his head.

The room was still. Melvin was the first to speak.

"Anything else before we excuse you so we can discuss this further?"

Adam placed his hands on the table, palms down. He looked around the conference table, making eye contact with each board member.

"You've known me for over a year. You know the kind of person I am. Nothing has changed. I made the mistake of going with a group of people to a casino, then drinking more than I should have. Those things really happened, things for which I am remorseful."

Adam stared at a spot on the table for a few seconds, then continued.

"I am fully willing to accept any disciplinary measures the board feels are necessary for those indiscretions. What I cannot do is accept responsibility for things that didn't happen. I ask only that you continue to believe in me as you have since I arrived. I haven't let you down before, and I will not let you down now."

#

Adam waited in his office as directed. It was ten-fifteen when Fletch Gordy knocked and stuck his head in.

"Rejoin the board please, Mr. Overstreet."

An hour and forty-five minutes after being excused, Adam returned. Most board members kept their heads down, studying their notes. Adam took his seat. Melvin cleared his throat and charged ahead.

"Adam, we have no idea what actually happened in St. Louis. Maybe we'll never know for certain." Melvin paused for a sip of water.

"Based upon what we've learned, we know that you traveled to a casino with a group of colleagues. We know that you drank to excess. We—"

"I'd like to see a show of hands from anyone at this table who has visited a casino or had too much to drink." Adam fired back.

"You've had the opportunity to present your testimony," Fletch Gordy interjected, before nodding at Melvin to proceed.

His face red, his breathing labored, Melvin continued. "We have a letter indicating that you spent the evening with a woman who was not your wife—"

"A lie."

"We have documented proof that you contacted the woman with intent to get her to change her story, and—"

"To find out why she was lying."

Fletch spoke again. "Mr. Overstreet, that'll be enough. If you persist in interrupting the chairman, we'll have you removed."

Adam searched the board members' eyes for any sign of support. There was none.

Melvin continued. "We've been presented with evidence that you left a sweater in the woman's room, and that you—"

Adam shot to his feet. "Who gave you that information?"

Fletch responded, "it doesn't matter."

"It matters plenty, Fletch. That's information known only to a few close friends and my pastor. There's no way..."

Realization set in. Someone from Surfside had told the board about the sweater.

"Just skip the rest, Melvin. What's the board's decision?" Adam remained standing.

"The board is placing you on unpaid leave pending further investigation. We have a security guard stationed outside who will take you to your office to pick up any personal items. He will then escort you to your car and ensure that you leave the premises. It needs to be understood that, until this investigation is concluded, you will not be permitted to return."

The short walk from the conference room to his office felt like miles. Les, a security guard whom Adam had often joked with, quietly and awkwardly led the way. Vicki was seated at her desk when they arrived.

"I guess I'm taking an unexpected vacation."

She said nothing.

After a quick glance around the office, he picked up a family picture from his desk.

"That's about it, Les."

His face florid, his eyes showing concern, the security guard stammered, "I need your cellphone, Mr. Overstreet. And your corporate credit card."

Adam fished the phone out of his pocket, then reached for his wallet and located the corporate card. He placed both in the big man's hand.

"I'm sorry, Mr. O., I didn't want any part of this," he said softly.

"Get me out of here, Les," Adam said, starting toward the door.

When they passed through, Vicki was standing.

"I hope we see you back soon," she said quietly. She reached for Adam uncertainly, wanting to hug him, but also aware of what was happening. Awkwardly she lowered her head and backed away.

Outside the office, Adam headed for the elevator.

"Mr. O., Let's go this way," Les pointed toward the hallway leading to the kitchen and laundry areas, sections of the hospital not as busy as the main corridor. Even in his despair, Adam was touched by the concern. When they reached the exit to the employee parking lot, Les silently offered his hand. They made eye contact while they shook, then Adam opened the door and exited into a media circus.

Both Salisbury TV stations had cameramen and reporters poised for attack. A half-dozen other reporters held out mini-recorders and cellphones or snapped pictures. Their braying was incessant.

"Mr. Overstreet! What happened in there?"

"A comment please?"

"Adam, what did the board decide?"

Resisting the desire to lash out, Adam composed himself before speaking.

"The Board of Directors has placed me on unpaid leave pending further investigation. I have shared with them the truth surrounding the incidents in St. Louis, but they have chosen to believe otherwise."

"What will you do now, Mr. Overstreet?"

"Is it true that you were involved in a tryst with a married woman?"

"How is your family reacting to the charges?"

"I can't comment further." Adam stepped around the reporters and headed for his car, cameras in tow. It wasn't until he pulled onto Ocean Boulevard that he started breathing again. Driving aimlessly, he considered where he should go. The previous night at home was tortuous. He thought about going to see Big Mike, maybe talking some sense into his friend. Then, with a clarity he hadn't felt in days, he made a left turn and headed north along the Boulevard.

It wasn't even noon, yet it was already turning into one of the saddest and sweetest days of Theresa's life.

Papa had picked her up just after midnight at the Cape Girardeau airport and taken her to Aunt Joy's house. Theresa had done little more than head to a tiny back bedroom and crash for eight hours. The smell of breakfast brought her back to consciousness, the morning sunshine beaming brightly through the open window next to her bed. Aunt Joy never splurged on air conditioning, and a sheen of perspiration was part of any summer stay. Theresa didn't mind. Having spent many summers with her grandfather, she was used to the humid extremes of this little spot near the Mississippi River.

Following a leisurely breakfast, they moved to the screened front porch. Theresa hadn't known what to expect after the tearful phone call the day before. Papa was ebullient, however, as he recalled fun times spent in Cape Girardeau during the summers he and Mama would visit between semesters at Penn State.

"Did you know that it was Aunt Joy who introduced us to Grandfather Meekins?" Theresa had known this, but always enjoyed hearing the stories again.

"Vance Meekins was one of the kindest people I ever met," Harvester said. "When you spend your life around a university, most of your friends are professors. They're smart, but they have tunnel vision. Biology professors know biology; literature professors know literature. But Vance Meekins... now there's a man who knew a little bit about everything."

Seated side by side, their attention was focused on the same spot: a vacant lot across the narrow street and three houses down. Grandfather Meekins' home had stood there until it fell in upon itself from neglect. Papa paid to have the debris removed and the lot cleaned up. He still paid a boy to mow it, warning him by phone to avoid running over the flowerbeds that Aunt Joy had continued to tend.

"Cookie, take a look at those pansies."

They were impressive, even in the June heat.

"It's like Aunt Joy has infused them with her spirit," Papa said.

"Maybe there's a little bit of Mama in there, too," Theresa replied.

"I doubt it," Papa laughed. "Your mama never took much to planting and caring for things. She was made for air conditioning, and air conditioning was definitely made for her. But Joy, that woman could coax roses from ragweed."

"It's ironic really," Theresa said, "because I don't remember flowers around the house when I used to visit Grandfather Meekins."

Papa shook his head. "Vance wasn't much on flowers, but he grew some of the best grapes I've ever had. He already had some good vines going when I met him. I helped him graft in some stronger varieties over the years. The man liked his wine, you know."

This she hadn't known. Her surprise must have been evident, as Papa chuckled.

"Certainly not to excess, but when we'd come to visit, he'd invite me over. We'd go out back to that little shed he had – you remember that shed?"

"Of course, he kept his tools in there."

"And his wine. He had a little closet in back. His own wine cellar. He'd say, 'Harvester, you pick the vintage.' He had bottles going back to the 1940's. Good stuff, I'm telling you."

Theresa shook her head. "Is there any left? I might need some to get through the next few days."

Papa belly-laughed. "Sorry, Cookie. As Vance got older, he couldn't bottle his wine anymore. After your Uncle Elijah passed, Vance and Joy took to enjoying an occasional evening drink right here on the porch. According to Joy, the stock gave out just a few weeks before Vance did."

"He really went downhill after that teaching job ended." Theresa smiled sadly. "What was that boy's name?"

"Chan Manning," Papa said. "Earl Manning's boy. People up there in Saxon County wouldn't let the little boy into public school because his mama was black; they paid your grandpapa to come work with him at the old schoolhouse on Grebey Island."

Theresa's heart warmed as she recalled the stories Grandfather Meekins had shared about his return to teaching. When integration came to the area schools in the 1940's, the local board of education fired him and the other black teachers rather than have them teach white children. Decades later, he was hired by the superintendent in Saxon County to teach Chan Manning, a biracial boy. Grandfather saw through the ruse, but took the job anyway. Then, after two years, he alerted the state department of education about what was going on, and young Chan was finally enrolled in public school. The experience had energized Grandfather, but soon after, his physical condition started to regress. Within two years, he was dead.

"How is Earl Manning?" Theresa asked. "Do you still see him?"

"I stop by when I can. He's better than he was a few years ago. His boy is still playing baseball someplace or other, but there's no contact between them. I keep telling Earl to reach out, but he feels bad about the way he raised the boy."

Theresa stroked his hand.

"I never want us to lose contact."

"That'll never happen, Cookie. You know better."

They sat silently amidst surroundings as familiar as an old friend.

"You know, Papa, I loved growing up on our farm and being close to the university, but the time we spent here was so special."

"How's that, Cookie?"

Theresa stretched her legs and shooed away a fly.

"When we were here, you weren't always getting called to campus or writing books. I always knew that for a couple weeks every summer, I had your undivided attention."

"Did you ever resent us sending you to stay with your Grandfather all those summers? Your friends back in Pennsylvania were swimming and going to parties, and you had to be out here in Missouri."

"Not at all. Grandfather Meekins was the only tie I had to my parents. He told me stories about them and made me feel like I really knew them."

Theresa's mention of her birthparents brought tears to Harvester's eyes.

"Sorry, Papa."

He shook his head, working to compose himself.

"Don't apologize, Cookie. It was important to your mama and me that you got to know more about your real mother and father. They died too young, and Vance felt he was too old to take care of you by himself. Asking us to step in was the ultimate act of sacrifice. Besides, you wouldn't be the woman you are without your parents, your Grandfather Meekins, and your mama."

She reached over and pecked his cheek. "And you, Papa."

#

Theresa accompanied her father to Sassman Funeral Parlor in Cape Girardeau. In an earlier day and time, Sassman was 'the colored undertaker.' Times change, but Sassman's clientele remained African-American. Aunt Joy used to say there wasn't a white undertaker anywhere who could give as fine a sendoff as Clarence Sassman. Theresa had to admit there was a certain palatial nature to the tired old funeral home's deep velour curtains and dark wood.

It had been Theresa's desire to secure the best casket available for Aunt Joy, but Papa nixed the idea.

"Simple and plain, just like she lived," he said.

Once arrangements were complete, they made their way to tiny Trowbridge AME Church, five miles outside of Cape. Theresa could see a sense of peace settling over her father as they drove up to the old church.

"We got married right here," Papa said, pushing open the church's front door and stepping inside. "Your mama wanted the ceremony here instead of Mississippi."

"Why, Papa?"

"It was after things got bad up on Grebey Island. We'd planned to be married two years before, soon as your Mama finished college. Then, they found your Aunt Thomasena and saw what had been done to her..." Harvester grew quiet, and Theresa knew she needed to steer the conversation in a different direction. His years on Grebey Island began with so much promise, but two white-supremacy groups, the Saxon County Knights and The White Covenant, had left a swath of destruction. Mama's father and sister were among the casualties. What little Theresa knew about that period came from scattered bits of conversation. Papa and Aunt Joy couldn't bear to talk about it.

"Do you remember your wedding day, Papa?"

Harvester lowered himself onto a pew in the middle of the church. Theresa sat beside him, hugging his arm.

"I remember everything. Your mama was so beautiful. Things had been going so bad at home..."

A few tears fell from his tired eyes. He did nothing to hide them.

"She came down this aisle right here, pretty white dress, white gloves. I was standing up front there when I first saw her. Just the sight of her about drove me to my knees."

"Papa, really?"

"She was so beautiful, Baby Girl." He turned and looked at Theresa, all tears and sweetness. "Just like you are today."

# # #

"Where is he?" Adam barreled into the reception area, startling Miles' secretary, DeeDee.

"If you mean Pastor Miles, he's in a meeting with Pastor Hatfield. If you want to wait I can—"

Adam threw open the door and barged in. Pastor Miles and Derby Hatfield were talking across the large desk. Both had their feet propped up when he entered. Their posture changed abruptly when he slammed the door.

"You talked to the hospital board." Adam pointed as he closed in on Miles.

"Get out of my office." Miles was on his feet quickly, not backing down. Derby jumped up and got between them.

"He told the hospital board things that were shared with him in confidence," Adam exclaimed to Derby.

"They needed to know!" Pastor Miles roared. "They need to know the kind of person you really are!"

Adam lunged for him, grabbing his outstretched arm before Derby could pull them apart.

"Adam, come with me, man. Let's talk—"

"What's to talk about, Derby? I was just put on unpaid leave because he made a call to somebody on the hospital board."

Derby glanced at Pastor Miles. The preacher's quick nod was all Adam needed to see. Adrenaline flowing, he shoved Derby out of the way and slammed Miles against the wall. Momentarily stunned, Miles called up the fighting skills he'd used as a teenager, sending an elbow to Adam's cheekbone, then delivering a hard punch to his midsection. Doubled over and trying to catch his wind, Adam didn't see the body block coming. Before he knew it, he was pinned to the floor. Miles threw a quick right to his head before Derby pulled the pastor off. Adam had nothing left.

Miles walked to his desk and picked up his phone, glaring at Adam the entire way.

"DeeDee, call the cops."

###

"Miles is a busy man, Baby Girl. Doing the Lord's work takes time. Don't be hard on him."

After a stop at a nearby grocery store, Theresa and Harvester had returned to Aunt Joy's front porch. The sun was down and cricket chirps filled the night air.

"Would you have sent Mama off by herself at a time like this?"

Papa was struggling to remain diplomatic. There was no way he would have done to Mama what Miles did to her, staying behind while she went home to be with her father.

"I never had that kind of responsibility, Cookie. I can't imagine the pressures that go along with it."

"Papa, don't diminish what you've accomplished. I was there. I saw how attached you became to your students. I saw the extra time and effort you put in, the books you wrote, the speeches."

"I was just doing what the Lord wanted, Cookie."

Miles notwithstanding, it had been a peaceful, soul-searching day. She and Papa had prayed together, bringing a closeness she hadn't felt in a long time. There was no rush. No next thing to get to. Just the two of them and God. Several times during the day, Theresa thought about a Scripture passage she had recently read. It was from Ecclesiastes, Chapter Three:

There is a time for everything, and a season for every activity under the heavens.

a time to be born and a time to die,
a time to plant and a time to uproot,

a time to kill and a time to heal,
a time to tear down and a time to build,
a time to weep and a time to laugh,
a time to mourn and a time to dance,
a time to scatter stones and a time to gather them,
a time to embrace and a time to refrain from embracing,
a time to search and a time to give up,
a time to keep and a time to throw away,
a time to tear and a time to mend,
a time to be silent and a time to speak,
a time to love and a time to hate,
a time for war and a time for peace.

She was struck by how completely Papa understood those verses. Miles always seemed to be pushing for more and bigger; unwilling to accept status quo. Theresa had to admit that she had much of the same drive and ambition as her husband. It was important to her that she'd become a rainmaker of sorts for the law firm, even adopting the stance taken by others in the firm that pro bono or discounted work was to be avoided. Sitting with Papa, a successful college professor who set aside his accolades to work with poor migrant families, she realized that her life was on the proverbial hamster wheel, spinning and spinning, but never getting anyplace that mattered.

"Papa, God is talking to me."

Her father reached for her hand.

"What's he telling you, Cookie?"

"That I'm just going through the motions. He wants more from me."

"How's he speaking to you?"

"Plainly, just as I sit here, but he came to me yesterday at the airport, and I didn't even know it at the time."

Theresa told her father about Adam Overstreet's trials, and how he had reached out to her at the airport.

"Do you think that man's innocent, Baby Girl?"

"I know he's run into some difficulties, but I don't think he's the bad person he's being made out to be."

Papa nodded. "Sounds like you got some work to do when you get home."

Tom McIlhenny's was the fifth number Adam tried. Thankfully it wasn't a busy day at the Worcester County Jail, and the duty officer was willing to let him use the phone.

First he'd called Brooke. No answer.

Then he called Big Mike. No answer.

Vicki answered when he called the hospital. She'd been advised to avoid contact with him, but she was willing to send her husband. Adam didn't want to get her in trouble, so he declined.

Derby Hatfield was next. It was a stretch, but they had been friends. DeeDee must have spotted the Caller ID, because Adam hadn't asked for Derby before she hung up.

That left Tom McIlhenny. On the phone, Adam poured out his story to the superintendent. An hour later Tom pulled up to the jail. Adam was waiting at the curb.

"Own recognizance, huh? I hope you got in a couple good licks before they took you to jail."

Little was said during the drive. Tom pulled into the Surfside parking lot to drop Adam off at his car.

"Thanks for your help, Tom."

"You're welcome, but I think its best we avoid each other. We're both fighting for our jobs. Surfside has us in its sights, Adam. We probably need to go our separate ways."

"I understand." Adam crawled out of Tom's car and walked across the lot to his.

Easy for Tom to say, he thought. He still has a supportive wife. I'm on my own.

He didn't fully understand how on his own he was until he arrived home.

The letter was short, to the point.

Adam, Jack and I are spending the evening at Eric and Denise's house. We will be home by nine-thirty. Please be out of the house. Take everything you can. After you leave I do not want you entering the house without contacting me first. Brooke.

It was six-fifteen. He thought about calling her, but knew she wouldn't answer. He went back outside and pulled his car close to the house, leaving the trunk open. Forty minutes later he had his belongings packed and loaded. By eight-fifteen he was checked into an extended stay hotel in West Ocean City, far enough away from the beach to get a halfway decent in-season rate. Glancing around the room, he spotted the phone on the bedside table. He moved toward it, feeling the need to call somebody. Anybody.

Then he realized there was no one to call.

FRIDAY

Day Fourteen

Twenty minutes until Aunt Joy's funeral, but no sign of Miles. Theresa had spent the past two hours standing next to the open coffin, greeting Aunt Joy's friends and marveling at how good Papa was at placing names with faces he hadn't seen in decades. Of their few remaining relatives, only two elderly cousins had made the trip from Alabama. "Most of them are up in years and can't travel," Papa had said.

At ten-fifty-five, Pastor Ludwick asked if they were ready to begin. They moved to the front row of the small church while Clarence Sassman, the undertaker, lowered the coffin lid and arranged the three photographs they'd chosen for the ceremony. Theresa's favorite was a picture taken years before at a Sears and Roebuck. A ten-year old Theresa sat on Papa's lap. Mama stood off to one side, her hand resting on his shoulder. Aunt Joy was on the other side. Theresa's teeth were crooked, but her smile spoke volumes. She was a happy child, posing with the three people who meant the most to her.

Fifty mourners half-filled the church. As the final notes faded from the church organ, Pastor Ludwick stepped forward and offered a greeting. The squeak of the rear door caused everyone to turn. It took Miles several attempts to push open the moisture-swelled door, then he made his way down the aisle to Theresa's side. His black suit was expensive and out of place in a church where few worshippers lived above the poverty line.

"I'm sorry, Tee" he whispered. "Plane was delayed in Philly." He squeezed her hand as Pastor Ludwick launched into an oratory about life and death.

"He's not much of a speaker," Miles murmured. Theresa slid away, keeping her attention on the closed casket.

After a church congregant sang a moving, if not pitch-perfect version of Aunt Joy's favorite hymn, *The Church in the Wildwood*, Pastor Ludwick returned to the pulpit. He glanced at the front row, where Papa, Theresa, and Miles were seated.

"In this time of distress and sadness, I call upon a true man of God. Many people have found their way to the Lord because of his tireless work; work done for God's glory."

Miles shifted in his seat, leaning over to Theresa. "You didn't tell me, Tee."

Theresa shook her head. Let him dream.

"He came from humble beginnings, yet rose above his circumstances to find his place in God's army. I don't know him well, but I know of his work."

Miles uncrossed his legs and moved to the edge of the pew.

"Will you please come forward and say a few words?"

Miles stood, taking two steps toward the pulpit before he realized what had happened. He quickly retreated to his seat while Papa made his way forward.

"Why did you let me do that?" Miles hissed.

"You needed to be here sooner."

For the next twenty minutes, Theresa and the others cried, laughed, and worshipped, hanging on Papa's every word. His speaking style was plain, but as Theresa had always known, his words were profound.

"I've never heard him preach before," Miles whispered. "His delivery's kind of flat, but he certainly speaks from the heart."

"Shut up."

"What?" Miles swiveled to look at her, drawing the attention of people seated in the row behind them.

"You'll never have the heart for people that he has."

Miles opened his mouth to reply, but thought better.

Most of the mourners stayed for the internment in the cemetery behind the church. The sign over the cemetery entrance, a reflection of a time long past, said, *Colored Cemetery*.

"Somebody needs to tear that crap down," Miles said as they moved through the gate. "It's an insult to our race."

"It's their history, Miles."

"Why would you bury your aunt in a segregated cemetery? It's wrong. This would never happen anyplace else."

"These are her people; don't you see that? Aunt Joy could've been buried anyplace, but she chose here."

"But—"

"But nothing." Theresa pointed at a neighboring plot. My grandpapa and grandmother are buried there. There's Aunt Joy's husband and one of her sons. It's home to them. I don't expect you to understand. Lately there seems to be a lot you don't understand."

Adam waited nervously while Jasmine reviewed Memorial's employee policies on the hospital website.

"Have you received any written correspondence from the hospital board?"

"Nothing. I went by the house last night. Brooke wasn't saying much, but she did give me my mail."

Jasmine continued reading silently, occasionally jotting on a legal pad while the printer under her desk spewed out several pages. Pulling the copies together, she turned to Adam.

"The hospital violated its own policies regarding hearings."

"How so?"

"You were supposed to receive notification of the hearing at least twenty-four hours in advance. Your secretary called you the afternoon before, right?"

"Yes, but she might have tried earlier. My phone died the night before."

"That's neither here nor there. Calling you wasn't enough. By not sending you a certified letter informing you of the hearing, they haven't met their obligation under the policy."

"That's encouraging."

"They might argue that it was an emergency situation. That allows them to skirt by to a point, but we would argue that if they wanted to rush this, they could've placed you on paid leave, at least long enough to allow you to prepare an adequate defense."

Adam nodded, waiting for her to continue.

"Then there's the issue of how they acquired the information they used against you, particularly regarding your trip to Kansas City. You're sure no one on the board knew you were going?"

"Positive."

"But they weren't forthcoming as to how they knew this information. As a result, you weren't allowed to face the individual making this claim."

"It was my church pastor."

"Your pastor not only violated an ethical responsibility, he also broke the law."

"Let's take it one step at a time," Adam replied. "First I want my job back."

172

Jasmine paused before continuing.

"Are you sure you want your job back?"

"Why wouldn't I?"

"Sometimes the environment becomes so tainted by situations like this that it becomes impossible to return and perform one's job."

It was the first time Adam had considered that he may never go back to Memorial. The thought made him nauseous.

"Jasmine, things are happening that are totally out of my control. What else can I do but fight for my family and my job?"

The hint of a smile played across her lips. "If you want to fight for your job, we have a good foundation to begin. Violation of their own policies, hearsay evidence, lack of written notification. Then there was the breach of your confidentiality when the Board Chairman appeared on television. These are points we can argue to at least get you moved from unpaid to paid leave."

"I don't have a job to go to, Jasmine. I have to make appointments to see my son. My friends think I'm something I'm not. I want to fight. Anything less makes me look guilty."

"We can get started first thing Monday. You'll have to pay a retainer of five thousand dollars. My hourly rate is three-fifty an hour."

"Oh, boy," Adam said with a laugh.

"You can find less expensive attorneys, probably a lot closer to home. Do you want to go that route?"

"Sorry, Jasmine, that's not it. I was just thinking; this is the first time I've ever paid an attorney out of my pocket. I guess there's a bit of sticker shock."

Jasmine smiled. "I understand what you're saying. I'll be prudent with your money. Still, I'll probably have to make some trips to Ocean City to get this resolved."

"How far do you think it will go?"

"Without knowing the parties involved, it's hard to say. I think we'll at least get your salary reinstated. Beyond that, it's anybody's guess. I'll go at it hard."

"I know you will. Do I pay with check or credit card?"

"Either. We don't usually take personal checks, but knowing you as long as I have, we'll make an exception."

Adam pulled out his checkbook, wrote the check, and handed it across the desk. Jasmine checked her watch.

"It's two o'clock on Friday. I'll see if I can get anything done today, at least place a call to the hospital's attorney. The heavy lifting will start Monday."

"You embarrassed me today. You embarrassed yourself too, for that matter." Theresa scooted away as Miles slid under the covers.

"Is that what the cold shoulder's about, Tee? You're bigger than that, aren't you?

Theresa glared at him.

"You..." Hearing her voice reverberate off the walls of the tiny bedroom, she took a breath before continuing in a quieter, but no less serious tone. "You couldn't take time off to be with me during a difficult period, then you barely show up on time—"

"It was the airline, Tee! The flight was late."

"There were plenty of flights yesterday and the day before. You chose to push it to the last minute."

"Don't you see how busy I am?" Miles' tone indicated he was not going to take her verbal onslaught.

"What's happened to you, Miles? The man I fell in love with wouldn't have stayed behind at a time like this. He would have been here. You couldn't even find time to drive me to the airport. I almost left the car at the curb with the ignition running. If it hadn't been for Adam Overstreet, we might not even have a car."

"Overstreet needs to work on helping himself," Miles replied, holding out his arm. "See these scratches. That man attacked me."

"Don't change the subject. I needed you and you let me down. That happens more and more these days."

"Theresa, I told you I'd be here and I was. Why are you beating up on me?"

"Because you're becoming someone I don't know. You're all about bigger and more and being in charge. Do you know how silly you looked this morning when you thought you were being asked to speak?"

"Why didn't you tell me?"

"Why should I? What made you think that anybody wanted to hear the high and mighty Miles Traynor?"

Miles snickered. "We both know I could've done a whole lot better than that old Pastor Ludlow—"

"Lud-wick. And you could learn something from him about humility and compassion. You could learn from Papa, too. He's more a man of God than you'll ever be."

"For crying out loud, Tee. I'm sorry. If I'd known it was such a big deal I would've come out last night."

Theresa stared at him for several moments, before turning over. It had been a big deal. A really big deal.

And he'd missed it.

SATURDAY

Day Fifteen

Theresa slept like a rock, despite the confrontation with Miles. The stress of the past several days had caught up with her, demanding that her body shut down long enough to recharge.

Rolling over, she dreamily reached out to touch Miles. He wasn't there. She lifted her head and looked around the room, darkened by the heavy shades he'd pulled shut the evening before. His suitcase was gone.

She got up and opened the shade closest to the bed, allowing bright sunshine to pour into the room. Squinting against the light, she spotted a note on the bedside table.

Tee, I'm sorry about yesterday. I will try to be there for you more. My flight back to OC leaves at nine this morning, and I had to get out early to make it back to St. Louis. Sorry I forgot to tell you. I didn't want to wake you up. Love, Miles.

Theresa read it again. Had he forgotten or was he too scared? It didn't matter. He couldn't spend twenty-four hours with her during one of the roughest patches of her life. She had hoped they could go home together on Monday. Riley was always happy to fill in for Miles on the occasional weekends he was out of town. Why not this one?

Theresa reached into her suitcase and pulled out a freshly laundered blouse and pair of shorts. Papa had insisted on doing her laundry, and she wasn't about to object. Straightening her hair in the tiny mirror on the room's single dresser, she considered the prospects of spending a couple more days with him. The thought made her happy.

Two days without a cellphone was interminable. Adam had finally succumbed the evening before, on the way back from Baltimore. The cellphone and prepaid plan set him back quite a bit, but he needed internet access.

The first call was home. His heart sang when Jack answered.

"Hey, big boy, I'll be there to pick you up in ten minutes."

"Yay! What are we doing today Dad?"

"How about going to see race cars?" This was a no-brainer. Jack's Hot Wheels were among his most prized possessions. Adam had heard about a stock car track on the Maryland-Delaware line that raced on Saturday nights. Jack was pumped. Adam was too. It would be the first quality time they'd spent together in over a week.

The feelings he experienced pulling into the driveway on Winterset Drive were familiar, yet hollow. After three nights at a hotel and the nights he'd been relegated to the guest room, it seemed like ages since he'd really been home.

He heard Jack bounding down the stairs when he rang the doorbell. Throwing open the door, the boy flew into his arms. Adam lifted and spun him around, inhaling his sweet little boy scent.

"Finish picking up your toys." Adam hadn't noticed Brooke's approach. He looked at her as he lowered Jack to the floor. She smiled, but her eyes were sad.

"It won't take him long. He's almost done."

Brooke waved him into the house, then followed Jack upstairs. Adam headed for the kitchen for a drink of water. Feeling every bit the visitor in his own kitchen, he leaned against the counter and waited for Jack's return. The smell and remnants of grilled cheese sandwiches made his stomach growl. He eyed the cookie jar, pulled off the lid, and helped himself to three chocolate chip cookies. A large box on the counter caught his attention. Pulling back the top, he saw a variety of food items including boxes of macaroni and cheese, assorted cans of soup, and other sundry items. A brightly colored card displayed the Surfside Church logo. Written below it was, *from our kitchen to yours during difficult times.*

Wow, they're acting like Brooke's down to her last fifty cents. What Adam saw when he turned the card over made his heart flip. A handwritten note.

Brooke, here are a few necessities to help you along. Your Surfside family is here for you. I'm here for you as well, as a pastor and a friend. I'll be out of town for a couple days, but my personal cell number is provided below. I hope you'll call anytime you need someone to talk to. Warm wishes, Miles.

"What are you doing?"

Startled, he turned quickly, still holding the card. Brooke was in the doorway.

"Brooke, what is this?" Adam held the card up.

"The church has been sending some food over. I think it's a nice gesture."

"You're not poor or homeless."

"Yeah, but you lost your job and—"

"I didn't *lose* my job." Adam felt his face flush. "I was put on unpaid leave, and it's because of this guy right here." He waved the card.

"Don't blame others for your shortcomings," she said, her voice rising to meet his.

"We're going to get to the end of this, Brooke, and you're going to realize that you should have trusted me instead of going along with everything Miles Traynor says."

"Right now, Miles Traynor is a providing a lifeline that I need."

"Fine," Adam thundered as he grabbed a pen. "I have a new cell number. I'll write it down next to Pastor Miles' number." He slapped the card and pen on the countertop.

An uncomfortable silence followed, the only sounds being the occasional bang of toys being placed in the large wooden toy box they'd bought for Jack when he was a baby. Adam worked to regain his composure.

"Brooke, let's put this behind us. We need to be a family."

"You're an adulterer, Adam. Repent of that and we can move toward reconciliation."

"I'm not an adulterer," Adam said, raising his voice again. "For the thousandth time, nothing happened. I'm a victim."

"We're not stupid, Adam. Give us more credit than that, and keep your voice down."

"Who is we? This is between you and me."

"You lost that chance. I have to depend on my friends and my church now. Until you admit to your failings, you can never live in this house again."

Adam couldn't tell what Jack liked better. Was it the sudden roar as twenty cars took the green flag, or the dirt and mud they spun into the bleachers? Maybe both. One thing was for sure; dirt-track racing was fun. As the cars made their way onto the track to begin each race, he and Jack would each pick two, then root like crazy. By nine-thirty they were covered with dirt, mud, and smiles from ear-to-ear.

As the night wore on, Jack started growing tired. His head started to nod, even when the noise was at its loudest.

"Ready to head home, buddy?"

"No, Dad, please. Let's stay. I like being with you."

His son's plea almost ripped his heart apart. Adam put his arm around him and held him close. Within five minutes he was dozing. Rather than wake him, Adam scooped him up and carried him to the parking lot for the ride home.

Adam was surprised to see several cars parked on the street in front of the house. Three of them belonged to The Group. One he didn't recognize.

It was Saturday. Small group day, but that was usually over before dinner. It was ten-thirty now. A sense of foreboding came over Adam as he carried a still-sleeping Jack up the steps and rang the doorbell.

Brooke answered quickly, looked at Jack, and pointed up the stairs. Adam carried him to his room, turned back the covers, and placed him in bed. Brooke pulled his shoes off and emptied dirt and sand into a small trash can.

"Dirt-track racing," Adam said as Brooke ran her fingers over smudges on the little boy's face.

Once they had Jack tucked in, they stepped into the hallway and closed the door.

"The Group's going late tonight," Adam said.

"They're here to see you."

Adam backed away, shaking his head. "I don't want to see them." He proceeded downstairs ahead of Brooke, intent on getting out the door as quickly as possible. Eric Stover was waiting.

"Can we have a word with you?"

###

On the final night of their time together, Theresa realized they'd developed a new routine over the past week. When the sun was setting, they moved out to the front porch to catch the southern breezes that helped beat back the heat and humidity. Sitting in the darkness, Theresa thought she could smell the Mississippi River three miles away.

"I'm taking a ride tomorrow on my way out of town, Cookie." Harvester said as she sat down. "I thought it would be good to visit Earl Manning. Would you like to go along?"

"How long has it been since you've visited Mr. Manning?"

"A couple years. We write back and forth, and talk on the phone some."

"Would you like me to go?"

In the dusk, she could see him contemplating.

"I think I would, Cookie. Good or bad, that island was a real part of this family."

Theresa nodded uncertainly. "Mama wouldn't approve."

"No, she wouldn't. 'There's too much blood spilt in that dirt,' she used to say."

"But you?" Theresa reached out for his hand and found him reaching for hers.

"Earl Manning was as much a victim as we were," he said slowly. "Grebey Island took his wife, and ultimately his son. It also cost him something inside. Unlike our family, he didn't get out. He's stuck there with his memories and losses."

Theresa squeezed his hand. "I'll be honored to go with you, Papa. And thank you for asking me." Then, she added, "There's no place else I have to be."

"Sure was sad that Miles left so quick," Harvester said. "I would've loved to talk to him some more, hear how things are going."

"I was sad too, Papa. He's got a lot on his plate right now."

"Doing the Lord's work, Baby Girl."

They sat quietly, listening as day sounds transitioned to night. Theresa was reminded of the many summer nights she had spent at her grandfather's house across the street. These same night sounds were her lullaby. They still had that effect, she thought with a yawn.

"Papa, have you ever heard of a church shunning people?"

She liked how her father took time to consider what she asked. It had been Theresa's experience in life and the courtroom that too many people charged ahead without thinking. Often they wound up talking a lot without saying anything. Harvester Stanley was not like that.

"A little. Some friends of mine live in the Pennsylvania Dutch country. They have Amish who shun people if they leave the church."

"I mean Protestant churches, like Trowbridge."

"Not really. I guess they could. There's some Bible verses that talk about it. Second Thessalonians says if somebody doesn't obey, you should have nothing to do with them. First Corinthians says something too, not to eat or associate with people guilty of sexual immorality, greed, or worshiping idols."

"What do you think?"

In the dim light of a crescent moon she saw him stroking his chin.

"I've kept my distance from a few people here and there," he said. "Occasionally there'd be a colleague at Penn State who was into things I couldn't condone. When I started working with the migrant workers, there was a man on a crew back in the Dakotas who'd made a baby with his daughter. I could hardly stomach being in the same field with him. I hope the Lord isn't too angry at me for that. There may have been one or two others."

"I've been hearing of churches that shun people, Papa. I don't think I like it." Theresa made sure not to mention that her husband was the pastor of one of those churches, but knowing Papa, he'd figure it out.

"Jesus certainly spent a lot of his time with sinners, that's for sure," her father replied. "I always liked his story about the lost sheep, about how we rejoice when we find them. Seems if we're not letting them be around us, finding them is that much harder."

Theresa sat back and gazed at the stars, reassured yet again that Papa could sum up in a couple sentences what others couldn't comprehend in a lifetime.

###

Adam tentatively entered the living room. Big Mike and Megan, the Delaneys, and Denise Stover were there. Eric followed him closely, as if he thought Adam might try to escape. He had actually considered it. One more tribunal with its sights set on him. Just what he didn't need. He'd faced this jury before, one week earlier. There was one difference, one more person in attendance. Surfside's Executive Pastor, Riley Wenger.

"Unless you're all here to apologize then we have nothing to talk about." Adam was in no mood for another lecture or further judgment.

"Tonight is a church matter, Adam," Riley said. "Pastor Miles and I thought it would be best if you were surrounded by your friends. Please sit down."

"No thanks. Say what you have to say, Pastor Wenger."

Riley pulled a sheet of paper from his sports coat. "When you and Brooke joined Surfside, you signed a covenant agreement. Do you remember?"

Adam rolled his eyes. "Not really, Pastor. It was shoved in front of me along with a bunch of other paperwork. I signed and moved on."

"There's one paragraph that I would like to share with you. Eric, will you read that section?"

"I agree to follow biblical procedures for church discipline in my relationships with brothers and sisters in Christ, to submit to righteous discipline when approached biblically by brothers and sisters in Christ, and to submit to discipline by church leadership if the need should ever arise."

"Adam," Riley said, "the need for discipline has arisen."

"So what are you doing, Pastor? Kicking me out of church?" Adam looked around the room, his patience at its end. "You've judged and convicted me of something I didn't do. You are supposed to be my friends. Why aren't you helping me?"

"We tried to help you," Big Mike said quietly. "We went to Kansas City and met with Mrs. Hardesty. Adam, you were in that hotel room. You were inebriated."

"But there was nothing sexual. Why won't you believe that?"

"Adam, you left your sweater there," Julie said. "And you kissed her."

"She kissed me."

"And what about the note you sent the next day?"

Adam stopped in his tracks.

"There was no note."

"We saw it, Adam," Big Mike said. "Mrs. Hardesty's husband showed it to us."

"I don't know anything about a note."

No one spoke.

"I don't know anything about a note," He repeated, his voice growing louder.

Riley stood up. "Adam, let's get back to why we're here—"

"There was no note!"

SUNDAY

Day Sixteen

Background Issues

- *Adam has admitted to participating in casino gambling and consumption of alcohol to the point where his judgment was impaired.*

- *Adam has been implicated, but not yet confessed to a romantic relationship outside his marriage.*

- *Adam's sins were brought to light only after letters were received by his wife and employer.*

- *The effects of Adam's sins have been widespread. He has been placed on leave by his employer and is the focus of stories in various local media.*

> • *Whereas Adam's transgressions are in direct violation of the Surfside Church Covenant he signed when joining the church, he will be under church discipline with the goal of full restoration upon demonstrating a repentant lifestyle.*

It was another mostly sleepless night, as Adam read and reread the church discipline contract Riley Wenger had given him. This issue could be behind us, Adam had said in an attempt to reason with Riley and The Group. Take out the statement about a romantic relationship and he would sign. He appealed to Forrest Delaney, relying on the concept of innocent until proven guilty, but Forrest mumbled something about the evidence being overwhelming. Even Big Mike, who had criticized Pastor Miles' wish that he close his business on Sunday, wouldn't step up. "There's no reason for her to make up this stuff," he said.

Then there were the consequences for his actions:

Plan of Discipline

> • *Adam will attend weekly meetings of Surfside's Freedom from Addiction program.*

> • *Adam will write out a list of all people he has sinned against over the past six months, including sexual sin, lying, and deception. He will share that list with Pastor Wenger and develop a plan to confess and ask for forgiveness from his sins.*

> • *Adam will meet weekly with Brooke and Pastor Traynor, during which time they will work toward reconciliation, with Adam reassuming his role as the head of his household.*
>
> • *Adam will not gamble, imbibe alcohol, nor put himself in any situation that could compromise his sexual integrity.*

The contract concluded by stating Adam would be excluded from church and small group activities until all items were fulfilled.

"What if I refuse to sign?" he had asked Riley. The pastor cautioned him that would result in his being permanently excluded from fellowship at Surfside.

"You don't want to make this journey alone," Eric Stover had said.

"I already am," Adam replied as he'd walked out the door.

At seven, he gave up on sleep, got up, and washed his face. Then, desperate for someone to talk to, he punched in a number he knew by heart.

"Hello," her voice was raspy.

"Mom."

"Hey, Adam, what are you doing calling on Sunday morning?" His mother coughed several times, trying gallantly, but unsuccessfully, to clear lungs ravaged by years of smoking.

"I hadn't talked to you in a while, Mom. I thought this was as good a time as any."

"It's a fine time. I don't go far these days."

Adam thought of his mother lying on the sofa in the same house he'd grown up in, oxygen tanks always close by. Her emphysema was diagnosed three years ago, and was now classified as moderate. Early on, she had hooked up the portable oxygen tanks and gone about her daily activities, but in recent months as her general health deteriorated, she left the house less and less. Adam and Brooke went to visit every three months or so. Seeing Jack was the incentive that always seemed to help her rally for their visits, but by the time they left, she was exhausted. Adam felt sad and a little guilty that he, her only child, wasn't closer. His father had passed away four years earlier from lung cancer.

"Everything good back home?"

Starving for friendly conversation, Adam listened intently as his mother chatted about the latest weddings, divorces, and other gossip. His hometown was small, and everybody knew everybody else.

"How are Brooke and Jack?"

He knew the question was coming and had rehearsed his response. In the end, he couldn't do it.

"They... are doing fine. Jack is excited to start school. Brooke is staying home with him for now."

"Any chance you might come back home before school starts? I'd love to see that little carrot-top."

"Maybe, Mom. I don't know yet."

For once he was thankful that his mother and her friends were not of the internet age. Had they been, they would've undoubtedly heard of his problems. Even so, it was a matter of time before word got back.

The call concluded with Adam making himself a promise that he needed to head to West Virginia soon. His mother's persistent cough seemed to have gotten worse, and her breathing sounded more labored.

After all, he thought to himself, if he wasn't allowed to be a father and husband, he could at least be a son.

"Grandfather Meekins made the trip five days a week for two years," Papa said as they crossed a rickety old bridge.

They were in Saxon County, two counties north of Cape Girardeau. When they'd passed through Adair, the county seat, a few minutes before, Papa made a detour to take her by an old church a couple blocks from the city square.

"This is where my Daddy, Aldus Dobson, and the rest decided to face things head on," Harvester said, going on to describe the day that twenty African-Americans took it upon themselves to integrate the Open Door Bible Church.

Across the bridge, the landscape was stark, yet beautiful. Green fields stretched in all directions, some planted with beans and corn, others growing wild with grass, weeds, and tree saplings. The road, rutted gravel and dirt, appeared untended.

"He lives out here by himself?"

"Has for years, since his boy left after high school. That's when he called me at the university."

At a crossroads, Papa continued ahead into the remnants of what had once been a small town.

"Grebey Township, they called this," he said, pointing out a building falling in on itself. "That was

Mr. Mauck's store. He was a good man, a Quaker. Very kind to our family."

Just past the store, on a side road, loomed two structures still in decent shape.

"That's the church up there, and that," he pointed to a two-story brick building. "That's the Grebey Island School, where your Grandfather Meekins worked with the Manning boy."

They pulled to a stop in front of the school. Overgrown weeds choked a path leading to the door.

"Can we...?" Theresa motioned to the front door.

"Certainly. Earl won't mind." They got out and made their way to the door. Papa put his shoulder to it and pushed, finally succeeding in getting it open. Seeing the effect this small effort had on him, Theresa was saddened by the fact that their time together was growing shorter. Aunt Joy's death was a reminder. She was several years younger than her older brother.

Theresa stepped past him and into the musty school house. Feed sacks and other farm items were stacked about haphazardly. The smell was a combination of moisture, burlap, and mouse droppings. But something stronger occupied the place.

"I can feel him here – Grandfather Meekins."

Smiling sadly, Papa nodded.

They stood for several moments. Neither spoke, but they shared something special.

"I haven't felt his presence since his house was torn down," Theresa said. "But he's here."

She hugged Papa tightly.

"Thank you for bringing me here."

###

He spent the afternoon in the motel. Sad, really, when Adam considered how beautiful the day was. Just a few miles away, families baked in the sun and played in the surf that made Ocean City the go-to vacation resort for the Mid-Atlantic. He remembered how excited he and Brooke had been when they moved to the area. A new beginning, made even better by sharing it with each other.

And a year later, he was alone in a business-class motel.

Despite the scores of people he'd come to know, the only ones he considered close friends were The Group. Socializing with hospital employees wasn't a good idea for many reasons. The same went for board members. "Never become too friendly with people you might have to fire or who might have to fire you," one of his MBA professors had stressed. Good advice for sure, but advice that left him with a dearth of friends.

There were the guys from college. Several times he'd picked up the phone to call his college roommate, Shad Sweeney. Shad was Vice-President of his father's construction company and seemed to spend as much time vacationing in exotic locations as he did working. Shad would help him out: advice, money, whatever. Shad was also the kind of guy who would often remind you how much you should appreciate his help.

No, it would be better to wait until tomorrow and talk to Jasmine. Perhaps she had more ideas. She'd know what to do about this letter he was purported to have written. It was stupid. There was no letter. For whatever reason, Penny was hanging him out to dry, adding evidence whenever the need arose.

And for what? He hadn't done anything to her. Their college breakup had been hard on her. She'd gone ballistic and made sure everyone on campus knew he'd dumped her, but that happened a lot when relationships went bad. Everyone at college knew Penny was mercurial, and eventually things returned to normal.

There had to be something more to it than revenge. After all, they'd been in each other's company a half-dozen times in the years since college. They'd both married and seemed to be doing okay.

Until now.

Earl Manning was a peculiar man. Dark hair and eyes, with a perpetual expression of fear and worry. Papa had told her what to expect, but he still seemed tragic.

Despite his pleasure in seeing Papa, Earl took some time to become comfortable in Theresa's presence. It wasn't until she took a chance and asked him about his son that he loosened up.

"Chan plays baseball. Played in high school and college. Even played major league ball for the Cincinnati Reds, up until a year or so ago. He's living in Louisville now. Got two kids."

"How often do you see him?"

Earl's face lost its animation. Theresa noticed a tremor in his hands.

"We don't see each other. Too much happened." Earl looked at Papa, their eyes meeting in a sad understanding.

"Earl's a dear friend," Papa said. "Back when he and Miss Cora ran this place, they were some of the best farmers anywhere."

"Wish I could say the same today," Earl said, glancing out the window. "Got the whole island now, but don't have it in me to do much." He turned to Theresa, a smile playing across his face. "I keep trying to get Harvester to move back. Maybe we can make things like they used to be, back before..." His voice trailed off.

###

Traffic was snarled as Theresa navigated her father's old sedan away from the ballpark. The Cardinals had defeated the Atlanta Braves, and the sounds of blowing horns were testament to the home team's solid play.

"How long since you last went to a ballgame?" Theresa asked.

"Stan Musial's last season," Papa said, going on to recount the entire game as if it had been yesterday rather than forty years ago.

It had been a spur-of-the-moment decision by Theresa to change her flight plans and leave from St. Louis rather than the small Cape Girardeau airport. The additional cost was worth it, as her father had reveled in seeing his beloved Cardinals play in person after his visit with Earl Manning.

"I wish you'd consider stopping in hotels a couple nights on your way back to Washington State," Theresa said. "It's a thirty-hour trip."

"I'll pull into some rest stops for a nap or two along the way. I like driving at night better anyway."

Theresa shouldn't have been surprised by her father's decision to head West so soon. His heart was with the migrant workers, and they would be transitioning from tomatoes to apples in the next couple weeks. The changeover required them to pull up stakes and move a few hundred miles. Papa had never been one to shy away from hard work.

"Papa, how did Mr. Manning come to own your family farm?"

The sudden change in the conversation didn't seem to faze him.

"When the situation out there got to be too much, my Papa and the others gave up and headed back down south. The organization that sold them the land took it over. They tried to find buyers, but had no luck. Eventually, they let it go. Earl's father, Levi, bought it for back taxes."

"I think Mr. Manning would let you have it," Theresa said.

"I've actually been thinking about that, Cookie. Let's just leave it at that for now, though. I'm still thinking through some things."

She beamed at him.

"Well, anything that gets you off the road would be great by me."

###

It was just after six when they arrived at Lambert International Airport. Theresa's flight left at seven-thirty, and she needed to get checked in. Pulling to the curb, she climbed out and walked around to the back of her car to get her suitcase from the trunk. Papa was quicker and was already setting it on the sidewalk. She looked at him closely. His eyes were still red from the tears they'd shed the past week, but there was something else there. He was at peace.

"I wish I could go with you," she said, pulling him into an embrace.

"You got your work waiting for you, little girl. Your mama would want us both to get on with our callings."

"I just wish my calling could come close to yours, Papa." Theresa placed her head on his shoulder, surprised at how fragile he felt. "Did I ever tell you how proud I am of you?"

Papa didn't respond and even though she couldn't see his face, she knew they were fighting the same emotions.

"I'll come see you and Miles this winter," he said as he pulled away enough to face her. "Who knows? I may even get on an airplane."

Theresa laughed at the thought. Her parents had always driven everyplace they went.

A few minutes and tears later, Theresa stood at the curb waving as Papa drove away.

Take care of him, Lord. Keep him safe on the road and let him continue to do Your work.

MONDAY

Day Seventeen

Weekends and weekdays now varied little, despite being less than a week since Adam had been placed on leave. Rising early, he decided to end the monotony. He might not be able to go to work or see his son, but he could take care of himself. He pulled on his running shoes and headed out. Forty minutes later he was walking through the hotel's modest lobby, sweaty and spent from a four-mile run.

"Mr. Overstreet, will you be staying a while longer?" Francisco, the front desk manager, asked. "I can put you on the weekly rate. It's fifteen bucks a night less."

"Yes, please do that," Adam said, heading to the area where the hotel provided a free breakfast. After a quick bowl of fruit and a glass of milk, he was back in his room looking up a phone number in a worn directory. There was no answer at the Ocean City branch of the Worcester County Library, but the recorded message said they opened at ten. He would put the downtime to good use, and the library's computer terminals would allow him to do his own legal research while waiting to hear back from Jasmine Fleece.

Miles hadn't stirred when Theresa arrived home after midnight. It was seven-thirty when she was awakened by his movement around the bedroom. She watched him go back and forth from the closet to the bathroom as he got ready for the day. He was slipping into a tan pullover when he saw she was awake.

"Welcome home."

"Thanks." Theresa smiled. "There's nothing on my calendar today, so I think I'll stay around here and clean up a little bit."

"How's your father?"

"Pretty good. We went to a Cardinals' game yesterday, then I flew home, and he headed back west. It was hard seeing him go."

"That sounds fun," Miles said, inspecting himself in the dresser mirror. "We had a good morning at church yesterday. Eleven people came forward. I preached from Philippians. I wish you could've been there."

"Like I wish you could've been there for me last week?"

Miles flinched. "Tee, I said I was sorry."

"I know. You want to have lunch today? I've been craving seafood."

"Let me check my schedule. I'll call and let you know." A quick peck on the cheek and he was off.

After a stop for legal pads and pens, Adam was waiting at the door of the library as it was being unlocked to begin the day. Moving past shelves of books and magazines, he located a bank of computer terminals in a quiet corner. He had just laid his new supplies down when his phone buzzed. He hurriedly made his way back outside, waiting until he was on the front steps before answering.

"Adam, Jasmine Fleece."

"Hi, Jasmine. Good news I hope?"

"Well, we've hit a snag. I'm sure you can take care of it, so I wanted to call you first thing."

"What kind of snag?"

Adam heard papers being shuffled, then Jasmine returned to the line.

"I'm sure it's just a mistake, but your check didn't clear."

By ten-fifteen Theresa had the house cleaned from top to bottom. The only area remaining was Miles' home office. After vacuuming, she dusted the areas of his desk not covered with stacks of paper or reference books. Miles spent hours each week preparing his sermons. Most of that time was spent at his church office, but he often applied the finishing touches at home.

Taking a seat, she fired up his computer to check her e-mail. Her shoulders sagged when she saw she had over three hundred. Maybe this afternoon. Remembering Miles' promise to call about lunch, she pulled her phone from the pocket of her shorts. She had forgotten to turn on the ringer when she got home and had missed a call; one of the partners at the firm asking her to cross-check some research. Searching the desk for a scrap of paper, she saw a file in the center of the desk labeled *Church Discipline*. She opened it.

Inside was a list of names under the heading, *Current Disciplinary Actions*. Beside each name was the alleged infraction. She was dismayed to see nineteen names on the list, mostly people she knew. The infractions ran the gamut. Two members, a man and woman in their early twenties, were cited for *Sexual Relations before Marriage*, with arrows connecting one to the other. Three others were listed for *Public Intoxication*. Further down the list Theresa saw Adam Overstreet's name. *Gambling, Alcohol, Infidelity* were the citations. Theresa's breath caught when she read, also beside Adam's name, in Miles' handwriting, *Refused Church Discipline – Excluded*.

Digging deeper into the file, she pulled out a copy of the contract Adam was asked to sign. Attached were notes with dates and times. Theresa counted three entries over the past week, *Meeting with B. Overstreet*. One of the meetings had been the evening before Miles flew to Missouri. All were after five in the afternoon. The inappropriateness of his after-hours meetings with Brooke Overstreet rankled her.

Theresa jumped at the ring of her cellphone. She closed the file quickly.

"Hi, Miles."

"Tee, I can't do lunch today. I've got a young couple coming in who want to get married in the church this fall."

"No problem. I'm busy cleaning anyway."

"I'll see you this evening. I have a meeting at five-thirty, but it shouldn't last longer than a couple hours. How about a late dinner?"

"Sure. Want me to pick you up?"

"Nah, that's okay. I don't know how long I'll be. I'll swing by home when I'm done."

"It appears a significant withdrawal was made late Friday afternoon. Mrs. Overstreet made it at the branch on Thirty-First Street."

"How much is left in the account?"

"Well, let's see," the young teller clicked a few keys. "There's... oh, it appears a transaction is taking place right now. OC Extended Stay Hotel?"

"Yes, that's mine."

"Well, they're charging... trying to charge... there's not enough money to cover the transaction. I'm seeing eleven dollars remaining in the account."

###

Brooke's SUV was gone when Adam arrived at the house. He sat down on the front step and called her cellphone.

"Brooke, call me as soon as you get this. It's important."

Adam dialed another number.

"Jasmine Fleece."

"Jasmine, my wife has removed all the money from our checking account."

"I'm sorry, Adam. I can probably help you get some of it back."

"That would be great. How quick can you start?"

"We still need the retainer. We can take a credit card."

Adam was reaching for his wallet when reality struck him between the eyes.

"Jasmine, I don't have a credit card. Only a debit card tied to the account."

"No credit card? Really, Adam?"

"Nope. Brooke and I try to avoid credit. I had the card the hospital issued me, but they took that back."

Silence.

"Jasmine?"

"Adam, how much can you pay? I want to help you, but my firm has a strict policy about collecting retainers."

"I've got eleven bucks. And another three hundred and fifty in my wallet."

More silence.

Jasmine took a deep breath. "I'm afraid I can't proceed without a larger portion of the retainer. At least a thousand. Can you borrow it?"

Adam raced through all the people he knew, aware that his circle of friends was pretty much limited to The Group. Calling his mother wouldn't do any good, as she lived on her social security check.

"Jasmine, I've reached the end of my rope."

Theresa pulled into the church parking lot at six-twenty. The church offices closed at five, and there were only two vehicles in the parking lot. One was Miles'. The other, a non-descript white SUV.

Using the key Miles had given her months ago, Theresa quietly unlocked a door leading through a side entrance. The entryway lights were off, but the area was illuminated by late-day sunlight coming through windows high on the wall. Outside the office area, she pulled the handle but found it was locked.

Pulling out the key again, she unlocked the door and pushed it open. The outer office had no windows and received only residual light from the entryway. Careful not to make noise, she crept to her husband's closed office door and pressed her ear to the thick oak. Inside she heard two voices, male and female, but was unable to make out what they were saying.

She stayed close, considering what to do next. She imagined how this would look to someone coming in. On several occasions, she'd represented clients who were brought down by eavesdroppers. She'd found the practice classless and unnecessary. Until now.

Divided between pushing open the door or retreating to the parking lot, she settled on the latter.

Moments later she was back at her car. The entire adventure took less than ten minutes.

With nothing else to do, she decided to sit and wait.

A sharp rap on the window startled her awake. It was Miles, alone, grinning at her through the window. The other car was gone. She lowered the window.

"Asleep at the wheel," he said with a laugh.

Shaking away the cobwebs, she looked at the dashboard clock. Eight-fifteen. She had dozed for almost two hours.

"Jetlag," she said as Miles crawled in the passenger side.

"Still hungry?" he asked.

"Definitely. How was your meeting?" Theresa started the car and steered out of the parking lot.

"Just a meeting. Where are you taking me?"

"Hooper's shouldn't be too crowded," she said.

Miles rubbed his hands together. "Whoo-whee! I'm gonna be digging into a bucket of clams for sure!" Even in her pensive state, Theresa couldn't help but laugh at his enthusiasm for seafood. She considered asking whom he'd met with, but that would be out of character. Perhaps there was a better way of finding out.

"I called your father this afternoon," Miles said.

"You did?"

"Don't be so surprised, Tee. I'm not always a schmuck."

"How was he?"

"Good. Really good. He was someplace in the Idaho Panhandle. I apologized all over myself for leaving so quickly. He was good with it; said he understood."

The gesture touched her. She had hoped early on in their relationship that Miles and Papa would grow close. For some reason, most likely distance, that hadn't happened. Still, her father encouraged and prayed for him just as he did for everyone in his life.

"So what's new around here?" Theresa said, reaching for his hand, suddenly feeling guilty for her subterfuge.

"Well, let's see," Miles replied, launching into an account that took them through most of dinner, an account that included everything that had happened the past week, but noticeably left out any mention of Adam and Brooke Overstreet.

After leaving for a quick supper on the Boardwalk, Adam returned to the house. Brooke's car was home. He rang the bell. Her face fell when she saw who it was.

"We need to talk."

"I got your message, but I've been in a meeting the past couple hours."

"Dad!" Jack rocketed into Adam's outstretched arms, clinging to him like one might a tree in a tornado. Adam started to tear up, but willed himself to stay upbeat.

"You guys play for a while," Brooke said cheerfully as she headed to the master bedroom. For the next hour, they played rough and they played soft. Jack was particularly excited to show off his new baseball glove. "I just got it today. Pastor Miles gave it to me."

Adam felt his stomach tighten as he inspected the glove from all angles before following his son into the backyard for a game of catch in the waning daylight. It was almost nine when Brooke called Jack into the house for his bath.

"Will you tuck me in before you leave?" Jack asked. Brooke nodded her assent.

"Of course. I'll not leave until you're tucked in." Jack bounded up the steps to his room.

"Let's talk in the kitchen," Brooke said.

Adam wasted little time. "Why did you take all the money out of our checking account?"

Brooke pressed her lips together, looking over Adam's shoulder, unwilling to meet his gaze.

"I need money to support Jack and me."

"All of it?"

"How was I to know you wouldn't take it all and leave us in the cold?"

Adam was incredulous. "Brooke, really? Do you honestly think I'd do that?"

"No, but I never thought you'd do what you did in St. Louis."

Adam fought against rising frustration. "Someday, hopefully soon, I can make you see that nothing happened."

When she didn't respond, he charged ahead.

"I hired an attorney to help me prove my innocence, but the check bounced. When I go back to the hotel, the desk clerk is going to tell me my debit card was denied. Brooke, what were you thinking?"

"Adam, we have no money coming in. I have to do what I think is best for Jack and me. If that means you giving up the high life in a fancy hotel, so be it."

"Fancy hotel? I want to be here. Say the word and I'll give up the hotel. One way or another I'll be giving it up tomorrow anyway. I have three hundred and fifty bucks and no credit card."

"Please, Adam, sign the discipline contract from the church, and we can move toward reconciling."

"I guess when I'm panhandling on the Boardwalk, I may have to sign it, even though I'd be confessing to something that didn't happen." Then, eyeing another box of food on the counter, he said, "It looks like you and Jack are pretty well set. You've got our life savings, the house, food from church, and a special relationship with Pastor Miles—"

"What's that mean?" Brooke was on her feet, moving away from the table. "You need to go, Adam."

"I can't go. I promised Jack I'd tuck—"

"Go! I'll tell him you got called away." Her tone left no doubt that he should leave, so he did.

TUESDAY

Day Eighteen

Adam put his luggage in the trunk of his car and drove away from the hotel for the last time. He would look for a cheaper place a few miles further from the beach. His first stop was at the bank branch closest to home.

Adam approached a teller.

"Is Larry available?" Larry Stevens was the branch manager. They had become acquainted through Rotary. Larry appeared and waved Adam back to his office. There would usually have been the exchange of pleasantries, but Adam wasn't feeling pleasant.

"Larry, I need your help," he said before launching into the Readers' Digest condensed version of his recent problems.

"I'm a divorced man myself," Larry said, shaking his head. "Valerie took me for everything, and I'm supposed to be a financial expert."

"I'm hoping it doesn't come to that," Adam said. "Right now, though, things aren't going well."

Larry turned his computer screen so Adam could watch as he accessed the Overstreet's checking account.

"Yep, Mrs. Overstreet wrote a check to withdraw all except a few hundred dollars. Some of that went to cover outstanding charges."

"Is there anything I can do to get some of it back? Both our names are on the account."

"Let's see." Larry's fingers raced over the keys. "It looks like she took the money with her rather than opening a new account." More strokes of the keyboard. "She deposited the funds into another bank Monday morning. Sorry, Adam, but I can't help you. Since it was a joint account, either of you could access the funds."

"How about our savings account?"

"Thirty bucks."

"What? We had seventy-five hundred in there!"

"Transferred to the checking account last Thursday," Larry said. "It appears Mrs. Overstreet planned this a couple days in advance."

"Larry, she's taken all our money. Any suggestions?"

Larry sat back in his chair and rubbed his chin.

"You can file suit, but that takes time."

"And money."

"Oh, yeah, there is that," Larry said, shaking his head. Then, brightening, he added, "How about a loan? We can do a short-term loan. The rates aren't great, but we can probably do twenty-five hundred on a signature loan."

"How quickly can we make it happen?"

Larry pulled a single-page form from a desk drawer. "We can do it right here. All I need is some basic information."

Larry started asking questions. Adam, feeling the first ray of sunshine in several days, provided the necessary answers.

"That's it," Larry said, getting up from his desk. "Let me go process this with headquarters. I'll have your check in about ten minutes."

Adam picked up a *Sports Illustrated* from the corner of Larry's desk and started reading. After flipping through several pages, he dialed the number of the hotel he'd checked out of to see if they accepted cash. He had just disconnected when Larry returned. He scanned the hallway before closing the door.

"I didn't know you'd run into problems at the hospital."

"It's only temporary. They received some incorrect information. I plan to take care of it now that I can pay my lawyer's retainer."

"That's the problem. When I called the bank president he said we can't make the signature loan since you're on unpaid leave at the hospital."

"I won't be after my lawyer talks to the hospital board," Adam said, offering a pained smile. "They were wrong to put me on unpaid leave to begin with."

Larry massaged his temples. "I've got my marching orders. I can't make the loan without a paycheck coming in. Trust me, man, if I could I would."

Adam got to his feet. "I'm three hundred bucks from being broke, Larry."

"Can't you call one of your friends? Surely somebody around here will tide you over."

"I don't know who," Adam said glumly. "I feel like I'm watching a movie about some poor down-on-his-luck drifter. The only difference is, I'm starring in it."

Larry offered his hand. "Good luck."

"Thanks. Just don't be surprised if I'm wearing a ski mask the next time you see me."

###

As he pushed through the entrance of Big Mike's Produce, a large poster board sign grabbed Adam's attention.

Effective the first week of August, we will be closed on Sundays. We hope we can meet your fruit and vegetable needs the other six days of the week.

He moved past the registers to a rear corner of the store. When he wasn't stocking shelves or helping customers, Big Mike could usually be found in his office. Sure enough, he was seated at his desk, engrossed in paperwork. He didn't hear Adam enter.

"Will you give me just five minutes?"

Big Mike looked up and flashed a smile that faded quickly.

"Adam." His voice was flat. He didn't get up.

"Closed on Sundays. He got to you too."

"Who?"

"You know who, Mike. Miles Traynor."

"It was our decision." The concern on his face belied the certainty with which he spoke.

"Quite an about-face from that day at the ballpark."

"Yeah, you know, the more we thought about it, the more we realized it was dishonoring God for us to open on Sunday. We'll get by."

"I'll be rooting for you, Big Mike."

"Thanks." Big Mike scanned his desk, avoiding eye contact. "I'm awfully busy here, Adam."

"I know you're not supposed to associate with me. I won't take more than a minute. I have one question and nobody else can answer it."

Big Mike didn't respond, but he didn't ask him to leave, either.

"What did you see or hear last Monday night that led you and Julie to leave Kansas City without me?"

"Look, Adam, I'm not comfortable getting in the middle of this. Can't you talk to Brooke or Pastor Miles? Julie and I came back and shared everything with them."

"They've told me nothing, and, besides, I need to hear from someone who was there."

"Well," Big Mike said, rubbing his hands together. "You left your sweater in Mrs. Hardesty's room. She brought it home and showed it to us."

"It is my sweater, Mike. I left it in in the suite. I've never denied being there."

"Yeah, well, then there was the letter you sent her the next day. We saw that too."

"There wasn't a letter."

214

"Adam, Julie and I saw it. Mrs. Hardesty's husband found it in her suitcase when she got home."

"What did it say?"

Big Mike exhaled. "Let's not play games, Adam. She said you wrote the letter."

"Did it ever dawn on you that I might be taking the fall for someone else?"

Mike stood up. "Adam, that woman is scared. Scared and ashamed of what happened. She almost lost her marriage, and she's telling her husband everything in hopes of keeping it together. You should do the same."

"It's not true. How many more times do I have to say that?"

"You don't have to say it anymore, Adam. Confess to your sins. Sign the church discipline plan and move ahead. Your family needs you, man."

Big Mike nodded at the door.

"Now, if you don't mind, I'd like you to leave."

WEDNESDAY

Day Nineteen

The Lexus's diagnostic system indicated it was time for a service call. Fat chance of that. After buying a cheap supper and paying for the night at his new home away from home, Adam had three hundred and five dollars.

Muscles were screaming, and he stretched as best he could while navigating the car across the bridge toward the beach. The Seagull Motel's advertised rate was forty-one bucks a night. Before checking in the afternoon before, Adam had negotiated it to thirty-five by paying cash and agreeing to take a small second-floor room next to the laundry facilities. Stale air, threadbare carpet, and a lumpy mattress greeted him when he'd opened the door to Room 215.

With his dwindling resources, having enough money to get by was becoming almost as important as getting his family back. Entering the library, he had two goals in mind. First was to continue the work Jasmine had started to get his leave changed from unpaid to paid. He had jotted down some of the irregularities and breaks with hospital policy she'd mentioned in their last conversation. Using the resources of the public library, he hoped he could craft an argument that would get the paychecks reinstated.

The second, more urgent goal, was to go by the payroll department to see if he could get his last paycheck. Even if the unpaid leave remained in force, he was still due a paycheck for the last two weeks he'd worked. Paycheck funds were electronically transferred on Fridays, and if he could head off the transfer, he would have enough money to pay a portion of Jasmine's retainer and get by for a couple weeks.

He made a beeline for the bank of computers located against a far wall. All occupied. Four elderly library patrons, three women and a man, were busily scanning the internet. Three of them were on Facebook. There was a sign posted above the terminals.

Please sign up at circulation desk to use computers. One-hour maximum signup.

Adam found the circulation desk, located the sign-in sheet, and added his name. Then, with fifty minutes to burn, he headed for the reference section.

"Hey, Tee, it's me."

"Miles. Why are you calling my office line?"

"I'm betting you left your cellphone in the car." She had.

"I need some help. Didn't you say you were going to Snow Hill for court today?"

"This afternoon. Why?"

"I can't say much right now. I'm at breakfast with Riley, and there are other people close by. A member of the congregation has asked the church for legal help. They're dealing with some issues and need a protective order."

Theresa's stomach clenched. Inevitably a protective order involved a woman or a child being abused by someone they trusted. She had filed quite a few over the years and never got used to the stories she heard.

"I can help with that. I'm tied up all morning. How about I hand you off to one of the secretaries? They'll get the information and prepare the paperwork. I'll meet you in Snow Hill at one. Court convenes at one-fifteen."

"That'll work. Thanks, Tee."

"I love you, Miles," Theresa said, hearing him disconnect.

#

Adam arrived during the noon hour, when many people were at lunch. Parking in the employee lot, he entered through a rear entrance and made it through a back hallway without running into anyone. When he turned the corner, his luck changed.

Vicki Passwaters bumped into him.

"Oh, I'm sorry... Adam?"

"Hey, Vicki."

"What are you..." the secretary looked behind her, checking to see if anyone was nearby. "Adam, you aren't supposed to be here."

"Wrong. I'm not supposed to be working here. I can still be in the building. After all, it is a public hospital, built and paid for with public money."

Vicki clutched her purse, her eyes darting around.

"I don't know, Adam. Melvin said—"

"Vicki, don't worry. I'm headed to payroll, and then I'll be gone. Ten minutes, tops. I even came during lunchtime so I wouldn't cause any problems."

Vicki exhaled, started to speak, stopped, reconsidered, and said, "Please be quick," before hustling back in the direction from which she'd come.

The half-dozen people he passed on his way to payroll either didn't know him or acted like they didn't. Entering the business office, he looked across the bullpen of cubicles and spotted one office with a light on. He approached and lightly rapped on the door.

"Cassie."

Looking up from her computer terminal, Cassie Mattis' smile faded when recognition hit.

"Mr. Overstreet."

"Cassie, I know you're surprised to see me. I just have a quick request, and I'll be on my way."

"Well," despite five years on the job, the petite brunette appeared flustered at seeing the ousted CEO standing in front of her. "Sit down."

Adam took a seat and laid out his request. Cassie listened, her eyes flickering from Adam to the open door behind him.

"Mr. Overstreet, you know as well as anyone that it's hospital policy to only provide electronic fund transfer. We try to avoid cutting paper checks for payroll."

"Yes, Cassie, but I also know that we've made exceptions in the past. You and I worked on a couple for employees who were new to the area and hadn't found a local bank."

"I guess that's right, but..." Cassie's eyes blinked rapidly.

"But what? It's as simple as a few keystrokes."

Cassie turned to her computer and started typing.

"Obviously, I'll have to get approval, just like I did from you when we made exceptions before."

Adam bristled. "Cassie, you don't need approval. If you look in the hospital's financial policies, you'll see that's only needed when you're expending funds that weren't appropriated. My paycheck is owed to me. I just want a paper check instead of having it electronically processed."

Nervously fingering a gold necklace, Cassie kept her eyes on the computer screen.

"I'll see what I can do, Mr. Overstreet."

Adam jotted down his number and handed it across the desk.

"Call me here," he said, standing up.

###

Theresa saw Riley Wenger enter the courtroom. She left the group of attorneys she was visiting with to meet him, pulling out the paperwork the firm secretaries had prepared.

"Theresa, sorry I'm late."

"No problem. Is Miles looking for a parking space?"

"No, he couldn't come. He had a last-minute meeting with a congregant."

"I've got the paperwork right here. I haven't had a chance to look at it, but orders of protection are pretty straightforward." Theresa opened the file and started scanning the order, her throat tightening when she saw the names.

"By chance, is the meeting Miles had come up so suddenly with Brooke Overstreet?"

Riley shook his head slowly. "You know I can't tell you that kind of thing, Theresa. We operate just like lawyers do, confidentiality and all that."

She could see in his face that she'd guessed right. Glancing at the clock, she motioned for him to join her on a bench.

"Riley, what do you make of everything that's happened with the Overstreets?"

Riley rubbed his neck. "The man made some mistakes that he's not willing to own up to."

"I've heard all that. I'm asking what *you* think."

A pained look crossed his face. "I like him; I really do. But facts are facts. He messed up. If he'd just come clean, they could move past this."

Theresa turned to face him. "Have you considered that he isn't willing to come clean because he didn't do all that he's being accused of?"

Riley held up his hands. "Look, Theresa. Miles feels strongly that the man has problems. I personally met and offered him a discipline plan, but he wouldn't sign it."

"So now we're shunning him?" Theresa felt her blood starting to boil.

"Don't use the word shunning, for crying out loud. It makes us sound like some nutcase religious sect." Riley's tone was whiny, almost pleading.

Theresa stood. "The fact that I've asked twice what you think and haven't gotten an answer tells me a lot." She handed him the file. "I can't in good conscience approach the judge about this matter. Find yourself another lawyer and start using the brain God gave you."

Adam was exiting the hospital when he spotted the notice on an employee bulletin board. Ocean City Memorial's Board of Trustees had a special meeting scheduled for Saturday, three days away. The meeting was posted as being closed to the public for the purpose of discussing employee issues. Adam had little trouble figuring out which employee's issues would be discussed. He read it again, pulled it from the bulletin board, and took it with him.

Returning to the library, he commandeered an open terminal, pulled up his private account, and fired off an email to Adele Sweet, the board secretary:

Adele, please consider this my formal request to appear before the Board of Trustees at their special meeting this Saturday. I wish to discuss legal and policy issues related to the board's decision to place me on unpaid leave.

He proofread the message and prepared to hit send when he had another thought. Moving the cursor to the bottom of the email, he added, *I reserve the right to bring along legal representation.*

Maybe that'll scare them, he thought, sending the message.

###

After leading the judge and court clerk through several continuances and orders, Theresa stepped away from the bench. It was late afternoon, and the courtroom was mostly empty. Gathering her files, she nodded goodbye to the two attorneys waiting their turn. Forrest Delaney was in the hallway.

"I thought you were in Georgetown today."

"I was," Forrest said quickly, straightening his tie and wiping sweat from his forehead. "Is there still time to see the judge?"

"A few more minutes," Theresa said, placing her briefcase on the floor. "What's so important to bring you all the way down here?"

Theresa spotted Riley Wenger rising from a bench at the end of the hall. Both men looked uncomfortable at having run into her. Good, she thought. Let them.

"Forrest, do you think Adam Overstreet is dangerous enough to warrant having orders of protection filed against him?"

"I think... things are..."

"Would you file this if Miles weren't asking you to?"

Forrest looked from Theresa to Riley, too tongue-tied to answer. Theresa picked up her briefcase.

"Have either or you prayed about this?"

Silence.

"What's next? Scarlet letters?"

Riley started to object, but Theresa had already turned and headed for the elevator.

Adam barely heard the knock at the door over the din of the television. He wadded up the wrapper from the sub sandwich he'd eaten earlier and tossed it in the trashcan on his way to the door. There wasn't a peep hole. He would have to peer through the curtain or open the door and take his chances. He chose the latter.

"Riley."

"You're a hard man to find, Adam."

"I'd be at home with my family if Surfside Church hadn't poisoned my wife against me."

Riley looked around uncertainly. His hands were shaking.

"Adam, I'm only here to deliver something to you. Hear me out, brother, and I'll be—"

"Did you just call me brother?"

His eyes widening, Riley stammered, "Sorry, it's just a word, I mean..."

Adam stepped back and opened the door wider.

"Come in, Pastor. Have a seat. You're the first guest I've had since moving in. Sorry I didn't clean up."

"Oh... it's okay," Riley said before noticing the grin on Adam's face. He entered and sat in one of the two vinyl chairs situated at a small table by the window. Adam took the other.

"So what are you springing on me now?"

"Broth—Adam, Brooke feels it's best that you don't come back to the house until you're ready to sign the church discipline agreement." He opened the folder he was carrying and pulled out several sheets of paper.

"What about Jack? I have a right to see my son."

"Arrangements are being made for you to meet him away from home." Riley flipped through the papers. "It looks like a third party will bring Jack to meet you each Sunday after church. Where would you like to meet?"

"What is that you're reading from?" Adam asked, peering over the table.

"It's just a document... a..."

Adam pulled the papers from his hands and started reading. After a few minutes, he laid them down, fighting back tears.

"I'm sorry, Adam. It's got to be this way."

Adam rested his head on the table, trying to get his wits about him.

"Please, Adam, sign the church discipline letter. We can walk out of here together."

Head still bowed, Adam considered the option. He missed Jack desperately. Despite everything, he missed Brooke, the way they had been. He imagined what it would be like to be home, playing ball with Jack or making love to Brooke.

It would be... good.

And it would be...

"Pastor, would you confess to something you didn't do?"

"Never." Riley didn't skip a beat.

"Even if it was the easiest way out?"

"The Bible is pretty clear on that. Verse after verse after verse, like Colossians 3:9, 'do not lie to each other, since you have taken off your old self."

"If I sign that agreement, I'll be lying."

They stared at each other. Riley appeared to be searching for the right words.

"If that's the case, prove you're telling the truth. Don't leave any rock unturned."

"Pastor, I have three hundred dollars to my name. My wife has closed our accounts. I have nothing left to fight with."

"I can't believe that. If you're right, God will help you."

Adam laughed harshly. "He's not doing very well so far."

Riley sighed. "It's hard to admit we've lied. I've seen the evidence and its overwhelming. Why don't you accept that?"

Bristling, Adam said, "the evidence is a sweater and a letter. The sweater is mine. I left it in the suite. The letter, I didn't write and still haven't seen. Shouldn't I have the opportunity to at least see the letter that's blowing my family apart?"

"Mike and Julie saw it."

"And because of that I lose my family. This letter I'm supposed to have written is turning into a scarlet letter, wouldn't you say, Pastor?"

Riley cringed at hearing that phrase for the second time in a day. Leaving the protection order on the table, he headed out the door.

"I'll meet you at the house tomorrow at noon. You can remove any remaining items you left behind. Brooke and Jack will be gone for a couple hours."

"You embarrassed me, Tee!"

The anger was immediate and real. Miles had barely entered the bedroom when he let loose. Theresa, startled by his vociferous approach, laid aside her book and eyed him warily.

Staring daggers at her, Miles stripped out of his t-shirt and headed to the bathroom. When he returned, anger still clouding his face, he grabbed the Bible he kept at bedside and flipped through until he found what he was looking for.

"Ephesians Five, Twenty-Two, 'Wives, submit yourselves to your husband as you do to the Lord.' Proverbs Thirty-One, 'A wife of noble character, who can find? She is worth far more than rubies. Her husband has full confidence in her and lacks nothing of value. She brings him good, not harm, all the days of her life.'"

He took a breath, then continued the barrage.

"First Corinthians, Eleven, Nine, 'Neither was man created for woman, but woman for man.' Do you need me to go on?"

Theresa looked intently at the man she'd thought she knew so well. Then she spoke.

"'But since you excel in everything – in faith, in speech, in knowledge, in complete earnestness and in the love we have kindled in you – see that you also excel in this grace of giving' That's Second Corinthians Two if you need to look it up."

Miles stood up, fists clenched.

"You may know the Bible, Theresa, but the bigger question is, why aren't you living the Bible?"

"You've changed," Theresa said softly. "You've become so intent on creating a perfect church that you've forgotten how important God's grace has been in your life."

Miles scoffed. "You have no idea what you're talking about."

"Miles, you're not willing to show the same grace to others that God showed to you when you were living on the streets of Detroit. You're making decisions that are destructive to yourself and others."

"What are you saying?" he thundered.

"I saw the file. You're shunning people. You're showing judgment instead of mercy. You're—"

"Tee, there are plenty of people who see what we're doing as the right thing. Just wait until tomorrow. You'll see too!"

THURSDAY

Day Twenty

"He don't look like a preacher."

"How many preachers do you know, Harry?"

"Not many, but he looks more like James Brown than Billy Graham."

Adam eavesdropped on the elderly couple as he devoured his two-ninety-five breakfast special.

"Is he in charge of that big church across from Cracker Barrel?"

"Looks like it."

"Can't even get into Cracker Barrel on Sunday no more. All them church people crowding in there."

"Excuse me," Adam said, turning around in his booth. "What are you reading?"

The couple looked his way. "*Surf Beat*," the woman said. "Article about the preacher at that big church across from Cracker Barrel."

"We used to go there every Sunday," her husband said. "Cracker Barrel I mean. Since that church opened, we drive up to Bob Evans."

"Where'd you get that?"

"They got 'em free at the counter."

Moments later, Adam was staring at a full-color shot of Miles Traynor. The picture was taken during a Sunday worship service; the spotlights shined through his dreadlocks, his face was sweaty. A white suit gave him a celestial aura.

While much of the article detailed Miles' rise from a poverty-stricken home in inner-city Detroit, there was a lot of attention paid to Surfside's strict code of conduct. *Our expectations are high*, Miles was quoted as saying, *but when you're representing the best, you need to be the best.* Several church members, including Denise Stover, offered laudatory remarks about his vision and leadership. *He's saved so many lives*, one member said.

And messed up one, Adam thought.

"Your husband's a rock star!" Keith Talbot held up the paper when Theresa entered the conference room.

"I'll say," another partner said, smiling at her as he took a seat. "Is there any way our firm can get some press for the work you do representing Surfside?"

"The plan for the Christian school is pretty ambitious," said Lloyd Enke, the firm's managing partner, seated at the head of the table. "A couple of school board members are not happy about it."

Theresa smiled and took her usual seat.

"Seriously, Theresa," Keith Talbot said, "a church as ambitious as Surfside should have a firm on retainer. Have you ever talked to your husband about that?"

"I haven't," Theresa replied. "So far I've been able to meet their needs in only a few hours a month."

"What did you think of the story?" Entering late, Forrest had taken the seat closest to Theresa.

"I haven't gotten a chance to digest it," she replied. Truth was, what she'd read left a bitter taste in her mouth. Too much breathy adulation. Too much about Miles' accomplishments and not enough about the Lord's work. She certainly understood how newspapers worked. They were looking for a story with mass appeal. A good-looking successful man like Miles fit the bill. Still, she'd shuddered when she saw the focus on his personal accomplishments.

"Sounds like your husband's church sets the bar pretty high." Dan Gallo, a junior partner in tax litigation said. "Certainly higher than I could maintain." Theresa was embarrassed by the laughter that filled the room.

"What happens if somebody falls short?" an associate asked.

Theresa glanced at Forrest. He was staring at his shoes, uncomfortable with the discussion.

"It depends on the person, I suppose. Hopefully church leaders help them find their way."

"And if they don't?" Dan Gallo asked.

"They wind up working in tax litigation for Talbot, White, and Enke," Keith Talbot said, drawing more laughter and bringing a deep red to Gallo's face.

Enke called the meeting to order, and the article was set aside for everyone except Theresa. Miles' parting shot the night before, before angrily heading to the guest room, had stayed with her. 'There are lots of people who see what we're doing as the right thing,' he had said. 'Just wait until tomorrow.' She hadn't known what he meant until she showed up at the Salisbury office and was greeted by a copy of *Surf Beat*, placed there by a well-meaning colleague.

Somehow Miles believed that type of publicity affirmed the church's work. The stringent discipline, the shunnings. Everything was part of a plan to achieve a greater good. Theresa wondered if the other side of the story would ever be told. Someone like Adam Overstreet might have a lot to say about Surfside's member agreement. She thought back to the last time she'd seen him, at the airport. He'd had so much on his plate, yet he stopped to help the wife of the man who was making his life miserable. Then she remembered the talk she'd had with Papa, about how she felt God leading her to do more.

But what?

After a half-tank of gas and another night at the motel, Adam had less than two hundred and fifty dollars.

Riley Wenger's was the only car in the driveway when he arrived at the house. His hopes that Brooke might have stayed around, that he might see Jack, were dashed.

At least he had a plan.

It was apparent from his demeanor that Riley had steeled himself for this confrontation. There was no smile, no referring to Adam as brother. He was all business.

"You can take clothing and personal items, nothing else."

Adam wanted to put him up against a wall.

"Says who?"

"Says this court order," Riley answered tersely. Holding it in front of him. "You have an hour."

"You're some pastor, you know that, Riley? I'm trying to imagine Jesus forcing an innocent person from their house. That picture isn't coming to me. Are you seeing it?"

Riley said nothing.

Adam returned to his car, coming back with several boxes he had picked up that morning. He headed for the master bedroom first, grabbed his remaining clothes, and tossed them in a pile near the front door.

"Want to check the pockets, Riley? Might want to make sure I didn't hide any jewelry."

Riley remained quiet, but did follow him back to the bedroom. Adam pulled two boxes from the closet and carried them past Riley and out to the car.

"Baseball cards," he said.

"Let me make sure that's—" Adam's stare stopped him in his tracks.

On his second trip, Adam grabbed his golf clubs from the guest room. He hardly played anymore, but like the baseball cards, the clubs would have some value.

Next was his grandfather's pocket watch. It meant a lot to him. Grandfather Overstreet had been a streetcar conductor in Baltimore during the Great Depression. The watch had the streetcar company's insignia etched into it. Certainly some value there, though it killed him to think of parting with it.

On subsequent trips he carried out an old laptop, a Brooks Robinson autographed baseball, and assorted items of jewelry, most probably cheap and worthless, but you never knew. Stopping in the utility room, he eyed his twelve-speed bicycle, considering ways to get it into the Lexus. It was a barely used two-thousand-dollar bike. In the kitchen, he located several bungee cords and carried them and the bike to the driveway. Soon he had jerry-rigged the bike on top of the Lexus.

When everything was loaded, Adam walked through the house a final time. He had seven minutes to spare. In the master bedroom, he looked at the family picture taken just a month before. Three Overstreets beaming at the camera from under a shade tree. It was a beautiful photograph he had happily paid four hundred dollars to have enlarged. He was removing it from the wall when Riley entered.

"You can't take that."

Ignoring him, Adam removed the picture and put it under his arm. When he got to the door, Riley put his arm out to stop him.

"That's not part of the order."

Adam's steely gaze moved from the preacher to the arm impeding his exit.

"Riley, get your hand off me or find yourself on the floor."

"Adam, I not going to let you walk out—"

Riley found himself on the floor.

Adam stepped over him and moved to the front door. He stopped at the hall closet, remembering something. He rooted around until he found it. An old two-person tent he'd had since college. Tucking the picture under one arm and the tent under the other, he walked out, closing the door behind him.

Theresa went through her day mechanically, hollow with the realization that the man she'd married had changed in ways that she'd barely noticed until now.

Forrest passed by her office several times, but didn't stop. Theresa knew he disliked confrontation, but she'd decided there would be one anyway. It was almost time to leave when she cornered him in his office.

"I'm really busy, Theresa. The partners want this brief by tomorrow morning and I—"

"I need your advice, Forrest."

She saw him relax with the understanding that she wasn't bringing up yesterday's encounter at the Snow Hill courthouse.

"Sit down. What are you working on?"

"Tough case. It involves a person who I believe is being falsely accused of something."

Forrest nodded sagely. "Defense clients usually say they're being falsely accused."

"Yeah, but the difference is, I think this one's telling the truth."

"Did he pay the retainer?"

"Not yet. But I know I can get the money when I get him off. He has a lot of earning potential."

Forrest looked at her strangely. "Wait a minute. If this is Adam Overstreet, I'm not—"

"It's not Adam."

"Okay, sorry. I know you do some pro-bono work for Surfside, but are the partners okay with you going off on your own like this?"

"I don't really care what they think, Forrest."

Pursing his lips, Forrest looked at the ceiling for a moment. "Theresa, you're certainly entitled to do what you think is best, but is it worth it? Getting on the wrong side of the partners just to represent some lowlife who may or may not be guilty?"

Theresa slumped back in her chair and sighed heavily.

"You're probably right. I guess I need to let this go."

"Yeah, probably," Forrest said, smiling. "Plenty of high-dollar work to do around here. Is he local?"

"Real local," Theresa said. "Poor guy. Student at one of the third-tier law schools. Trying hard to make it through. Now he's up against something and can't get out."

Forrest sat up in his chair, suddenly interested. "Which school?"

When Theresa threw out the school name, his eyes widened.

"What did he do?"

"Some of his classmates accused him of cheating. He swears he didn't, but the evidence is against him. The guys accusing him are a bunch of white boys from the Main Line in Philly. Guys who partied their way out of Penn or Temple. The last thing they wanted was to be outperformed by a black boy from some little Eastern Shore fishing town."

Forrest looked like he might be having a heart attack. Mouth falling open, hands going to chest, he gasped then tried to compose himself. He stood up shakily and closed the door.

"How..." He appeared lost, unable to express what he wanted to say. Theresa helped him.

"How do I know?"

Forrest nodded. He breathing was ragged.

"It's not that hard to figure out. You had a reputation when we started here of being a lion in the courtroom. Quite frankly, I never saw that. Neither did the partners." Theresa nodded at the brief he'd been working on when she came in. "That's why they give you work like that; stuff a paralegal should be doing."

Forrest stared at her, mouth agape.

"When a lion becomes a pussycat, one wonders why. I figured something along the way scared you. It turns out, it did. Later, when you got here and started enjoying the big salary, you paved a path for yourself that would never set you to be scared again. Am I right?"

Forrest shook his head slowly, seeming to barely comprehend what Theresa was saying and emboldening her to continue.

"I did a little digging; people I know who went to law school with you. They told me. Face it, Forrest, you and I both know that part of why we work here is that our black faces look good on the firm webpage. We would have to really screw up for these guys to get rid of us. The difference between us is the direction we took that freedom. I decided to pursue justice in places where I saw it lacking. You took the safe route. Now I'm in court five days a week, doing what I love. And you... you're pushing paper."

"So... why now, Theresa? Why today? I'm guessing this has to do with Adam Overstreet."

"You bet it does. That man was your friend. Then, when he needed help, you and the others turned your backs on him. I think it's—"

"Hold on, Theresa." Forrest's voice was stronger. "We're following the direction of our church. Our pastor, your husband, thinks—"

"He thinks, Forrest! He doesn't know, he thinks!" Realizing her voice had grown loud, Theresa dialed it down. "You know Adam Overstreet better than anyone in this town, yet you dumped him. Now I can understand a busybody judgmental know-it-all like Denise Stover doing that, but you, Forrest? After all you went through? After those rich white boys set you up to take the fall for their cheating?"

Forrest hung his head as Theresa continued.

"I understand there was a man who helped you get through those dark days."

"Clem Sabine. I worked at his firm between first and second year." Forrest smiled at the memory.

"He stood by you, even when the law school faculty was ready to send you packing."

Forrest nodded sadly.

"Who is being Clem Sabine for Adam, Forrest?"

The Lexus was attracting attention for all the wrong reasons. The bicycle, haphazardly strapped to the top. The back seat, full of clothing and other possessions. Brooke would have called him a 'looky-loo.' That was what she said when they saw someone at Walmart whose outfit was particularly garish or ill-fitting, or whose car was being used for things other than transportation. He laughed at the recent memory of a man driving one of those PT Cruisers, rear hatch open, seats removed, with two lawnmowers stuck in back.

"Looky-loo," Brooke had said with a laugh.

What if she saw him today?

Two West Ocean City pawnshops weren't particularly generous with their offers. He did unload the used laptop for forty dollars, and surprisingly, a couple pieces of jewelry netted a hundred and sixty. Neither broker knew what to do with his grandfather's watch. One offered him a hundred bucks for the bike, but Adam decided to try some of the shops in Salisbury first.

In between visits to the pawn shops, he ran by the motel and grabbed his belongings, careful to avoid the lobby. Technically he owed another thirty-five dollars, since it was well past the noon check-out time. Pursuing him probably wasn't high on their priority list, though. Besides, with word already out about his alleged misadventures in St. Louis, and word about to get out about how he'd assaulted a local preacher, skipping out on a night's room rental was nothing.

Remembering the tent was a stroke of good luck. There were places he could set up camp without paying anything. He'd seen the homeless that squatted at Sunset Park and knew he had to avoid that scene. He'd take his chances someplace more remote.

Remembering an area where he'd once gone hunting with a hospital board member, Adam ventured down a series of increasingly narrow roads to a secluded spot off Isle of Wight Bay. He parked the car in an isolated area, unloaded the tent and some food he'd purchased, and made his way through the woods. A quarter mile in, he found a level spot perfect for setting up camp. Within a few minutes, the tent was in place.

After a meal of turkey jerky, an apple, and a day-old slice of raisin bread, he moved through the gloaming to the point where land met water. His campsite was on a narrow tributary, but a few hundred feet beyond, he could see the open waters of Isle of Wight Bay, separating Ocean City from West Ocean City. Across the Bay, the lights of Ocean City's condominiums, high-rise hotels, and shops beckoned like a muse. The vacation spot of the Mid-Atlantic loomed just a mile away.

And as the stars and moon began their illumination of the sky, he returned to his campsite. Alone, chilly in the July evening air, but not cold, he sat alone. The irony was not lost on him.

He was homeless in Ocean City.

FRIDAY

Day Twenty-One

The breakfast meeting was filled with negative energy. Theresa wished she was anyplace else.

"More juice, sweetie?" The Pepper Pot waitress was an old-school, gum-smacking platinum blonde. Theresa said no thanks.

"I should never have put my hands on him," Riley said.

"You're lucky he didn't break your jaw." Derby said, examining the swollen left-side of Riley's face. "That shiner's gonna look real good in church on Sunday."

"I'm calling the cops," Miles said angrily. "He needs to be in jail."

"You can't press charges, Miles," Theresa said. "That has to come from Riley."

Miles slammed his coffee cup to the table, attracting the attention of breakfast diners at surrounding tables.

"Riley was doing church business, Theresa. There's got to be some protection for a man doing his job."

"It isn't his job," Theresa said quietly. "You sent him. We recommend having a representative of law enforcement if the threat of violence exists." She nodded at Riley, silently watching their verbal volley. "Riley was unprepared for that situation."

"I never would have thought in a million years Adam would get physical," Derby said. "I know him better than any of you, and I've never seen that."

"Derby, do you think he might be innocent?" Riley's unexpected question brought them up short.

"We can't go soft," Miles said loudly. "We found evidence that the man sinned. A plan is in place and will be followed." His tone left no doubt Miles was finished discussing it.

Theresa wasn't receiving the message.

"There's more there than we know. I can feel it."

"I agree," Riley said.

"Seriously, Riley? Even after he decked you?" Miles' eyes were on fire. "Take it from a guy who's run some mean streets, that's the sign of a guilty man."

"Or an innocent one," Theresa said.

Miles rose from the table, his glare never leaving his wife. For a moment, she felt something she'd never experienced. Fear coursed through her, a shaky feeling that made her consider fleeing the crowded diner.

Miles tossed a fifty on the table.

"Riley, call the police. File a report. Tell them that Pastor Traynor expects them to find Adam Overstreet and take him to jail. A Lexus full of junk with a bike strapped to the top won't be hard to miss, even in Ocean City."

He'd awakened a couple times, but otherwise slept well. The sleeping bag was comfortable enough, and the tent provided enough coverage to feel safe in the desolate location. The anger and humiliation of Riley watching his every move had ebbed away, and, try as he might, he couldn't remain angry at Brooke. This wasn't at all the person he'd married, he told himself. Brooke cared for people, even those who others might turn their backs on. Something was changing her.

Or somebody.

Walking through the woods, he rounded a corner and noticed immediately that something was different.

The bicycle was gone.

How had somebody spotted his car? Despite being within sight of Ocean City, he was far-removed from civilization. There hadn't been a sound all evening, at least that he'd heard. No noise of approaching cars, no voices. But somehow, they'd taken his bike.

Hurrying his pace, he was a hundred feet from the Lexus when he saw there was more.

The driver's door was open.

So was the trunk. Open and empty.

Now he was running, closing the distance in seconds.

The contents from the back seat were scattered. His clothes were everywhere, wadded in the dirt and mud, strewn like wreckage from a plane crash.

His golf clubs, gone.

The boxes of baseball cards, gone.

His grandfather's watch, gone.

They'd taken a crowbar to the dash in an attempt to start the car. Unsuccessful, they'd chosen instead to slash the seats and tires.

Then he remembered – and panicked.

The photograph. The family photograph.

Would they take something so personal?

Adam backed out of the car, looking in all directions. He picked through a mound of his own clothes. Nothing. Then moving toward a pile of debris, he almost stepped on it.

Upside down, in the dirt and wet moss.

He picked it up, turning it over carefully. The first thing he saw was Jack's face beaming at him from the picture. That alone made things better.

Brooke's face was obliterated by some sharp object jammed through the canvas, like some sadistic nut for whom ransacking the car wasn't enough. He needed to make it personal.

Lost, unsure what to do next, Adam gently placed the picture on the back seat of the car and closed the door. From a pile of clothes on the ground, he picked a pair of grubby shorts and a light green t-shirt. Turning the shirt around, he grew nauseous at the screen print on front.

Surfside Cares!

"Theresa, do you remember several months ago, when I asked if you'd noticed a change in Miles?"

Derby had left soon after Miles marched out of the restaurant, leaving Riley and Theresa.

"Of course. I asked if you'd mentioned it to him and you hadn't."

Riley nodded sadly. "I never did."

"So why bring it up now?"

Riley rubbed at the side of his face that had connected with Adam Overstreet's fist.

"I gotta tell you, Theresa, I don't think Adam did everything he's accused of doing."

"Have you told Miles?"

"I just..." The tears brimming in his eyes provided the answer.

"He's... different," he said, daubing at his eyes with a napkin. "When I came on staff, it was a joyous place. Theresa, I absolutely loved that man. Just being in the light that illuminated from him was intoxicating."

She understood. She'd seen it many times. Miles had a way of pulling people into the excitement of his vision.

"But now... lately we seem to be focused on all the wrong stuff. A school, bigger buildings, more services, double-tithing," he stopped for a moment. "And this Surfside code of conduct..."

Riley's lip started to quiver. Theresa remained quiet.

"And then there's... the way he's meeting with her... at night... Theresa, I..."

He was unable to continue. The tears turned to wracking sobs. Theresa was uncertain what to do next, but knew she had to get him out of the restaurant. She said a quick prayer before grabbing his hand.

"We're going to my office. We can talk there."

With nothing else to do, Adam started walking. He'd pulled out the Auto Club card he carried in his wallet, but his cellphone had died. It probably didn't matter anyway, as the Auto Club membership was one of the hospital fringe benefits that had undoubtedly been discontinued. Besides, replacing the tires and repairing the damage done with the crowbar would cost ten times more than what he had in his wallet.

He'd packed a change of clothes and some basic toiletries in a backpack. It was the first time in months he'd gone without shaving. This compounded the homeless feeling.

Four miles of walking brought him to Route 50, the east-west highway leading to Ocean City. At a convenience store, he picked up a couple protein bars and the biggest, cheapest bottle of water available. The sideways look and wrinkled nose he received from a lady behind him in line spoke volumes.

"You go to Surfside?" The kid cashier said, pointing to Adam's shirt.

"Used to."

"That pastor, what's his name? The guy with the cool dreads. He stops in every few weeks." The tone of the kid's voice afforded Miles the type of status usually reserved for movie stars. Adam wished he hadn't worn the shirt.

He remembered hearing something about a shelter and hoped one of the homeless people in Sunset Park might know something about it. Seeing his car trashed and his stuff strewn around had scared him, and the thought of camping in a secluded spot didn't seem as smart as it had the day before.

Then there was the issue of his check. With no cell phone, Cassie from the hospital couldn't get hold of him. Perhaps his check was ready. That would certainly make things easier. He could get the Lexus repaired, pay Jasmine, and get into a cheap motel. Despite the happenings of the past day, the thought of continuing the fight to get his family back energized him. He approached the Ocean City bridge stepping a bit lighter.

Theresa escorted Riley to her office. It was mid-morning, and most of the attorneys were in court. She was certain, however, that one of her colleagues would be in his office. She stuck her head in his door.

"Forrest, come to my office, please."

"Look, Theresa, I've got nothing else to say to—" Forrest's eyes widened when he saw who was accompanying her. Silently, he got up and followed.

After closing her door, she wasted no time.

"You gentlemen need to talk. I'm due in court, and I'm going to leave you here. Don't leave until you've told each other everything that's troubling you."

"What things are you—"

"Don't play dumb with me, Forrest." She glared at him, daring him to continue. "Riley, you have concerns and I think Forrest might share them."

With a final look that said she meant business, Theresa left.

Sunset Park was busy. Mothers with children. Elderly couples on their morning walks. People everyplace.

But none who appeared homeless.

Probably too early, Adam thought, returning to the street. Ocean City Memorial was seventy blocks north, almost four miles. Typically, he covered that much ground on his morning runs, but he'd already walked six miles. The city bus was air-conditioned and would only cost a couple bucks. Easy enough decision.

Taking a seat near the back, a couple seats away from the closest passengers, Adam cringed when he caught a glimpse of himself in the bus window. His hair was unkempt and the day-old growth of beard gave him an almost sinister quality. How the magazine models made the five-o'clock shadow look sexy, he had no idea.

As the bus travelled north, more passengers boarded. Vacationers mostly. Younger people who used the bus to get around without giving up their treasured parking spaces. At the intersection of Coastal Highway and Winterset Drive, Adam craned his neck to catch a glimpse of his house. Brooke's car was in the driveway. From a hundred yards away, all looked good. It was a mirage.

"Mind if I sit?" He was startled by her question. A young woman, dark hair, probably no more than twenty. He hadn't noticed the bus had filled. Smiling slightly, he moved in and left space.

"Thanks."

She sat down, inadvertently rubbing her arm against his and smiling apologetically. Her fragrance was the first thing he noticed. Fresh and pretty, like Brooke.

"Beautiful day," she said. "Rain coming later, though."

Adam smiled, but said nothing, remembering how he looked and smelled. He hoped she wasn't riding far.

"Do you go to Surfside?"

That darn shirt again.

"I used to."

"I saw it on the Boardwalk. Beautiful."

Adam nodded.

"I'm visiting from West Virginia. Eleven of us. We're on a mission trip. I'm Cathy."

"A mission trip to the beach? How lucky can you get?"

She laughed. "We went to Nicaragua last year. Money is tight, so we stayed closer to home."

Adam didn't respond. All he needed was for somebody to preach to him. Besides, they were just a few blocks from the hospital.

"How long have you lived in Ocean City?"

Adam tried not to let his irritation show.

"How do you know I live here? Maybe I'm vacationing like everybody else."

She shook her head, turning so she could make eye contact.

"No, you live here. I saw the way you were looking down that street when I got on the bus. You live there... or used to."

"Look... what was your name again?"

"Cathy. What's yours?"

"Cathy, I appreciate your concern, but we're approaching my stop, so if you'll excuse me..." Adam stood, making her turn so he could get by.

"Take these," she said, sticking several small slips of paper into his hand in such a way that he couldn't refuse.

Adam lurched toward the exit as the bus came to the stop closest to the hospital.

Why hadn't she pressed Riley about Miles' frequent night meetings?

The thought dogged Theresa as she left the office. Didn't she want to know? Didn't she already suspect something?

And who? Brooke Overstreet, of course. She could tell from the way Miles looked at her. On a whim, she made a quick detour. The Overstreets lived in Ocean City. She called the church office and got Miles' secretary, DeeDee, who quickly provided her with an address on Winterset Drive.

She waited for a city bus to load and unload at the corner of Ocean Highway and Winterset, then made the turn. The address was several houses down, and in front she spotted the same non-descript white SUV she'd seen in the church parking lot. She wasn't sure what to do with this confirmation. It probably wasn't anything more than just a pastor meeting with a troubled parishioner. Happened all the time, right?

Right?

But not in the evening. And never just the two of them. That was taboo. Introduction to Pastoring 101, right? Don't meet alone with a woman, married or otherwise.

Right?

How strange it felt to be left waiting in his own office.

Vicki had gasped when he walked in, despite undoubtedly being alerted of his arrival by Cassie in Human Resources. She was tight-lipped, but Adam saw the concern in her eyes.

"Is there a check or not?"

"I was told to have you wait until Melvin gets here."

"I'm owed this money, Vicki. I worked for it and I want it."

"Please Adam," she pleaded. "It's not in my hands. Melvin said he would be here in a half-hour."

He waited, flipping through magazines and watching the clock inch ahead. Just before noon, the outer office door opened, and Melvin strode in. Following in lock-step was County Sheriff Whit Masters.

And Miles Traynor.

"Really, Melvin?" Adam said, getting to his feet. "Do you need this much firepower to hand me a check?"

Melvin waved him into his former office. The others followed. Melvin took the chair behind the desk, Adam's chair. Adam moved to a seat across from him.

"Don't sit," Melvin said brusquely. "You won't be here that long."

Adam straightened and glanced behind him. Sheriff Masters and Miles were stationed at the door like sentries.

"There won't be a check," Melvin said. "There might have been, but after you assaulted Pastor Wenger, the Board didn't see fit to reward you for such a savage act."

"You're lucky you're not in county jail," the sheriff said. "If I have my way, you still might be there before nightfall."

When Adam turned to face the sheriff, he caught his smooth reach for the butt of his sidearm.

"Maybe I should just come with you now, Sheriff. It would give me a place to stay tonight. Want to know where I slept last night?"

"I'm guessing you were in the woods near Buck Island Pond," the sheriff said. "Your stuff's strewn everywhere. I ought to give you a ticket for littering."

"Yeah, you do that, Sheriff. And maybe try to find the people who vandalized my car while you're at it."

It was evident that Melvin hadn't heard this.

"Yeah, Melvin. I'm officially homeless now. I slept in a tent last night. I'm down to two-hundred bucks, no car, no phone. Somebody ransacked my car while I slept and took what little I had left. I came here by bus, and about the only friendly face I've encountered is the girl who sat next to me and tried to save my eternal soul."

Adam pointed at Pastor Miles. "This fine example of the clergy is counseling my wife at all hours of the day and night. He provided you with private information that you used to get rid of me. He's closed all doors that might have been open. There's God's love in action for you, Melvin."

"Hold up a minute, Overstreet." Sheriff Masters moved closer, his right hand resting on his sidearm. "You have no right to insult Pastor Traynor, especially after the way you beat up one of his colleagues."

Miles had remained quiet, but Adam noticed that he never took his eyes off him.

"Adam," Melvin said quietly. "How can you allow yourself to fall this far?"

"Because," Adam said, angrily jabbing his finger in Miles' direction. "That man wants me to sign a piece of paper saying I had sex with Penny Hardesty. You and the board say I had sex with her. The local

TV and radio stations say I had sex with her. The newspapers, people on the street, everybody says I had sex with Penny Hardesty.

"The only problem, Melvin," Adam shrugged past them and flung open the door. "Is that I didn't!"

Court dragged, and it was almost five as Theresa drove back to Ocean City. She checked her messages. Nothing from Forrest or Riley. She prayed they'd demonstrated courage, but wasn't optimistic.

That meant the confrontation would fall to her. She couldn't go on acting like everything was the same as it always had been. What would Miles' response be to her suggestion that he step back from the Overstreet situation? Anger? Hostility? And how about other issues, such as double-tithing? Was she getting too much into his business? It was times like this when being a pastor's wife put her at a real disadvantage. Who was there for her to talk to? Certainly not anyone at Surfside. There were other pastors' wives, but her career kept her from that orbit.

When she heard her phone buzz, she hoped it was Forrest or Riley. Instead, it was her father, the one person she could talk to without judgment.

"Hello, Papa, you don't know how happy I am to hear from you!"

"Cookie, I am always glad to hear your voice, too."

"I have to talk to you." They said the words at the same time, giggling when they realized what happened.

"You first," Harvester said. "Mine can wait."

"No, Papa, you first."

Harvester took a deep breath. "I'm settling down, Cookie. No more following the harvest with the migrants."

The words made her joyous.

"Papa, really? Why? Where?"

Harvester chuckled. "Yes, really. Let's just say I got an offer I couldn't pass up. I'll be settling on Grebey Island."

Oh, my. Grebey Island? With all the history?

"Are you sure, Papa?"

"Been praying on it since leaving St. Louis. Earl Manning's been offering to return our family farm to me for years. The time didn't seem right. Now, it does. I'm going to rebuild the old house and live right there."

"What about our home in Pennsylvania?"

"I put it on the market this morning. The fellow who's been renting the land will probably make a good offer."

Theresa shook her head. "Wow, so fast."

"Yeah Cookie," he said, his voice full of excitement. "Earl and I are going to divide up the entire island into small farm tracts. We'll offer some of the migrants I've met a chance to settle down and have their own places."

"Papa, are you sure that's wise? Saxon County isn't the most tolerant place on earth."

"Things might be changing up there, Cookie. Earl introduced me to the County Commissioner for that part of Saxon County, a real strong old lady they call Miss Bertie. She's related to Earl's mama someplace way back and reminds me a lot of her. Anyway, she's on board and there's a local church that's going to pitch in and help, too. Pastor named Duke something or other, he's all for it."

Theresa listened as Papa effused about his plans. She'd almost forgotten this side of him, paled as it had with age and loss. It took her back to her childhood when Professor Harvester Stanley was known nationally as an enthusiastic and brilliant scholar and teacher. She was excited, proud, and more than a little envious.

"I know your Mama never wanted to set foot on that island again, Cookie, but I can't help but think she'd approve."

It was true. Mama couldn't mention Grebey Island without shedding tears. The bigotry and hatred of 1930's Saxon County had gutted her family, driving them away in despair. Still, Papa had never completely gotten the place out of his system. Even during his heyday at Penn State, she sensed sometimes that his heart was back in Missouri.

Finally, breathless and reaching the end of his story, Harvester paused.

"Now tell me your news, Cookie."

"Oh, Papa," she said, certain it wasn't the time to bare her soul, "I want to wait and tell you another time. It's nothing compared to what you're doing."

Usually, he would have insisted, but it was obvious that the excitement of the day was starting to crash in upon him. When he spoke again, his voice was weary.

"Sweetie, just know I'm here whenever you need me. For now, I think I'm going to take a nap."

Oh, Papa, she thought as she laid the phone aside. Just when she thought he'd reached a point where he was finally going to relax, he was taking on a project as big as anything he'd done before. Thinking about him made Theresa sad for the distance that separated them. If she had her way, she'd chuck the workaday life at the law firm and move west to help him with his dream.

But it wasn't as easy as that. There was so much more to consider.

There was Miles.

She wondered what he was doing right now. Was he in his office? Visiting with Riley or one of the other staff members?

Was he meeting privately with Brooke Overstreet?

Across the divided highway, something caught her attention. A man, haggard, walking alongside the busy highway in a *Surfside Cares!* t-shirt. He looked vaguely familiar, but with his cap pulled low and scruffy appearance, she wasn't sure.

She was about to turn to see if he needed help when he ducked behind some old buildings onto a side road that led to the remote Worcester County countryside. Turning her attention to the road ahead, she continued toward home.

###

He should never have left the tent behind.

It was probably gone. If not, he would pack it and take it with him.

Adam was exhausted. After the meeting at the hospital, he'd set out walking. Seven miles later he still had a way to go to reach the campsite. Why hadn't he thought to pack the tent and bring it with him?

He'd considered hitching a ride, but knowing how he looked, it was doubtful anyone would pick him up. Once he got to the campsite, assuming the tent was still there, Adam had resigned himself to one more night in the wilderness. After all, how much more damage could be done?

And what about tomorrow? He still had a couple hundred bucks. A bus ride from Ocean City to Wheeling was a hundred and twenty and took twenty-five hours and two transfers. At least at his mother's house he'd have a roof over his head while he figured out his next move.

But wouldn't that be like giving up? He would have a bed to sleep in and a hot shower; he would also be hours from Ocean City. What if something happened to Jack? How could he make Brooke see the mistakes that were being made if he was in West Virginia?

A car whizzed by on the narrow road, slowed, and backed up. A nice car, luxury type, even nicer than his Lexus. The driver stopped thirty feet in front of him and pushed open the passenger door. The late afternoon sun was in his eyes, and Adam couldn't see the driver. His heart started to race. Hitchhiking was dangerous, everybody knew that.

Like he had something to lose, he thought as he approached. When he was a few feet away, he felt the air conditioning wafting from the interior. He leaned down to speak.

"I've been walking for a while and don't smell very good. If you don't want—"

Miles Traynor.

Adam recoiled like he'd spotted a snake.

"What do you want?"

"To talk."

"Why should I talk to you?"

"What have you got to lose by talking to me, Adam. Get in. If nothing else, I'll drop you off at your car."

Adam backed away, reconsidered, and got in.

"How do you know where my car is?"

Miles pulled from the curb and drove toward the country, ignoring the question. Several moments of silence passed, as Miles navigated the narrow back roads leading to Adam's campsite.

"Looks like somebody did a number on your car," he said, pulling to a stop a few feet from the rear bumper of Adam's battered Lexus.

Adam eyed the preacher skeptically. "Why did you show up when you did?"

Miles smiled slightly.

"You need to get that car fixed and get out of here, Overstreet. Taking the bus to West Virginia ain't no way to get home."

Adam felt a coldness deep in his gut. This man knew stuff he had no business knowing.

Miles reached across Adam's lap and opened the glove compartment, brusquely shoving his leg in the process. He removed an envelope.

"Brooke is done with you. She contacted an attorney today and started divorce proceedings. I thought you needed to know."

"She can't do that."

"Of course she can, man. You got caught with your pants around your ankles. She'll get everything."

"She already has everything," Adam said icily. "Thanks to you."

"It wasn't me that got slobbering drunk and forced myself on that Kansas City skank," Miles said. "You got no chance in this one, man. The woman puts you there and your wife wants out. Surfside's putting its resources into making sure Brooke has what she needs to move on."

Adam considered decking him, but the limited space of the car's interior would mute any damage he could do. Besides, how could he know for sure that the preacher wasn't packing a gun? He decided to remain cool and see if Miles had more surprises.

He did.

"To help move things along, the church wants you to have this." Miles held out the envelope. "There's a rental car waiting for you back in town. I've got a church member who runs a body shop in Berlin who's going to get your car fixed up and delivered to your Mama's place in West Virginia, good as new. There's ten grand in the envelope. That'll get you back on your feet. In West Virginia."

Adam opened the envelope. Inside, a set of keys with a rental car keychain, a business card for a West Ocean City body shop, and a thick stack of hundreds and fifties.

"The church wants me to have this?" Adam said sarcastically. "Did they take a vote?"

"Overstreet, you know how things work. You've run big organizations, or at least tried to. When it comes to Surfside and how things are done, I am the church."

Adam nodded. "Hmmm. Guess I missed that part, Miles. Must be from a book of the Bible I haven't read yet."

Miles laughed like they were two old friends cutting up. Then, just as abruptly, turned serious.

"You'll get joint legal custody of Jack. A few weeks in the summer, alternate holidays, that kind of thing. Child support will be five hundred a month, but you can swing that as soon as you get back on your feet. No alimony. Brooke was generous in that area. She wants to get by on her own."

"You've done well, Miles. Those late-night counseling sessions at the church, you and Brooke alone together, have really helped."

Miles' face turned stony. His right hand formed a fist.

"I think we're done. That rental car needs to be picked up first thing tomorrow. My boy will come and get your car tomorrow, too. It's time to get on with life, Adam. You screwed it up the first time around, and it cost you the love of a good woman. You're young, though. There's still time to get it right."

Miles dropped the gearshift into drive.

"Now, get your ass out of my car."

262

Miles was distracted during dinner, and Theresa's attempts to get him to talk were rebuffed.

"I've got a meeting at eight," he said, getting up from the table.

"I was hoping to tell you Papa's news," Theresa spoke to his back.

"How long will it take?" Miles asked, glancing at his phone.

"Longer than you have." Theresa sighed, her tone not lost on him.

"I'll be home by ten-thirty, Tee. Tell me then."

Theresa ate slowly, stewing as Miles left the house. She considered driving by the church, but didn't have it in her. She'd expected to hear back from Forrest and Riley, but there'd been nothing on that front. At least Papa had some happiness in his life.

She was cleaning up the kitchen when her phone buzzed.

"Riley?"

"Can we talk tomorrow, Theresa?"

"Of course, or tonight, unless you're going to be at the meeting at church."

"There aren't any meetings tonight. I just locked up and left."

Theresa's stomach flittered. "Miles had something going tonight. I assumed it was at church."

The line grew quiet for a moment.

"Tell you what, Theresa. I'll call home and let Leslie and the kids know I'm going to be late. I'll meet you at the Dough Roller up north."

###

Thankfully, the tent was untouched.

Adam downed a protein bar with his last bottle of water. It wasn't much, but it would have to last until morning. Sitting outside the tent, he allowed a northwesterly breeze to cool his face. The temperature had dropped several degrees, signaling the likely arrival of a summer storm. He hoped the tent would do its job and keep him dry.

The Ocean City skyline took on an ominous appearance in the graying skies. The water was choppy and boats were sparse. Birds in the trees above him were restless. Stormy weather was coming.

But nothing like the storms in his life. Adam played the encounter with Miles through his mind a dozen times. He had come close to taking the money and the rental car. So close. Then, coming to his senses, he'd considered throwing it at him, maybe accompanying it with an elbow to the mouth. In the end, he'd placed the envelope on the seat between them and walked away. "You'll regret it," Miles had threatened. "We're coming after you."

Hoping to get some sleep before the storms arrived, he crawled into the tent, zipped the flap, and stretched out on the sleeping bag. Outside, the birds quieted, and the wind grew calm. Perhaps the bad weather had turned north. He thought about tomorrow.

Tomorrow.

He had to go back to Ocean City. If it was over between them, he wanted to hear it from Brooke.

Maybe he could convince her otherwise.

In the silence, he cringed at the reminder of something he hadn't done in days. Like many in times of crisis, he'd turned his back on prayer. It wasn't like he was a regular at it, but he tried to remember to thank God when good stuff happened.

But recently, he'd forgotten. And there hadn't been much good stuff.

Lord, you see what's going on. I'm about to lose my wife and little boy. God, I love them so much and want to keep them. I'm sorry for the sins I've committed and ask that you help the truth come out. Father, there's evil happening, and I can't deal with it on my own anymore. Can you please—

Was that a noise? Footsteps?

Adam raised up, listening.

Nothing.

Silence.

Then, yes! The sound of someone approaching.

No voices, just footsteps.

Better to meet them standing up than have them come upon him and be surprised to find a tent in the woods.

And why was someone out here in the first place?

He unzipped the tent, making more noise than he intended, and crawled out. Looking behind him, in the space between the tent and the road, he saw only darkness.

Then, the *whoosh* of something cutting through the air.

Then, nothing.

"Forrest is out. He wants nothing to do with this."

Theresa hadn't gotten seated before Riley made his proclamation.

"And you?" she said.

"Me? The bigger question should be, why are you jumping in the middle of this? Theresa, you're going against your husband."

She nodded. "You're going against your boss. What's *your* motivation?"

"That still small voice," he said quietly, his reference to scripture not lost on Theresa. "I condemned Adam too quickly, and God made sure I knew it. Two days ago, I went to his motel and gave him the court order kicking him out of his house."

Riley stopped and took a deep breath.

"I offered him every opportunity to make this go away. 'Just sign the form,' I said—"

"The discipline agreement," Theresa said irritably. "Don't minimize what it is and what it means."

"Yeah," Riley smiled sadly, "but he refused. Then, yesterday I met him at his house. That's when he decked me."

Theresa smiled despite herself. "You've gone through a lot for Surfside."

"I have," Riley replied, laughing. "And I still can't make myself believe Adam is guilty."

The conversation stopped while a server took their order.

"How about Forrest?" Theresa said, after the server had moved on.

"It sounds like you pounded him pretty hard. He feels like you're persecuting him for supporting Miles and Surfside."

"Oh, please." Theresa said, blowing air through her mouth. "Forrest is just a shell of the man he used to be. He's allowed himself to be emasculated and wants to pin it on me."

They sat quietly as a large party of diners made their way toward the exit.

"So, what's next?" Riley said.

"We find Adam, though I'm not sure how easy that's going to be."

"It will be very easy. Do you want to go now?"

#

When he awoke, he thought he was paralyzed. He was in more pain than he'd ever felt.

Then footsteps in the darkness. They were coming back.

They'd probably been waiting for him to stir so they could finish him off.

But that was dumb, wasn't it? If they wanted to finish him off, they would have gone ahead and done it.

The way he was feeling, he kind of hoped they did finish him off. He lifted his head from the muddy ground, turning toward the approaching footsteps.

"Adam?"

The voice, it was familiar, wasn't it?

I'm right here, he wanted to yell. Struggling to get up, he rolled over on his left arm. The pain seared like a branding iron, then nothing.

SATURDAY

Day Twenty-Two

The headache was piercing; his left arm, numb.

The rest of him felt like he'd been dragged across the Route 50 bridge from the back of a truck.

Concussion, they said. More tests were needed.

A broken arm. Broken in two places.

The kicks to his midsection were likely delivered by steel-toed boots, Dr. Wong had explained. "We would've gotten to you sooner, but we're short on staff and supplies." The ER doctor's cutting comment wasn't lost on Adam.

Fortunately, Adam remembered little from the night before. The whooshing sound he'd heard was, according to Chauncey, the X-Ray Tech, most likely a piece of rusty pipe before it made contact with the back of his head. The rest of the damage came after he was knocked out.

It was five-forty in the morning when he woke for good. The E.R. staff seemed uncertain how to deal with their former boss; beaten, filthy, and reeking of outdoors and expended adrenaline. At seven, Dr. Wong was replaced by Dr. Lettie Dickerson, a recent hire. She informed Adam that they wanted to keep him a few days for tests and observation. He refused. His clothes were brought to him by an aide he'd been in the process of firing. Happy for a little retribution, she held the smelly bag at arm's length like a dead animal.

By nine, he was back on the street, hungry and in pain. Hunger trumped pain, and he walked a few blocks to a pancake house. People he passed on the street gave him ample berth. He hadn't seen himself in a mirror; it was probably better that way.

Entering the restaurant, he reached for his wallet.

Gone.

Where was it?

The tent.

Back in the woods.

Miles away.

###

"This is Jasmine Fleece. Who's calling? How did you get my personal number?"

"Ms. Fleece, my name is Theresa Traynor. I'm an attorney in Ocean City."

The line grew quiet.

"You're calling about Adam, aren't you?"

"We found him in a wooded area near here last night, beaten and unconscious. Your card was in the tent where he'd been sleeping."

Theresa could hear her uneven breathing.

"I should have done more."

###

He had no money, but the bus pass was still in his pocket. He'd crawled onto the south bus intending to get off near the Route 50 bridge. He was awakened by the bus driver.

"Buddy, you can't stay on here any longer."

Adam looked around, groggily.

"What time...?"

"Eleven fifteen." He'd been riding for two hours. As he pulled himself up from the seat, every bone in his body protested. Over the thumping in his head, he heard other passengers' whispered comments as he staggered down the aisle.

"Homeless."

"Drunk."

"Junkie."

And worse.

A wadded up five-dollar bill hit him on the side of the face and fell to the floor.

"Buy yourself a shower and a bottle," a kid in a muscle shirt said. Adam looked down, trying to spot the bill, but the dizziness from the effort caused him to almost lose his balance. Somehow he made it off the bus and began stumbling down Dorchester Street, in the direction of the beach.

Just a quick rest in the sand, then he'd make his way to the campsite. The effort proved too much.

###

They'd ridden in silence for most of the three hours from Ocean City to Baltimore. Both knew what was at stake.

Jasmine Fleece met them at the front entrance, escorting them through a deserted reception area to a third-floor office.

"I've been reviewing the information Adam provided me when he was here. I've already contacted a friend at a law firm in St. Louis. They have an investigator who might help."

Theresa pulled a checkbook from her purse.

"Don't worry about that yet," Jasmine said, waving her off. "We can settle later. I'm going to pitch in a third. I should never have turned my back on him."

The meeting ended with Jasmine's promise to move quickly and stay in touch. Outside, Riley, who had said little during the meeting, cleared his throat.

"Let's find a place to talk. Since I'm probably out of a job anyway, there's more you need to know."

###

As afternoon became night, Adam awakened several times from the same dream. He was in a soft comfortable bed, being spoon-fed soup. The stifling heat was mitigated by the soft hum of an air conditioner. He shivered, pulled a down comforter up to his chin and nestled in. Then the headache would overcome him again, sending him off to darkness.

Their phones rang in quick succession, like the volley of a tennis match. Twice each. Three times.

Miles.

They didn't answer.

"He's figured out we're together," Riley said somberly. Theresa didn't respond. She was still grappling with what he'd told her after leaving Jasmine's office.

They were a few minutes from home when Riley spoke again.

"Do you wish I hadn't told you?"

Did she? She'd suspected there was something there, but the girl was only nineteen. She'd seen it before. Miles' persona pulled them in. He was counseling her, he'd told Theresa at the time.

Just like now, with Brooke Overstreet.

Riley's phone, silent since the earlier calls, chirped.

"He wants me at church," he said, reading the message and putting the phone in his pocket. "I guess this is the end."

"Maybe he doesn't know—"

"He knows," Riley said grimly. "It probably went like this: Forrest told Eric Stover. Eric told Miles."

"Don't go. Go home. I'll go to the church."

"Are you sure you don't need..." Riley trailed off, unsure what he could offer a woman who was about to confront her husband.

"You're not going to shoot him, are you?" His gentle poke at humor fell short.

She knocked on his office door.

"Get in here, Riley! I've been trying to call you—"

Snatching open the door, Miles went slack-jawed when he saw his wife, but recovered quickly.

"You and Riley—"

"You and Shelby Canter."

The name brought a frightened look to his eyes. She remembered the stories he'd told of being cornered and whipped by older kids. She felt a bit of sympathy for him.

It passed quickly.

"Look, Tee. I don't know what Riley's been telling you, but he doesn't know—"

"Did you give her family fifty thousand dollars?"

"I... they were..."

"Yes or no?"

"No... well, yes, but I never—"

"Church money, Miles. Given by people who trust you during one of your infamous double-tithing periods."

"Look, Tee. You know I would never—"

"Never cheat? Is that what you're about to say?"

He nodded.

"I thought I knew that, but I also thought you'd never misappropriate church money. There's apparently a lot about you I don't know."

Miles didn't hide the tears.

"Tee, she was in trouble. That family of hers was a mess."

"So you gave them fifty thousand dollars. Did that clean up the mess, Miles? And what about the meetings you had with her?" Theresa formed quotation marks with her fingers. "The counseling meetings you had after hours, when nobody else was around."

"There wasn't anything to that, Tee. I was helping her plan—"

"It doesn't really matter now, does it? You gave them the money under the table, and you made Riley be party to it."

"Riley believes me, Tee, unlike you, my own wife." His voice grew louder, his eyes hardened. "Maybe I should be asking you the same questions. What's with you and Riley? You gettin' a little on the side now, Tee? Am I not enough for you any—"

She slapped him hard, causing him to recoil and clench his fists.

"Nobody hits me!" He roared, taking a menacing step toward her. When she didn't retreat, he hesitated. The old street ploy hadn't worked.

"You will tell the church. Tomorrow. Then you'll take a leave of absence and allow the church board to decide what to do. During that time, you'll repay the fifty thousand."

They stood silently, staring at one another. Neither blinked. Then Miles pulled out his cellphone.

"Derby. It's me. I know its late, but I need you to call the church elders right now. Tell them we need to have an emergency meeting in an hour. My office."

He listened for a moment.

"I don't care what they're doing. Tell them to be here. You too… no, not Riley. Just the board, you, and me."

He clicked off and placed the phone in his pocket.

"Don't expect me home tonight."

SUNDAY

Day Twenty-Three

The light was dazzlingly bright, causing Adam to wonder for a second if he'd died and was seeing the illumination people associated with near-death experiences.

It was only the sun, streaming through a window to his right.

He turned his head away, taking in the surroundings. A large bed in a small room. Blue wallpaper. White sheer curtains.

A nightstand with a lamp and a glass of water. He suddenly felt parched and reached for it with his right hand. The pain of the movement caused him to flinch and sink back into the soft mattress.

It was the room he'd seen in his dreams, which meant they weren't dreams.

The door opened. An elderly woman with white hair and a kind face entered.

"Good morning, Mr. Overstreet."

He gazed at her, warily.

"Whaaa—"

His throat was dry and speech seemed impossible. The woman sensed that, picked up the water glass, and held it for him. He noisily slurped it down.

"I'm Hilda Watson," she said. "Miss Ocean City, 1960."

She picked up on his confusion.

"This is my house. Well, mine and Carl's. You passed out in our front yard yesterday. Carl recognized you and had some of the people next door carry you in."

1960?

Passed out?

Carl?

"We found your discharge papers in your pocket. Knowing what's been going on between you and the people at the hospital, we figured you wouldn't want to go back, so we decided to let you rest. And here you are."

She turned toward the open door and yelled, "Carl, he's awake." A few moments later, Carl poked his head in.

"G'morning, Mr. Overstreet."

Adam tried to remember his face, but had no luck.

"Carl Watson," the old man said, attempting to be helpful. "Last winter I was in the hospital for a heart bypass. You came by my room when I was watching *The Price is Right* and guessed the price of the Showcase."

Adam smiled faintly, a glimmer of remembrance playing through his mind.

"I'm better now," Carl said. "Walking a mile and a half every day."

"When we heard about your problems on the TV, Carl said, 'there ain't no way Mr. Overstreet did what they're saying he did,'" Hilda said. "Then, when we saw you in our yard, Carl said we needed to help you like you helped him. So here you are."

"Where are we?" Adam's voice was scratchy.

"Dorchester Street. We've lived in this house for fifty years," Hilda said proudly. "Last house on the block that isn't rented out to vacationers."

"Yeah, they get on our nerves sometimes," Carl said, motioning to a building next door. "They can be loud and leave trash strewn around, but mostly we like living here."

"Right in the middle of everything," Hilda said.

"Is there anything we can get you before we leave for church?" Carl asked.

"Do you have something for a headache?"

Hilda left the room.

"We'll be gone for a couple hours, but you'll be okay," Carl said.

"Do you go to Surfside?"

"Nah," Carl said dismissively. "We go to the Presbyterian Church around the corner. Same place where we got married. We don't much care for those big churches."

#

The phone buzzed, Papa's Sunday morning phone call. They didn't come every week, maybe once a month or so, almost always when Miles had left for church, and Theresa was getting ready.

And they always seemed to come at a time when she needed to hear his voice.

"I'm sure you're getting dressed up to head to church, Cookie. I just wanted to tell you that I love you." The kindness in his voice almost brought her to tears.

"I'm finishing up some things here in the Northwest, then heading back to Pennsylvania to get the house ready for showing."

"You're really going through with this, aren't you?"

He chuckled. "I already have a handful of migrant families wanting to settle down on Grebey Island. There's no grass growing under my feet. I've got a man tearing down the old place. A contractor says he can put a new house up for me starting this month on the same spot. I think it'll bring some peace and closure to an ugly period."

He was right. Theresa knew it. Though he'd derived great pleasure from his work with migrant families and, before that, at the university, she'd felt there was a hole in his life. Grebey Island had been out of his possession, but never out of his heart.

"You okay, Cookie? Something's troubling you, I can tell."

Theresa breathed deeply. She considered telling him, but what? Miles stole from his church. That she knew for certain. Had he cheated on her with Shelby Canter? She may never know for sure. Something had happened. You didn't give people that much money for nothing, especially when the money really wasn't yours to give. And how about Brooke Overstreet? What was going on there?

And what about the two of them, her and Miles?

Were they going to weather this?

Did she want to?

So much would depend upon how he'd addressed the situation with the elders the evening before.

And how he would address the situation today in church.

Would he even be there?

The last thing she wanted was to appear at Surfside today.

But there was one way to find out.

"Papa, I'm going to have to run. It's time for church."

# # #

It had seemed such an unnecessary expense, broadcasting Sunday church services over a local cable station and streaming via internet.

Miles was certain it would pay dividends in terms of lives saved for the Lord. The elders agreed, and seven months before, they'd started broadcasting live.

Theresa had never watched a Surfside service from anyplace other than her usual spot.

Until today.

The music was joyous as always. Derby was a master at working the congregation into a frenzy for the Lord. His heart was in the right place, too; but when the camera moved in tighter, she saw pain in his face.

He knew.

There was no sign of Miles as cameras panned the auditorium.

Had they put him on leave?

Could the elders pull that off? She had always felt they were little more than puppets doing Miles' bidding.

The music reached a crescendo, then quieted. A clear signal to everyone that it was time for the message.

And then, there he was.

Dressed in black, rather than his usual colorful attire, Miles moved slowly to the center of the stage. His eyes were red and tired. His posture, stooped. He appeared to be a man defeated.

Then he began to spin his story.

Each sentence struck Theresa like a gut-punch.

He described problems at home.

A wife who didn't respect him or the church; who chose to be married to her career.

A wife who wouldn't give him children.

As he spoke, he became overwrought with emotion. After two breakdowns, the elders came on stage and surrounded him, praying for the strength to continue.

Theresa remained still, shocked at what was taking place. For some silly reason, as Miles recovered from each breakdown and was pulled to his feet by the elders, she thought of the James Brown concerts she'd seen on television as a girl. Brown would appear exhausted from his performance. His assistants would come out and place a royal robe on him, only to see it shucked off as the Godfather of Soul rose to perform again.

Miles Traynor - James Brown of the Pulpit.

If there were questions about the future of their marriage, Miles was answering them for the entire world.

Then, he turned even darker.

Riley Wenger became the target of his wrath. His friend and confidant, Riley had given church money to a young girl for reasons Miles never understood. He produced the signed checks, careful to cover Buck Canter's name while displaying them for the cameras.

Then, if that wasn't enough, he asserted that Riley and Theresa had recently started spending time together. Alone.

Miles had begged them to break it off, but they hadn't.

Just the day before, they had been spotted together in an Annapolis park.

There were pictures. Those were put on camera, too.

Riley was no longer associated with Surfside. Congregants were encouraged to turn their backs on a man whom Miles described as a thief and adulterer.

And Theresa?

Fortunately, the church has members who are willing to help in times of need, Miles said. Forrest Delaney was one of those members. Called to the stage, he appeared bewildered as Miles announced that he would be assisting their pastor in pursuing appropriate legal measures.

Criminal charges against Riley.

And the "putting away" of Theresa.

That was how he said it – putting away. Theresa would have laughed if she weren't so numb. He wouldn't use the 'd' word. Divorce was a sin, associated with all kinds of unsavory things. Nope. Because of her adultery and unwillingness to change, Theresa was being *put away*.

She bolted from the room, missing the end of the sermon.

Adam awakened to a soft knock on the door.

"Feel like some lunch, Mr. Overstreet?" Hilda opened the door slightly.

He did, but first... "May I use your restroom, Mrs...?"

"Call me Hilda. Sure. I'll help you get there."

Adam was surprised how steady he felt. The headache had been reduced to a dull throb. In the hallway, they were met by a young woman.

"I was just coming to help—Hey, it's you!"

Adam looked at her, unsure where he knew her from. A pleasant fragrance reminded him.

"From the city bus, Cathy, from West Virginia, right?"

She beamed. "Good memory! Especially after..." she pointed at the bandage on the back of his head. "It looks like you've had a rough couple of days."

"You don't know the half of it," he said, entering the bathroom and closing the door.

Come to think of it, he thought, smiling to himself, he didn't know the half of it either.

#

Years of practicing law had taught Theresa when to charge ahead and when to wait. This seemed like a good time to wait. Eventually Miles would make a move.

She didn't have to wait long.

At one o'clock, she heard the garage door going up. She'd spent the past couple hours considering her next step. Miles had already revealed his strategy – go on the offensive. She would have a few surprises for him.

"We need to talk," he said bluntly, entering the living room and standing a few feet away. "Things have changed."

Theresa chose not to reply.

"In thirty minutes, some people are coming to remove my clothes from the premises. You've proven yourself an unfit wife, Tee. I'm moving out."

She remained quiet, not taking her eyes off him, but not taking the bait, either.

"You got nothing to say?" He asked, after several moments locked in a stare-down.

Theresa shook her head.

"You changed, Theresa. You used to be the most loving, supportive woman a man could ask for. Now, you're focused only on yourself."

Again, no response.

"Keep the house... and the payments. I took a lease on a place on the north end of the beach. Keep what's yours. I'll take what's mine. I don't want to fight about bath towels and silverware."

Theresa picked up a small voice recorder from the coffee table.

"What do you want to do about this?"

"Never seen it before."

"No, not the recorder," she replied. "The recording."

When she pushed a button, Miles' voice filled the room.

"I need you to prepare a check, Riley. Fifty thousand."

"May I ask what it's for?"

"It's a church issue. Buck Canter is trying to get a fresh start, and Surfside's going to help."

"Buck Canter's not a Surfside member, Miles. Shelby is, but —"

"Exactly. And the best thing for Shelby is for her old man to be far away."

Theresa watched the arrogance drain from his face as the tape played on.

"Have you taken a vote of the elders, Miles? That's required for expenditures over five thousand."

"Remember who you're talking to, Riley." Indignation dripped from his voice. *"I talked to Eric Stover. He's taking care of the others. This is time-sensitive and I want the check ASAP."*

The recording was quiet for a moment, then Riley spoke.

"This whole thing with Shelby, Miles. I just don't want to be in the mid —"

"Take care of it, Riley!"

"Turn it off." Miles voice was chillingly cold. When Theresa made no move to comply, he grabbed the recorder, heaving it against the brick fireplace.

Then, the doorbell rang.

"They're here to get my stuff."

Theresa nodded. "Do what you came for."

Miles looked hesitantly toward the front door, then back at Theresa. Her recitation of Jesus' final words to Judas before his betrayal were not lost on him.

"Maybe we can figure something out. Maybe I reacted—"

Theresa held her hands up. "There's no working anything out. You're grooming Brooke Overstreet the same way you tried to do with Shelby. You were planning on replacing me with her, weren't you?"

Miles froze.

"That's what I thought."

Over a late lunch of oyster fritters and coleslaw, Adam told them everything. At least everything he could remember.

Even the unpleasant things, about the night in St. Louis.

The drinking, the gambling.

The kiss.

But he didn't tell them anything beyond the kiss, because there was nothing left to tell.

And they believed him.

Completely.

For the first time in two weeks, someone believed him.

Theresa remained seated, in plain sight, as a half-dozen Surfside members carried Miles' clothes and other possessions to a borrowed panel truck.

She wanted it that way. She wanted them to pass her each time they made another trip through the house.

Five of them lowered their heads, offering little more than mumbled hellos. Their embarrassment was obvious.

Only one dared make eye contact.

Denise Stover, Elder Eric Stover's haughty wife shook her head when she spotted Theresa. Her disdain was obvious and only added to the discomfort of the others. At one point, Theresa overheard her talking to another woman in Miles' study.

"She certainly has some gall. Just sitting there watching as that poor man's life falls apart."

Theresa wanted to tell her the truth. She also wanted to deck her. Denise Stover was a judgmental social climber, happy and willing to assume a position as one of Surfside's Grande Dames. Theresa had warned Miles about her several times.

She was certainly having her day today.

Enjoy it while you can, Theresa thought.

After two hours, they were gone. Miles walked them out, then returned to the living room. Theresa hadn't moved.

"You don't know as much as you think."

"I know enough," she said.

"I can explain that tape. People will believe me."

"Did you have someone beat up Adam Overstreet?"

Theresa's misdirection brought him up short. For a moment.

"Don't be ridiculous, Tee. I went out of my way to help him. I picked him up and gave him a ride to the place where he was camping. I even offered him some money to get back home to West Virginia."

"But he didn't take it, did he?"

"How do you know so much?"

"I know Adam Overstreet a little bit, but I know you very well."

Miles waved her off like he might a fly.

"I'm outta here. You're crazy if—"

"When are you planning to begin seeing Brooke? Outside the privacy of your office, I mean?"

Miles slammed the door on his way out.

They'd spent so much time talking about him that Adam had learned little about Cathy or the Watsons. Cathy and her friends were hosted by Carl and Hilda's church. They rotated through the various homes for Sunday lunch. The fact that this was Cathy's week at their house was nothing more than coincidence.

"Mission work at a beach resort was a lucky draw," Adam said.

"You'd think," Cathy replied. "But there's also a lot of sadness, Mr. Overstreet. This week, I met a girl about my age who moved here to be with a boy she dated back home in Pennsylvania. The best she's found is a couple part-time jobs. Now he's kicked her out of the apartment, and she's living in one of the city parks."

Ouch. He didn't mention how close he'd come to the same thing.

Carl had retired from the sanitation department a decade before. They'd raised four kids who now lived all over the country. After the kids were out of the house, Hilda went to work for a local flower shop, before joining her husband in retirement two years earlier. Over the years, they'd had many offers to sell their house, the most recent approaching a million dollars.

"We figure we'll stay here until we can't, then sell," Hilda said. Similar houses that surrounded theirs back in the 1950's and 60's had been replaced by larger structures built as rental units.

"We miss the neighbors, but there are some nice renters," Carl said.

After lunch, they moved into the living room and continued their visit. Cathy fit in well, despite her youth. Though they were from different areas of West Virginia, she and Adam discovered they knew a few of the same people, not a rarity for the Mountaineer State.

At one point Cathy's phone buzzed. She excused herself to the kitchen where she took the call. A few minutes later, she returned.

"Mr. Overstreet, did you know you're a wanted man?"

Adam's stomach knotted up.

"There's a man asking around town about you. A preacher."

Adam groaned. "Let me guess. Miles Traynor."

She shook her head. "Nope," she glanced at a text message. "Pastor Riley Wenger. Does that name mean something?"

"Unfortunately, yes."

"He's putting the word out around town. He wants you to call him ASAP." She again consulted her phone.

"He says not to worry.

"He wants to help you."

MONDAY

Day Twenty-Four

They were waiting when she exited the courtroom. Four of them. Two that Theresa expected, two she hadn't.

Riley and Adam were together, seated on a long hard bench. Neither got up. They knew they would be waiting in line.

"Theresa, we need to talk." Keith Talbot got right to the point, which was one reason his name was on law firm's masthead. Dan Gallo trailed behind, trying to hide his smirk.

Theresa said nothing. She nodded at Riley and Adam, holding up a finger as a sign that she wouldn't be long. She followed her law firm colleagues to a small meeting room. The door was barely closed before Talbot got started.

"Surfside has signed a retainer for our firm's representation."

It wasn't even noon yet. Miles had certainly been busy. Talbot continued.

"Dan will take over your cases, effective immediately. Until we can sort through what's going on between you and Pastor Traynor, you'll be on paid leave."

Theresa nodded.

Dan Gallo nudged his boss and looked toward the hallway.

"Oh, yeah," Talbot said. "I almost forgot. You're forbidden from doing any pro bono work for Overstreet and Pastor Wenger. If you choose to go against this directive, consider yourself terminated."

For a few moments, they stood quietly, locked in a standoff while Talbot waited for an acknowledgement that wouldn't be coming. Theresa went in a different direction.

"It must have been a handsome retainer."

Dan Gallo nodded slightly, caught himself, and stepped behind his boss.

"The size of the retainer has nothing to do with this decision." Talbot looked down his nose at her. "Your indiscretions have put our firm in a precarious situation. We need to make sure our integrity isn't compromised by your problems."

Theresa bit her tongue. This was a fight best delayed. Talbot opened the door, motioning for his flunky Gallo to walk out ahead of him.

"Leave any case files in your possession with the receptionist at the Ocean City office by five today," Talbot said.

###

Riley hadn't said much since picking him up early that morning, and Adam was still uncertain about what was going on. One thing was for sure: the two guys from Theresa's firm hadn't driven all the way to Delaware for a social visit. Within ten minutes of showing Theresa to a room down the hall, they came out, passing without a word. It was another five minutes before Theresa emerged. She came toward them, stopping a few feet away to survey the empty hallway, then pointed to the same room she'd come from.

Adam became emotional when told that Jasmine Fleece had reasserted herself into his life. Then, with Jasmine on the phone reporting that a St. Louis investigator was also on the case, his lip started to quiver. He quickly turned away.

"The investigator thinks there might still be video from that night, but he has to follow the chain of command to get it."

Don't get too optimistic, Jasmine cautioned. It was highly irregular for a hotel to keep video for more than a few weeks. The Gateway Hotel had been exposed to two high-profile lawsuits in the past eighteen months, and their legal team had recommended archiving surveillance footage for longer periods.

Adam could finally have some hope. But first, the air needed to be cleared. Theresa leaned forward, resting her arms on the table. She didn't usually care whether or not a client was guilty, but this was different.

Adam was starting to regain his composure when she leveled him with her gaze.

"How much of her story is true?"

His throat grew dry. He glanced around for a something to slake it, but there was nothing available.

"We need to know," Riley said quietly.

He opened his mouth to respond. Once, twice, but nothing came out. He'd spent the past two weeks defending himself, and there wasn't much left in the tank. But Riley was right. They deserved to know.

"The truth about what really happened," he began, carefully choosing his words. "Is that nothing happened. She kissed me and I left."

Adam halted again, shaking his head. "I only wish I could remember the time between leaving and waking up in my room. I've wracked my brain, but nothing."

"And the letter?" Theresa asked.

"There's no letter."

For several moments, the only sound was the whoosh of air conditioning from an overhead vent. Theresa and Riley were looking at him, their faces full with concern.

Concern for him?

For themselves?

The absurdity of the situation gnawed at him. Why were Miles Traynor's wife and second-in-command suddenly in his corner?

What was going to happen? And did it matter anymore?

Why were Theresa and Riley so concerned? Were they really here to support him, or out to finish what Miles had started?

Adam raised his head and took a deep breath.

"I guess I have some questions for you."

Riley went first, initially holding back some of the more sordid details. It was at Theresa's prompting that he let down the veil he'd become accustomed to maintaining as a pastor. Theresa followed suit. They told Adam everything, their disclosures sucking the air from the room.

And then they were done. Theresa wouldn't have felt more fatigued if she'd run a marathon. Riley looked battered and worn.

Adam eyed them across the table. "So... you're both unemployed? Tell me again why I should want to hang with *you guys*?"

His simple declaration might have seemed callous or mocking to some, but given all they'd been through over the past hour, it brought a much different response. One Adam was aiming for when he said it.

Laughter.

Cleansing, therapeutic laughter.

And then, a plan.

TUESDAY

Day Twenty-Five

A rattling boom roused Adam from a deep sleep. He glanced at the 1970's-era clock radio on the nightstand. Not even six.

Outside, the guys on a trash truck tossed empty cans to the sidewalk, repeating the racket that had awakened him. The old bed in Carl and Hilda's spare room invited sleep, wrapping itself around him, but Adam missed the comforts of home. His home.

Riley had offered his guest room, but Adam chose to come back to the old house on Dorchester Street. Carl and Hilda had saved his life, and he didn't want to leave just yet. When he'd returned last evening, they wanted to know everything, so he told them.

With further sleep unlikely, Adam pulled on the gym shorts and t-shirt he had rescued from the campsite the night before. Theresa had insisted they return there, and the three of them spent a half-hour gathering anything worth salvaging. Theresa took a trash bag of his clothes home to launder. This simple gesture had pushed Adam's emotional buttons. Theresa Traynor was in the midst of her own personal tempest, but was reaching out to help him.

And Riley? There was a man operating solely on the Lord's promptings. All of them had lost something over the past few days. Riley could have avoided his losses by doing little more than staying in lockstep with his boss. He'd chosen not to.

Adam laced his running shoes as best he could with his arm in a cast. He couldn't run, but a walk on the beach sounded glorious. Grabbing his water bottle from a dresser, he stopped to look at the family portrait. Though it was badly damaged from the elements, he'd insisted on bringing it back. He missed Jack so much.

And he missed Brooke.

He picked up the cellphone Riley had given him, debating a call home. Was it too early? What would Brooke say when she recognized his voice?

Was it too late?

She answered on the first ring.

"Brooke."

Silence.

"Brooke, it's—"

"I know. What do you want?"

Short, words clipped, but what was different?

"I just wanted to call… to make sure you're all right."

He heard her take a deep breath.

"You mean Jack. You just want to know if Jack is all right."

"Well... yeah, but you too. How are you, Brooke?"

Her breathing sounded ragged.

"Brooke?"

Silence.

"Did something happen? Is Jack okay?"

"He's okay." Her voice was breaking. He could tell she was fighting to keep from crying.

"I'm coming right over. Don't go anyplace."

"Cookie, I need a favor."

Papa didn't waste any time getting to the reason he'd called. That was fine with Theresa. She wasn't sure she could keep up her end of the conversation. She'd stayed strong for Riley and Adam, but Papa...

"His name is Oscar Bolden. Oscar *Everett* Bolden. His half-brother is also Oscar, but his middle name is Manley."

Papa went on to explain. Oscar Manley had a warrant for his arrest in Pike County, Missouri. Oscar Everett, one of the migrants who was relocating to Grebey Island, had been mistaken for his half-brother when he applied for a Missouri driver's license. One thing led to another, and Oscar Everett was being held in the Pike County jail.

"Do you know any lawyers out this way who can help?"

"Maybe, Papa. Let me do some checking." Theresa had only slept an hour or two, as the weight of the past two days pressed in from all directions. She hoped the ache in her chest didn't carry through to her voice.

But it did.

"What's wrong, Cookie?"

It wasn't his question as much as the tenor of Papa's voice that did it. She could feel his concern through the cellphone. Nobody could read her like he could. Not even Miles.

When Brooke opened the door, she seemed strong; a new resolve sweeping away whatever had been bothering her on the phone. She displayed the guarded front of the past couple weeks.

"I'm sorry you came for nothing. Everything is fine."

Adam shook his head. "You're not doing that to me, Brooke."

"I'm not doing anything. You're the one who did something."

They stood in the doorway, waiting for the other to say or do something. Adam considered asking if Jack was up, but it was six-thirty, an hour before he usually stirred. He turned to leave, then changed course.

"What did he do?"

The question startled her, he could tell.

"Who?"

She knew who. Adam could see it in her eyes. He waited.

"Adam, you need to go." She tried to close the door, but Adam stuck his foot in the jamb. When she realized what he'd done, the tears came. Hard. She retreated into the house, Adam close behind, following her down the hallway. She reached the bedroom door, locking it before he could turn the knob. Through the thick wooden door, he could hear her sobs. He knocked gently, then harder.

"Go away!"

Adam leaned against the door, hopeful she would reconsider. After a few minutes, he started to leave, but was brought up short by what he saw on the kitchen table. He'd blown through too quickly to see the large floral arrangement the first time. Beside it was a single sheet of folded stationary. He couldn't help himself. He unfolded it and began to read.

"Cookie, Baby Girl, I'm coming to you. I'll fly out of Seattle today."

Theresa's crying turned to blubbering, then to laughter at the thought of Papa getting on an airplane.

"Papa, you haven't been on a plane since Nixon was president." She wiped away the tears from her cheeks.

"It doesn't matter. I can do it. I'll take a pill or something." His response made her laugh harder. It felt good. Papa was useless when he got higher than the second rung of a stepladder. The story of his first and only airline flight, from Pittsburgh to Milwaukee to accept an award, was legend, and Mama had reveled in telling and retelling how Papa had screamed so loud during takeoff that a physician on board offered him a sedative. Papa took a double-dose, slept through the landing, and rented a car for the return trip to Penn State. Since then, even for meetings on the West Coast, Papa drove.

And now he was willing to get on an airplane. For her.

"I'll tell you what, Papa. How about I meet you halfway? You drive back to Missouri, and I'll catch a plane to St. Louis. I'll get Mr. Bolden's situation straightened out and then take care of a little business of my own."

They gathered at Theresa's dining room table. There was new information to share, but Riley insisted they pray and eat the light lunch Theresa had prepared before charging ahead.

As they ate, Adam was reconsidering if he should share the photos. The last thing he wanted was to drag Theresa and Riley further into despair, but then again, they'd agreed to put all their cards on the table. The pictures would be damaging cards.

"Do you think it's worth it?" Adam asked as they finished lunch.

"What do you mean?" Riley said.

"I know exactly what he means." Theresa took a sip from a water bottle. "Miles has buried you, Riley. Your chances of getting another job in this town are almost nil."

Riley shrugged.

"And me? My marriage is over. I could fight to get my job back and probably win. The partners exhibited a major conflict of interest and have probably violated a few state bar regulations. If none of that worked, I could throw out the race card. Black female attorney, good work record, great evaluations…"

Adam picked up where she left off. "The question would be if you even *want* to work here after everything that's happened. I'm in the same boat as you, Theresa. When I'm cleared, I could fight to retain my job, but—"

"The drinking," Riley said.

"Yep. That's always going to be there. If I can beat the rap of being a philandering hospital administrator, they can always maintain that I'm a drunk. I'm not, but the evidence begs otherwise."

"You do have a problem with it."

Theresa raised her hands, her eyes shooting daggers at Riley. "It's not the time."

Chastened, Riley said, "But it does beg the question, where do we go from here?"

Adam answered quickly. "I want my wife and little boy back."

They finished their lunch in silence, Adam's words hanging in the air. The irony was evident. Of their newly-formed triumvirate, the only one with something worth fighting for was the one who's problems had brought them together in the first place.

After Theresa cleared the table, they forged ahead. Theresa went first, telling them of her planned trip to St. Louis.

"I'm hopeful I can help Jasmine's private investigator access the surveillance tapes. The hotel has been dragging its feet."

"Would it help to get a subpoena?" Riley asked.

Theresa shook her head. "There's no criminal investigation. Our best hope is to run into someone in hotel security who's willing to do a good turn for a stranger."

"Do you need our help?" Adam asked.

"Not really," Theresa said, apprising his appearance. "Besides, you still look pretty beat up. It might be best for you to rest."

Adam couldn't disagree, the throbbing had eased to a dull ache that returned with a vengeance when he expended too much energy.

"I have something to share." Adam pulled out his new cellphone, opened the photo app, and laid it on the table. Riley picked it up; Theresa leaned over his shoulder to look.

"Flowers," Riley said, looking at Adam for clarification.

"On my kitchen table," Adam said. "There's another photo, but Theresa I have to caution you it might be hard to take."

Adam saw her shudder, then throw back her shoulders. The lady certainly had resolve. Riley flicked ahead to the next photo and they took a few moments to examine it."

"It's a letter. To my wife. It was on the table, next to the flowers."

Riley remained stoic as he read. Theresa, not so much. Tears appeared; she stopped reading and looked away. Riley moved the photo out of her sight-line, but she pulled it back.

"No. I need to read all of it."

"Does Brooke know you saw this?" Riley asked.

Adam told them about his visit.

"I think she was struggling with Miles' overtures," he said. "I caught her on the phone at a weak moment, but by the time I got there she had shut down."

Theresa clutched herself, as if she were cold.

"There's one more." Adam looked at Riley as he spoke. The pastor took a deep breath and forwarded to the final photo.

A signed check from a Surfside account. $15,000. Made out to Brooke Overstreet.

Signed by Riley Wenger.

WEDNESDAY

Day Twenty-Six

The early flight got Theresa to St. Louis by nine. Harvester was waiting at the curb in his road-weary sedan. By noon they had made their way to Pike County and helped the prosecutor clear up the case of the two Oscar Boldens. Discussion on the return trip centered on Miles. While Papa drove, Theresa told him everything.

"He should go to jail." Papa's response wasn't what she'd expected from a gentle man who sought out the good in others.

"In most places he would," Theresa said as she stared at the ribbon of interstate. "But, Papa, he's bulletproof in Ocean City. Even the police seem to buy what he's selling."

Papa shook his head slowly. "What happened, Cookie? Of all the boys you brought home, I never saw potential like I did in Miles. He could do just about anything..."

Papa's voice trailed off, leaving a silence that lasted the rest of the drive.

Riley rose from his seat, preparing to make a hasty exit from the diner. It was the third time since lunch had arrived.

"I respect Theresa, but it's my reputation on the line. I'm going to the police."

And for the third time, Adam talked him off the ledge.

"Won't it be better to take them an account of everything, Riley? Rather than a piece at a time."

"Look around. You're not the one getting the evil eye from half the people in here." Riley's eyes darted about the diner. "When I walked in here a week ago, everybody wanted to buy my lunch."

"Yeah, I wouldn't know about that." Adam's sarcastic response brought a puzzled look before Riley realized what he was saying. For the first time all day, he smiled.

"Yeah Adam, but you're last week's news."

"I'll wait here." Papa scanned the parking lot for an open space.

"Nonsense. You have a way with people, Papa. I'm not sure what I'm going to run into here. The investigator has tried going through hotel management, but hasn't gotten anywhere."

They entered a hotel service entrance, catching sideways glances but little else from uniformed hotel staff they encountered. A few wrong turns later, they found their way to the basement location of hotel security. Theresa knocked.

"Help you?" The reply came through a speaker beside the door. Theresa assumed they were also being watched.

"I'm Theresa Traynor. We were told you could help us."

"Who told you that?"

Theresa hadn't thought that far ahead. Papa stepped toward the speaker.

"Young man, I'm Professor Harvester Stanley, Penn State University."

"So?" The disembodied voice responded.

Papa's eyes took on a glint Theresa had seen before. He was about to take control of the situation.

"So...? So how about you knock off the foolishness and open this door, young man. I'm considering this hotel for future business that will greatly impact its bottom line, and quite frankly, your demeanor over this tin speaker isn't helping at all."

Silence.

"C'mon, Miss Traynor." Papa took her arm and started to move away, his tone similar to what he'd used when he lectured her as a child. "Let's go upstairs. Miss Correnti will want to hear about this."

Click. The unmistakable sound of the door being unlocked.

"Who's Miss Correnti?" Theresa whispered as they returned to the security entrance.

"Hotel Manager," Papa said with a wink. "I saw her name and picture on the wall by the service entrance. Pretty young thing."

Inside, a burly man with a crewcut eyed them suspiciously. Papa stepped in front and offered his hand. "Professor Stanley, and my associate, Miss Traynor."

"George Garber. Sorry for the attitude, Professor. It's been a day."

Papa nodded. "I'll get right down to it. We're considering two St. Louis hotels; this one and the Spirit. The security guy from the Spirit said this place had a problem with security, and I wanted to come check for myself."

Garber's face tightened. "That's Rickson. He's a jerk. We got no problems here."

Papa took a few moments to check out the surroundings. Subdued lighting, an obese woman seated in front of a bank of monitors acting as if she weren't listening to them, the smell of corn chips or foot odor stagnating the air.

"Your set-up looks good enough, but there's another concern. On second thought, maybe we should just go see Miss Correnti."

Papa was bluffing, but Garber didn't call him on it.

"Try me first, Professor. Miss Correnti is already on my butt. I'd rather keep it between us men."

"Fine, Mr. Garber. My concern involves an associate who stayed here a couple months ago. Do you have an office where we can visit?"

###

Adam was relaxing in a saggy easy chair in the Watsons' living room when his phone buzzed. He excused himself and stepped into the kitchen, so as not to interrupt Carl and Hilda's enjoyment of *Jeopardy*.

"Hello?"

"It's Theresa."

"Hey. Any luck?"

"Maybe. Get some sleep. You need to be at the airport first thing in the morning. You're booked on a six-fifteen flight to Kansas City."

"What? Seriously? What happened?"

"I'm still working on this end, but I need you to get here."

"I don't even have the funds for a bus pass." Adam mindlessly patted the wallet in his pocket. "Let alone an airline ticket."

"It's all taken care of."

"But what about Riley. He was a mess today. I had to—"

"I've already talked to him. His wife is there for him. Don't worry about him; just catch that plane."

THURSDAY

Day Twenty-Seven

The route was the same he'd taken a couple weeks before, from Kansas City International Airport south into the city. This time, rather than a rental car, it was an older four-door sedan with squeaky springs and a passenger seat that sank when you sat down.

The driver was Theresa's father, Professor Harvester Stanley.

Spotting the dignified gentleman in the baggage claim area, wearing a natty suit and holding a wrinkled sheet of notebook paper with Adam's name on it, he was reminded of the Morgan Freeman character in Driving Miss Daisy.

"Cookie is waiting for us downtown," he said after introducing himself. When he reached for Adam's overnight bag, Adam waved him off. On the way into downtown, Professor Stanley offered minimal responses to Adam's questions about what had happened.

"She's meeting with an attorney about some information she uncovered yesterday in St. Louis," he said. "We're headed there now."

Forty minutes later, they were seated in the waiting area of a large law office. Adam had counted forty names on the directory out front. It was a busy, but not an ostentatious place, probably deriving much of its income from slip-and-falls and rear-end collisions.

The wait seemed interminable. The clock swept past ten and eleven. Adam was edgy and spent his time absently plowing through a pile of outdated magazines. Professor Stanley had an e-reader and remained silently engrossed. The few times he looked up and their eyes met, he nodded at Adam. It's going to be okay, his eyes said.

It was quarter to noon, and Adam's stomach was starting to growl. The bag of peanuts and diet soda on the plane had run their course. He stood up.

"I'm going to look for something to—"

"Adam."

Theresa appeared from around a corner.

"Come with me."

Theresa took his elbow and led him through a maze of hallways.

"What's going on?" he asked.

She said nothing, but the thumbs up she gave him said plenty. Near the end of a busy hallway she knocked softly and entered a conference room. Waiting for them was a boyish looking man whose ponytail contradicted his two-thousand-dollar suit.

"Adam, this is Mick Fray. He's Penny Hardesty's attorney." Mick stood and offered his hand.

"I assume at this juncture, it's okay for me to talk to Adam openly in your presence," Theresa said as they situated themselves around a small conference table. Fray nodded.

Theresa placed her right hand on Adam's left, squeezing it slightly.

"She admitted that she made everything up."

Had he heard correctly? Could it be?

Suddenly, he felt overheated, despite the air conditioning running full blast. He searched for what he wanted to say, but the words came up missing.

"Mr. Overstreet, my client has put you through a terrible ordeal, and she's remorseful for every—"

"Cut the lawyer-speak, Mick." Theresa waved her hand at him. "Adam's been to hell and back the past month, and doesn't care about your client's remorse." She turned slightly in her chair, placing a small stack of papers between them.

"The closed-circuit cameras at the Gateway Hotel showed you leaving her room at twelve-thirty. You made it about fifteen feet and passed out in the hallway. A few minutes later, another man, Mrs. Hardesty's secretary—"

"Personal Assistant," Fray interjected.

"—stepped over you and entered the room." Theresa forged ahead as if Fray hadn't spoken.

"They've been... involved for several months now. He had a room on another floor, and as soon as you left, Penny called him."

Adam leaned forward, cupping his head in his hands. Could it be over? Then, another thought.

"I need to call Brooke." He was getting to his feet when Theresa put her hand on his shoulder and gently guided him back to the chair.

"Let's finish here," she said as she picked up a single sheet of paper and handed it to him. "Here's a statement, signed by Mrs. Hardesty and Mr. Fray this morning. It's already been faxed to the hospital board members in Ocean City."

Statements I made in recent weeks involving an extramarital relationship between Adam Overstreet and me were false. On the evening of June 19-20, Mr. Overstreet remained in my suite at the Gateway Hotel after other guests had left. He stayed at my request. Both of us had been drinking, but it was me who initiated intimacy with Mr. Overstreet. He immediately rebuffed my efforts and left the suite, leaving his sweater behind. Later, to cover up a relationship I was having with a work associate, I told my husband Mr. Overstreet had forced himself upon me. At my husband's insistence, I shared this falsehood with Mr. Overstreet's wife and employer. I know now how much my behavior has impacted others and sincerely regret the grief I have caused Mr. Overstreet and his family.

Adam laid the statement on the table. Nauseous, he stood and lurched toward the door.

"Second door on the left," Fray said. When Adam returned ten minutes later, the attorney was gone. Rather than taking a chair, he slumped on the floor against a wall. He looked up at Theresa and motioned for her to proceed.

"She resigned from her job this morning. I don't know what's going to happen between her and her

314

husband. Apparently, he has a history of being controlling."

Adam nodded, but said nothing. He felt like he hadn't slept in weeks.

"We can still sue her for libel. The news accounts speak for themselves. The police department in Independence, where she lives, isn't going to be happy about enforcing a restraining order under false pretenses. If you want to proceed, you won't have any problem—"

"I just want to go home."

FRIDAY

Day Twenty-Eight

Brooke refused to see him. Even as he exclaimed over the phone, "It's over. She admitted she lied."

She wouldn't believe Theresa either.

Or Riley.

"I know what you two have been doing. Pastor Miles told us everything."

It took Derby Hatfield, Miles Traynor's music minister and Adam's friend, to get Brooke to listen, but it took Big Mike and Megan Lusk to get her to agree to a face-to-face meeting. Megan even arranged for one of the Lusk children to pick up Jack and take him to their house. Riley had spent the prior evening meeting with Derby and the Lusks. Though he'd remained loyal to Miles, his friend and boss, Derby couldn't overlook the evidence - Miles' letter to Brooke; the check with Riley's signature.

On the drive from the Salisbury airport to Ocean City, Theresa's phone buzzed continuously with calls from Ocean City Memorial's Board Chairman, Melvin Proffer. She let them go to voicemail.

Within an hour of Theresa and Adam's return flight from Kansas City, they arrived at the house on Winterset Drive. The others were waiting. Brooke's eyes grew wide when she opened the door. Adam, Theresa, Riley, Derby Hatfield, and the Lusks. Megan hugged her as they made their way to the living room. When they were seated, Big Mike spoke.

"Brooke, you've been leaning on Megan and me since this all started. You know we love you and wouldn't do anything to hurt you, right?" Brooke nodded.

"We're going to listen to what Adam, Theresa, and Riley have to say. They've gotten to the bottom of the situation with the lady in Kansas City." Big Mike nodded at Adam.

"Brooke... it's been... Theresa and I went to Kansas City..." he was unable to get the words out, as the emotion of the past month spilled over. Big Mike put his arm around his friend as Theresa took the lead.

"She made it up."

Brooke's posture became stooped, and her eyes teared as she pushed her fist to her mouth. She looked from Theresa to Megan Lusk. Megan nodded.

"I read her statement. She apologized and quit her job."

Brooke's eyes darted about the room. A day before, she wouldn't have trusted three of the people seated around her. But now...

"Why?"

"She was having a relationship with another man," Theresa said. "She used Adam to cover it up when her husband found out."

"But... Pastor said..."

"Pastor Miles has his own problems," Riley said.

"The deacons are meeting as we speak," Derby said. "Did you cash the check he gave you?"

"How did you know..."

"It was forged," Riley said. "Miles had a policy of never signing checks for the operation of the church, so he forged my name."

The room grew silent. Adam, more composed, moved to a spot on the floor in front of his wife. When Brooke looked down at him, Theresa could see the change in her eyes. They were going to be okay.

"It's time for us to go."

SEVEN MONTHS LATER

"Miss Traynor, you have a call holding on Line Four."

"Thanks Lexie. Hello, this is Theresa Traynor."

"Cookie!"

"Papa! Where are you?"

"I'm in town. Can you break away?"

"For you, always."

#

There weren't any beaches in Pittsburgh, and he wasn't a CEO anymore, but Adam was happy.

The position was new, Vice-President of Patient Care, with no shoes to fill, big or otherwise. The hours were decent, and Adam spent much of his day visiting patients and their families, making sure all was well.

He'd chosen to be upfront during the hiring process. After all, the stories were easy enough to find online. A couple hospitals hadn't given him a second look. Pittsburgh Regional did. The CEO knew people who knew Adam. They freely attested to his abilities as an executive. When contacted, Theresa, Riley, and Derby Hatfield explained the final weeks in Ocean City. Though he'd stepped down as Board Chairman, Melvin Proffer offered a heartfelt recommendation that the Pittsburgh CEO said made the difference.

Adam's Tuesday schedule was punctuated by a long lunch break away from the hospital. It began in a church basement a few blocks from work. Alcoholics Anonymous was a promise he'd made to Brooke. He'd dragged himself to the first few meetings, but now felt something was missing if he didn't attend.

The garage door was up when he pulled into the driveway of the rented condominium. Despite the blustery conditions, Jack was riding his bicycle up and down the sidewalk. Brooke was sitting on the front stoop, a down jacket protecting her from the cold. Both waved when he pulled in.

"I've got chili ready," she said, kissing him tenderly on the cheek. They went into the house, Jack close behind. The lunches were the marriage counselor's idea, one of many that had helped mend the tear in their relationship. It had taken time, but Adam finally felt they were at a point close to where they were before. They were still on a high from the cruise they'd taken two weeks before, leaving Jack in the loving care of Adam's mom, now just an hour away. The closeness had helped forge a relationship between grandmother and grandson that would have been impossible in Ocean City. Mom's friends said they noticed how she perked up whenever Jack was coming to visit. Adam hoped to have her around for a few more years.

As always, Papa drove. Theresa studied him as he watched the road. He looked tired. Older than a few months before.

"Papa, have you been taking care of yourself?"

He shrugged and smiled. "The last few weeks on the road were hard, Cookie, with saying good-bye to my friends, and the drive here. I'm not as strong as I used to be."

And Theresa's pending divorce.

He didn't say that, but she knew it lingered under the surface. The Stanley family didn't have divorces. Until now.

Oh, he understood. Theresa knew that. There was no possibility of reconciliation after Miles had publicly put her away.

"Riley said he'd heard attendance at Surfside is only a quarter of what it was."

Papa's face clouded. He gripped the steering wheel like it might try to take off on its own.

"Why in the world those church elders kept him on is beyond me."

Theresa had been surprised too. Miles had taken a two-month sabbatical, citing exhaustion. She never expected him to return, but Eric Stover stood by him.

When two other elders objected to his return, they were voted off the board and left the church, taking many members with them. Miles' grand idea for a church school had been shelved, and word was they were behind on the church mortgage.

"How is Riley doing?" Papa asked as he steered his trusty sedan down a country road.

"He and Derby are doing okay. Their church start-up has about seventy-five people coming each week. Derby does music and preaches. Riley still prefers to be behind the scene. They said money was tight, but they're getting by. The forgery case against Miles is dragging along. They don't even have a court date yet."

"When they find him guilty will that be the end of Miles in Ocean City?"

"Never underestimate Miles Traynor, Papa. I wouldn't be surprised if he rises from the ashes."

The car rocked as they crossed the wooden bridge. It had been months since Theresa visited Grebey Island. Papa drove past the old church and school. Theresa gasped when the homestead came into view. The ramshackle house had been demolished. In its place was a neat yellow bungalow that made her smile.

"Mama's favorite color."

"Took those boys four months to build. It's got to be a record." Papa pulled close to the house. "Come see."

Though lacking furniture, the small sunlit kitchen welcomed them. Off to one side were two bedrooms. A living room adjoined the kitchen, and beyond that, a front porch that seemed larger than the house itself.

"My papa and the others allowed me to join them on the front porch of the old house each night as they planned how to handle the attacks against our families," Papa said, lowering himself onto the steps. "I figure to do plenty of planning of my own right here."

Theresa sat beside him and closed her eyes, trying to imagine a teenaged Harvester Stanley. What had he been like? As she considered it, she began to understand that he was probably not much different from the man he'd become. Considerate. Passionate about a cause. Dedicated to family.

"Furniture comes this week," he said. "I've got a room for you."

She hugged him. "Thank you, Papa, but this bird's gotta fly. I figure you want to put Aunt Joy's place on the market, and I've started looking for my own place on the Cape Girardeau riverfront. I need to be close to work."

Harvester squeezed her hand. "It's a joy to me, Cookie, that after all these years, we're living so close. I hope you're as glad as I am."

She nodded, tears filling her eyes. The offer from the Cape law firm included the possibility of a partnership after three years. Her salary was a third larger than Ocean City, and pro bono work wasn't just tolerated, it was encouraged. In the two months since arriving, she'd already been assigned a couple of high profile cases.

"Someone's coming this way," Papa said, nodding at a cloud of dust rising in the southwest. A few moments later, a rusty gray pickup pulled up. Earl Manning got out.

"Good to see you, Harvester." Like when they'd met before, Theresa noticed the hesitation in his eyes.

"First migrants arrive in five months, Earl. I figured I'd better get my place set up and get about making this old island home again."

Earl didn't speak. His eyes scanned the land beyond the house.

"Remember the time old Levi shot at you?" Papa asked. Right out there by that pine tree?" He pointed to a spot on the road. Earl nodded, a grin played across his lips.

"I'd spent the day eating mincemeat pie and playing with Mary."

Harvester chuckled. "Levi had no idea you were here."

And just like that, they disappeared into the past. Theresa listened to their tales of a much different time on Grebey Island. A time when race took a back seat to the Golden Rule. Where neighbor helped neighbor.

A place Papa intended to find again.

Want to read more about the life and times of Harvester Stanley, Theresa Traynor, and Earl Manning? Check out, Harvest of Thorns, *Paul E. Wootten's debut book, available only from Amazon.*

ACKNOWLEDGEMENTS

To everyone who read my first book, *Harvest of Thorns*, thank you! Your encouragement helped make *Shunned* happen.

To Living Stones Community Church in Blue Springs, our home church, and Pastor Dan Roye. Robin and I love you folks. Dan, you're as far from Pastor Miles Traynor as night is from day.

Thanks to Judy Falin Dellinger, my eighth and eleventh-grade high school English teacher and now my editor. Good job!

And thank you, Lord, for giving me the time, interest, and ability to write these words. Without you, I'm nothing.

Paul E. Wootten is a writer, educator, blogger, and former usher with the Kansas City Royals. His first book, *Harvest of Thorns*, was published in 2016. Paul and his wife Robin live in Bradenton, Florida and Kansas City. You can get in touch with Paul at his website, http://www.paulwoottenbooks.com or by e-mail at paul@paulwoottenbooks.com

Made in the USA
Columbia, SC
28 August 2018